Sulisa Publishing

Let Go of My Ear!
I Know What I'm Doing

Let Go of My Ear!
I Know What I'm Doing

An Anthology of Outstanding Undergraduate Short Fiction

Edited by Alison Shaw Bolen

Cover art by Elise Woodward ~ Auburn State University

Sulisa Publishing

Sulisa Publishing
625 SW 10th Avenue; PMB 388C
Portland, OR 97205-2788

This book is a work of fiction. Names, characters, places and incidents either are products of the authors' imaginations or are used fictitiously. Any resemblance to actual events, locales, or persons, living or dead, is entirely coincidental.

Text is set in Footlight MT Light
Book design by Amy Buringrud
Manufactured in the United States

First Edition

Cataloging-in-Publication Data
(Provided by Quality Books, Inc.)

Let go of my ear! I know what I'm doing! : an anthology of outstanding undergraduate short fiction / edited by Alison Bolen. -- 1st ed.
p. cm.
LCCN: 99-93885
ISBN: 0-9672126-0-X

1. Short stories, American. 2. College students' writings, American. I. Bolen, Alison.

PS648.S5L48 1999 813'.010892375
QB199-797

10 9 8 7 6 5 4 3 2 1

In memory of Frank D. Wilkins

ACKNOWLEDGMENTS

Many thanks to Tim Wagner for being the most awesome person in the universe; Alison Shaw Bolen for assistance and encouragement; Michelle Solinger for judging expertise; Ed Buringrud for art on the fly; Karin Jacoby for being a most valued source of inspiration; all the writers for obvious reasons; all the judges for their fantastic work; and all those with a kind word of encouragement.

This book is printed on recycled paper.

Contents

Preface

Having graduated from Ohio University not long ago, I am not far removed from the excitement and passion in the newfound talent of creative writing. Though many writers like myself, may have written in high school, or even at a younger age, it isn't until the first critique or the first difficult assignment bested, that we understand that this talent is bound to be a life-long passion. With this understanding, it is natural to want to display the work that wading through long nights, battling blank computer screens, and facing endless rewrites has produced. A mere, red 'A' at the top of a cover sheet is not sufficient, there must be something more. Which is exactly what led us to offer a stage to writers who have generally been barred from the publishing scene for lack of experience, years, or credentials; but certainly not for lack of talent. Sulisa Publishing's *Let Go of My Ear!* anthology is devoted to introducing a larger audience to these exciting new voices from the nation's colleges and universities.

Let Go of My Ear! stands apart from other anthologies because it is the collected work of writers who, though were previously unknown by the average reader, have bright writing futures to look forward to, based expressly on the talent and courage demonstrated in their writing. Many famous writers began their brilliant careers at a young age, and of course all writers were at one time "undiscovered." It is the writers who bragged their talents particularly early in their careers that I thought of often, while reading the submissions the contest generated. Rather than an age limit to filter out fresh talent, we required undergraduate status of those who chose to submit. A surprising number of excellent stories showed up in our mailbox, and although choosing the twenty winning entries was a daunting task, the judges and I were able to come to consensus on the stories you see in this book. After careful consideration and stimulating debate over the submissions, I can say with confidence that the work in this anthology is the best of what colleges and universities have to offer today.

I have read that Rust Hills, fiction editor at *Esquire*, feels that, "If one but stands back a bit and looks, one sees that it is no longer the book publishers and magazines, but rather the colleges and universities, that support the entire structure of the American literary establishment—and, moreover, essentially determine the nature and shape of that structure." With this in mind it is clear that it is not merely the work of Sulisa Publishing that has made these stories available to readers, but more importantly, the writing programs that have encouraged these new writers to contribute to and possibly alter the structure that is the American literary establishment. I applaud the work of the creative writing programs across the country, and eagerly look forward to the next wave of talent they will present us with.

One never knows what to expect when working with a bunch of wild undergrads, and I certainly did not predict a network among the writers, who live in every corner of the country. Now of course, it seems a completely natural development. My hope is that the connections the writers make with one another, through critique and comparison of their work, will survive past graduation; and with any luck, continue to provide a sense of community within the writing world when workshops on campus have been outgrown.

This process has been extremely rewarding for me, particularly because I have had the lucky experience of working with the wonderful people included in the anthology, something I will always treasure. The writers' enthusiasm often matched or exceeded my own and their commitment to the project also often rivaled that of the Sulisa staff! These are writers that will not only show up again and again because of their talent, but also because of their devotion to the craft and business of writing. I am very proud to be a part of their early careers and wish them the very best in their lives as writers and whatever else they may aspire to be.

Amy Buringrud
Publisher

If you know an undergraduate student who needs a place to display creative work, be it short fiction or art suitable for a book cover, please pass on our address and phone number, and encourage them to keep at it:

Sulisa Publishing
625 SW 10th Avenue
PMB 388C
Portland, OR 97205-2788

(503) 233-5232
sulisa@teleport.com

Let Go of My Ear!
I Know What I'm Doing

Katherin Nolte
WRIGHT STATE UNIVERSITY

Trying to Get Here

Junior is thinking about trilobites. He is sitting at the kitchen table, left palm pressed flat against the top of his head, using the corresponding elbow to prop open page 127 of *Fossils of Ohio: A Field Guide*, right hand jotting notes and making dark, detailed sketches. He is devoted to the fossilized remains of an organism that precedes our existence by five hundred and thirty million years. I'm watching him from the couch in the living room.

"Hey, Junior, babe," I say, patting the empty cushion beside me, "come over here."

Junior looks up from his notebook, lets the hand on his crown slide to his forehead. "Uhmm," he says, stalling, contemplating his options: fossils or wife. "Uhmm." He runs his hand through his dark hair, bites his bottom lip.

"Never mind," I say.

He exhales deeply, grateful, mumbles "Thanks," and returns to his book.

I continue to watch him for a while, thinking about what to make for dinner, thinking about Candy and her appointment tomorrow morning, thinking about Junior and how long he can make a summer evening seem, thinking about how even when we're together it feels like I'm alone. I lean into the couch and run the palms of my hands across the cushions, breathing in the silence that Junior and I so expertly create.

After dinner, Candy does her thing. Junior sits on the floor, back against the couch, legs stretched out in front of him, watching a documentary about the Cambrian Period. And Candy struts around the room, stepping over, and sometimes on, her father's long legs. She is dressed in matching powder blue undershirt and panties with my black, patent leather heels on her feet, and she is really going at it: thrusting out her tiny eight-year-old hips as she saunters back and forth across the room, one hand resting just above her waist and the other pushing her auburn hair out of her eyes, whispering, "Hey, baby. I look damn hot."

I stand in the center of the kitchen, dish towel in hand, taking it all in: the way Junior shifts his body right then left, trying to keep his eyes on the television as Candy steps over him; the way Candy's bony ankles buckle and twist as she tries to maneuver in my size-ten heels. And I think, *My God, where did she learn to walk like that*; and, *my God, where did she learn those words?* And, *please God, don't let this be my daughter.*

"Hey, Melinda," Candy says, noticing that I'm watching her, "don't I look sexy?"

"You need to call me Mommy, honey."

"No, your name is Melinda. Don't I look sexy?" Candy sticks out her lip and takes a shaky step towards me.

"Junior, can you help me?" I whisper to my husband.

"God, why won't you just answer me? I hate you!" Candy shrieks, pulling at her hair.

"Please be quiet," Junior mumbles from somewhere deep within another era.

I squeeze the towel in my hands. "Fine, honey. You look pretty, okay? Now let Mommy finish the dishes."

"Thank you, Melinda," Candy sings and begins to strut around the room again.

I press the heels of my feet hard against the kitchen floor, close my eyes, and take slow, deep breaths. *I will not let Candy upset me*, I repeat over and over in my head. When I open my eyes again Junior is staring at me. The credits on his program are rolling.

"Is something wrong?" he asks.

Candy and I are stuck in early-morning traffic downtown, trying to inch our way to the 111 building on First Street for her doctor appointment. Candy is excited. She grips her knobby knees which stick out from beneath her denim dress as she leans forward in her seat.

"When are we going to get there, Melinda?" she asks and pinches my arm with her nails.

I push her hand away. "Don't pinch Mommy. We'll be there in a little bit."

Candy rolls down the passenger window and makes exaggerated sniffing sounds. "I can smell the one-one-one building in the air."

"Roll up your window, please."

"I'm hot," Candy says, crossing her arms and looking at me belligerently. "The psychiatrist's office better have air conditioning."

The muscles in my stomach clench and I grip the wheel tightly. "Whose office?"

"The psychiatrist. Are you deaf?"

Candy reaches over and pinches me again, but I let it slide. "Who told you that you're going to see a psychiatrist?" I look at my daughter and she smiles at me brightly, pleased that she knows something she shouldn't.

"Junior told me. He's right, right? I'm going to see a psychiatrist because I'm cuckoo, right?" She sticks out her tongue and crosses her eyes and rolls her head from side to side.

"That's not funny, Candy. You're not cuckoo. Mommy just wants to talk to the doctor about some things."

"About me being cuckoo?"

"No. Stop using that word."

"I hate you," Candy says. She puts her hands back on her knees and tries to twist them like bottle caps. Then she sees it. "The one-one-one building," she cries and claps her hands.

And there it is, two blocks ahead of us: a huge, red brick building with 111 painted on its side in white, ten-foot strokes.

"Slow down," Candy says. "Slow down."

But we coast past it. "Hey!" Candy shouts and looks at me, mouth open, eyes wide. I ignore her and turn right on Main to head back home. She whips around in her seat and sticks her head out the window, her auburn hair flies around her face. "One-one-one," she calls to the building she can no longer see.

She turns back around and rolls up her window. She looks at me again, but I pretend that I'm concentrating on the road. She shifts her gaze to her lap. Head down, shoulders slumped: she is disappointed. But I make no apologies. I'm not ready for the building, the doctor; I'm not ready for any of it. At least not today.

Junior's Honda Civic is sitting in the driveway when Candy and I pull in. Junior took the day off of work to go fossil hunting at Caesar's Creek; he shouldn't be home.

Candy is pouting: sighs deeply as she climbs out of the mini-van, walks as slowly as possible from vehicle to house, makes me stand in the doorway, holding the screen door open, while I wait for her.

Inside, Junior is lying on the couch, hiking boots propped up on a decorative pillow, one hand covering his eyes, contents of a packed lunch spilled on the floor beside him.

"What are you doing home?" I ask.

"The fucking car wouldn't start." Junior keeps his hand over his eyes like he's shielding them from the sun.

"Junior said 'fucking,'" Candy says and laughs.

"It's not funny," Junior says, his voice loud and rough. "It's not funny."

"Why don't you play outside, Candy," I say. And Candy heads toward the front door, still laughing, but for presentation rather than amusement.

"What a waste of a day," Junior mumbles.

"We could all go somewhere in the van."

"No." He rolls onto his side so he faces the back of the couch. "I just want to sleep."

"Fine," I say, but I don't leave the room. I want him to ask how Candy's appointment went. I stand there and stand there and stand there, but he doesn't ask. I go outside to find my daughter.

Dinner time, and Candy refuses to eat. "I only want oatmeal," she says and pushes her plate of fish sticks and green beans to the center of the table. She crosses her arms and looks defiantly at Junior.

"You're going to eat what your mother has prepared," Junior says as he cuts his food.

"I hate fish sticks."

"Honey, try to eat a couple of bites," I say.

"Make me."

Junior sets down his silverware. "Fine. You can sit at the table then until you've cleared your plate." His face is red, his neck tight, muscles clenched, and his hands are fists on either side of his plate.

"Junior's face looks like a tomato," Candy laughs, covering her mouth for effect.

"I am so sick of this," he shouts and hits his fists hard against the table. The plates bounce. I hold my breath. "I am so sick of this!"

The legs of my chair scrape against the linoleum as I rise from the table. Junior and Candy stare at me. "You guys," I say, "you have to… to…" But I stop. I don't know what to say. Their eyes are on me, waiting. Candy licks her lips; Junior rubs his temples.

"Hey! You can't just leave—" Junior shouts. But I'm out the door before he can finish.

I walk around the block, breathe in the summer air, let it fill each limb, each portion of my body, until it feels like I'm floating. I walk quickly, and the sound of my shoes against the pavement, the sharp slap of each deliberate step, creates a soothing rhythm that my body glides to: a sound that I control. And then I am back at the house again, standing in the driveway, tracing the letters on Junior's license plate with the tip of my index finger. I move toward the house, hesitate when I am between screen door and main door, one hand on each handle, entire body cinched, prepared for what I'll find inside.

They are both crying: Candy rolled in a ball on the living room floor, knees drawn up to her chin, taking in quick, shaky breaths; Junior on the edge of the couch sobbing, head in hands, dark hair sticking up in tufts like he recently ran his fingers through it.

"What's going on in here?" I ask. No one moves. "Why are you both crying?"

"The cat bit her and then she bit the cat," Junior says, looking up at me. His eyes are wide and soft.

"You bit Sunshine?" I ask. Candy nods her head.

"I like how his fur felt in my mouth," she says. Then she starts to cry again.

"No you don't, honey," I say.

"This is too much. This is just too much," Junior breathes into the palms of his hands.

"It's too much," Candy whispers.

I sit down beside Junior and wrap one arm around his waist, pulling him close. He smells like after-shave and shampoo and soap. Candy watches me, her entire face trembling, both hands stuffed into her mouth. "It's going to be okay," I say, fooling no one, not even myself.

Two days later Candy and I are back at the 111 building, this time inside. I'm sitting in the doctor's office: beige carpet, large oak desk, two maroon chairs, a poster on one cream-colored wall with children from all over the world smiling and holding hands. Candy is in the waiting room, playing with blocks and badly worn stuffed animals and plastic dolls.

The doctor is telling me the results of Candy's tests: hearing, vision, IQ. And I am wishing for a window, a hole, a crack in the wall, anything so that I can focus on the city outside instead of the smooth, tan skin and perfect teeth that lean across the desk in front of me.

"An IQ of 158," he says, "you have a very gifted child."

And if I just had something to focus on, something my eyes could devote themselves to, everything would be okay.

"I think that what we're seeing evidence of is a very gifted, very precocious, but very spoiled little girl."

"Yes. But she bit the cat," I say. "I don't think that's normal."

The doctor smiles. "Believe me, I've seen worse, much worse. I think that what Candy needs is more structure, more discipline. This is a little girl who is begging for discipline; she wants her mommy and daddy to set limits, she needs them to. Do you follow, Melinda?"

I nod my head and we talk about ways that Junior and I can create guidelines, enforce rules, reward and punish appropriate and inappropriate behavior. And while the doctor is talking, I suddenly become desperate for my daughter. I want to touch her fine hair, her soft skin; I want to see her fat cheeks and bony legs, breathe in the sweet smell of an eight-year-old girl.

And then I'm shaking the doctor's hand. He wants to see us again in six weeks, next time with Junior too. And then I'm in the waiting room with Candy grinning up at me from the floor, bent over the kingdom she has created with multicolored blocks.

"Did I do good on my tests?" she wants to know. She slips her hand in mine. It is warm and soft and almost too much for me to take. I mouth the word yes.

On the way home, Candy talks about the doctor. "He said I could call him Doctor Steve," she says. She is pleased with him, the visit, her tests. She sings quietly to herself for the rest of the ride. I glance at her out of the corner of one eye, and sometimes I sing too, but for the most part I am silent. For some reason, the sound of her voice is enough.

Junior and I sit on the front steps after dusk. Candy is tucked into bed, asleep and already lost deep in a dream. And Junior is quiet, but he is happy; it has been a good day for him. This morning he had the Honda repaired, and then he drove to Caesar's Creek and spent the afternoon on his hands and knees, sifting through rock and dirt in search of fossilized treasure. And for once, he didn't come home empty-handed. When Candy and I came through the door, he was waiting for us, holding in his palm the back end of a trilobite. "It's something," he said.

Now, in the soft, gray dark, my bare foot rests on top of his, and we sip iced tea out of tall, clear glasses. I feel I could sit like this, in the quiet night with Junior, forever.

"We can start again tomorrow," he says, and it's almost a whisper so as not to disturb the air around us.

I lift my glass and ease an ice cube into my mouth. I slide it against my tongue, revel in its smooth perfection. I could hold it in my mouth forever—this ice cube, this night, Junior's silent presence—and never want anything more.

Eric Lundgren
Lewis & Clark College

The Automatic Writer

Automatic Writing: Writing which is attempted without conscious control. It is more likely to be possible in states of hypnosis or under the influence of drugs. When Dadaism and Surrealism were fashionable, the disciples of the creeds 'went in for' automatic writing. It produced the equivalent of a 'happening.' Nothing of any importance survives.

-*A Dictionary of Literary Terms,* J.A. Cuddon

Like most men, impotence frightened Charlie more than anything: lack of creation, or procreation, exposed the old existential blank. At eighteen, Charlie thought mostly of writing and women, or of women and writing, and he was failing miserably at both. He sat at his kitchen table, brooding over an overstuffed ashtray, four empty coffee cups and a single white page. The kitchen light droned above him like a fat electric insect, while a ceiling fan circled monotonously, circulating the dull shafts of air through the room. The lone sentence of his story for fiction class glared at him, an uninspired epitaph: "Had I been flawless, the whole thing would have been impossible." Crusty, bearded, in his girlfriend's pajamas, Charlie dropped his pen to the desktop and staggered down two flights of stairs to the mailbox. Since it was four a.m., there was no one around to witness Charlie and mutter "poor bastard." A word of sympathy would have consoled him much, but his roommate was shooting up heroin somewhere in Sellwood and his girlfriend wasn't answering his calls.

Thinking four a.m. thoughts, thoughts that slouched wordlessly through his brain, Charlie undid the lock on his mailbox. Electric bill, phone bill, heating bill, utility bill. He hadn't really expected a handwritten letter from Heaven or anything, but why not a few kind words from some idle philanthropist, or at least a note from Meghan? (In his mind he pictured her whispering: "It's all right, Charlie. You're tired, I know. Will you touch me instead?") Under the stack of computer-processed, impersonal missives, he noticed a small scrap of paper with these words scrawled on it:

BLOCKED?
We can help.
817-4231
Ask for Calliope.

In his stupor, this little ad seemed like a *deus ex machina* to Charlie. He climbed the stairs, sure somehow that he had discovered the cure for his verbal constipation. A bad dream had been recurring the last few nights: Charlie would open a newspaper box and find the front page blank, except for the headline NO NEWS TODAY. His short story was due for Friday's class, in forty-eight hours. He sunk into his bed, the seconds and minutes clicking past him in the dark, until he receded into a long, blank sleep.

Charlie woke up coughing. His discovery of the crumpled phone number in his palm was, in truth, little consolation, but at least it gave him a reason to get up. Still half-asleep, he tripped through the waste land of his apartment to the phone, and dialed the number.

A frazzled voice answered, "Department of Psychoanalysis and Literature."

"I'm a writer," Charlie muttered plaintively. "Is Calliope there?"

"Speaking."

"It's terribly important," said Charlie. "I need a story for class by Friday, and I've got nothing."

"Nothing, yes. I understand. Look, Mister…"

"Charlie."

"Now that I look at it, Chuck, I'm expecting a return sometime today. Anne Rice, you know. I've told her, 'Listen, Anne, stick with the vampires. It's what you do well. Sex, fangs, impalement. People eat that stuff off the page.' But *no*: 'I'm concerned about my integrity as a writer.' Integrity, for chrissakes. Anyway, you've come to the right girl, Chuck. See me at four. Wait—no, four will be all right."

"Whereabouts?" asked Charlie.

She sighed audibly into the receiver. "Back door of Portland Typewriter on Barbur Boulevard. Back door, mind you. Be punctual."

At ten minutes to four, Charlie stepped off the Tri-Met across the street from the typewriter shop. His nerves were wrecked. He had just held a ten-minute discussion with a shifty meth fiend on the virtues of William S. Burroughs' "cut-up" method of writing. This involved a random juxtaposition of words and phrases from miscellaneous sources, resulting in sentences like "proxy white rabbit shat a clamor high." *Maybe all I need is a large infusion of illicit drugs and a few months' continuous sex with Moroccan boys*, thought Charlie. Then again, he figured his classmates might not appreciate the erotic (auto-erotic?) nature of all creative work.

He stood in front of the shop's rotting back door, which hung at a desultory angle from its hinges. Tacked to it was a scrap of sallow paper bearing a quote:

> "HE IS HAPPY WHOM THE MUSES LOVE. FOR THOUGH A MAN HAS SORROW AND GRIEF IN HIS SOUL, YET WHEN THE SER-

VANT OF THE MUSES SINGS, AT ONCE HE FORGETS HIS DARK THOUGHTS AND REMEMBERS NOT HIS TROUBLES. SUCH IS THE HOLY GIFT OF THE MUSES TO MEN." — HESIOD

He worked his way up a grimy old staircase, hemmed by peeling walls which were stained as if by an immortal chain-smoker. He had an urgent desire to flee, but curiosity egged him on down a narrow hallway. Behind milk-glass windows with the words "Calliope Longhand, Ph.D." inset in black marble, a voice chattered indecipherably. Somewhere a grandfather clock struck four, and the woodwork rattled. Charlie slumped to the floor, his eyes locked on the blank, yellow wall.

Calliope answered the door in a cherry-red, satin dress and black, stiletto heels. She motioned Charlie in without interrupting her cell-phone conversation.

"J.D., just listen to me. Hold out one more year and we'll publish the works. Yes, *Holden Grows Old* and all the rest. Yes, I know, but you've got to realize how much this hermit bit is doing for your image! Right... Jerome, I know forty years is a long time, but... don't hang up on me now! I mean it, I'm through with you if—" Calliope threw the phone across the room and it uttered a cry of pain as it met plaster. The room was crammed wall-to-wall with text: manuscripts, books, atlases, newspapers, journals, magazines, loose sheets.

"I've been swamped lately, Chuck," she said. "Absolutely swamped. Used to be, I'd handle only epic poetry. That I could do. A few centuries ago they figured out that nobody *writes* epic poetry anymore, and now I'm serenading every moronic fuck with a Macintosh and an ego. No offense, Chuck. Here, sit down."

She heaved a huge stack of volumes from the only chair in the office. Reclining on a large, mahogany desk across from Charlie, she crossed her stockinged legs and took up a brush. She pulled it slowly through her lustrous, black hair.

"Remind me, Chuck. What was it you wanted?"

He studied the slope of her thighs momentarily before answering, "I'm taking this fiction writing class, you see, and I need a story for Friday. So far, I've got nothing."

"Ah," she said, grinning slyly, "anxiety of influence got you down, eh, Chuck?"

"I'm doubting my chops," said Charlie. "Feeling a little… impotent."

Calliope uncrossed her legs, approached Charlie, and pressed her finger along the fly of his pants. "No… I don't think you're impotent. A little weak, maybe, a little confused. You were right to come to me, Chuck. You know how much a woman can do for you when you're feeling weak. I might have just the thing you need."

She pointed to a case on her desk, about twice the size of a typewriter.

"W-what is it?" stuttered Charlie, straining to pronounce the words.

"W-w-well, it's the Automatic Writer, of course."

"The *what?* Ms. Longhand, you've got me all wrong. I just need some help getting started on this story. I have the feeling that one word, one sentence…"

Calliope shook her head, and pleaded with someone high and invisible.

"How many novels do you think James Michener wrote, Chuck?"

"Oh, I don't know. One every year for about half a century."

"Seventy-four, Chuck. Each one of them the width of your fist. How do you think he pulled that off?"

"I have no idea."

"Well, Chuck, the answer sure as hell isn't 'the spontaneous overflow of powerful feeling,' if that's what you were thinking. No. I helped him. I'm the *muse.* And I want to help you too, Chuck, because I've always been drawn to the young and naïve. But you've got to get off this 'I'm-the-Progenitor' trip."

She paused and took a breath, fixing on Charlie the teasing stare of the unattainable. "The Automatic Writer doesn't create its own stories. It culls them from your head, that's all, culls 'em and lays 'em out in rows of flawless font. I tell my customers that its output is only as interesting as your psyche. You can't doubt your id, Chuck. Otherwise, all is lost. Trust me. I've worked with all the biggies, though you'd never know it—homage isn't fashionable anymore, you know. This job might seem glamorous to most, but I'll tell you, sometimes it's hell to be a working woman in this world!"

She slid her elbows back on the mahogany and pressed a Cambridge into a golden cigarette holder.

"Got a light?" she asked. "Oral fix, you know."

Charlie sheepishly fumbled for his Bic.

"How much does it cost?" he asked, pointing to the machine she caressed lovingly with her free hand.

"It's an old model," said Calliope. "I'll cut you a deal."

At midnight Charlie crouched over the Automatic Writer in the dim silence of his apartment. Calliope's words had really chilled him: *"Its output is only as interesting as your psyche." What if this machine spat out weird ink-blot configurations? Or only blank pages? It could be seen as a minimalist experiment*, thought Charlie. The composer, Cage, had, after all, written that piece, "4:33," where the pianist just took the stage and sat in front of a grand piano for the duration, without touching a key. Someday, Charlie Dick would write the Great American Novel, and there wouldn't be a single word in it. Just five hundred pages of space.

When Charlie cracked the lid, he found only a cord, an instruction manual, and what looked like an obsolete computer. He knew he had been scammed: the thing just looked too ridiculous to be the instrument of a righteous muse. Nevertheless, he plugged it in and pored over the instructions. They were printed on the same shabby paper he had seen tacked to the door.

1. SITUATE THE AUTOMATIC WRITER NEAR THE BED.
2. ENTER ALL REQUESTED PERSONAL INFORMATION.
3. ENTER GENRE OF WRITING, LENGTH, STYLE, ETC.
4. GO TO SLEEP.
5. REMOVE WRITING FROM FEEDER UPON WAKING.

Charlie went by the book, typing in his name, date of birth, and social security number. Then he typed: *Short story. 1250 words.* Asked to choose a style, he added: *Joycean*, laughing. Charlie listened to the quiet slurs of passing cars on the street outside, and switched off the light, chuckling at himself and his folly.

The Automatic Writer did not occur to Charlie again until he was half finished brushing his teeth the next morning. "'Remove writing from feeder upon waking.' Yeah right!" he told the mirror. What crazy doubts he had! The cool morning sunlight declared his nightmares null and void. Charlie waltzed around the apartment in his boxers, doing Mick Jagger pelvic thrusts to "Satisfaction." But when he saw a thin stack of paper jutting from the machine beside the bed, he tensed. His limbs froze. Trembling, he reached for the cover page:

THE MISFORTUNES OF ERIC LUNDGREN
by Charles M. Dick

Clearly, it was a lousy title, largely due to the prosaic, Scandinavian name. Charlie sensed that this "Eric Lundgren" character was only a thinly veiled replica of himself, and was already vaguely offended. But he read on:

> He strolled along the beach, along the mudslopes and sandhills, under the manycolored palette of sky hanging loose and fuzzyclouded over his spinning

head. He wandered on and on and on and on, in tune only with the impulsive throbbings of his wildheart and the magic concussive breaths of wavelets.

A girl stood before him in mid-stream, washing her sleek limbs in saltwater. Her thighs, softhued and flowerlike, effused currents of heat that electrified Eric's heartchamber. Her lyrical movements were hymns to the sea, songs of praise to the vast, wide, impossible bluegreen.

Heavenly God! cried Eric's heart, in an outburst of profane joy. He wandered on and on in a silent buzzing bliss of the soul, drunk with sunshine and seasmell and pisswater. The girl became aware of his juvenile reverent eyes on her swanlike flesh, and met his gaze. *To live, to lose, to fail, to fornicate!* he thought.

Eric Lundgren tripped and tumbled into the mudslime and bogwater.

"Where'd you learn to walk?" cried the laughing, pitiless girl, still daubing her glimmering, goddess-like flesh. "I'm calling the cops, you lousy *voyeur!*"

After falling on his face thricemore, Eric scampered away like a gutless, childish hare. *O Great Artificer,* he thought, *I am fallen before you, humiliated, a failure, Icarus scorched...*

Charlie, unable to read more, threw down the manuscript with rage and indignation. He smarted from the initial blow of this cruel parody, though its full import remained hidden. Sure only that this wicked contraption had pegged him as a second-rate mimic, he jerked its cord from the socket and slammed down the lid. Charlie hurled the bulky machine toward the window; the glass collapsed and the Automatic Writer plunged into an open dumpster two stories below, raising little flurries of tinfoil and styrofoam on impact.

Crumpled on the bed, Charlie lapsed into one of those sessions of prolonged introspection that usually undid him. He saw, more clearly than he wanted to, the Automatic Writer's revelation. Joyce (or Dedalus) had engaged in a selfless vision of beauty; the girl on the beach was, for him, both woman and goddess. In her he had seen Helen, Aphrodite, beauty personified, and had realized his duty as her scribe, her disciple. Charlie's gazes at the female flesh, however, were furtive, self-conscious, rueful ones. His artistry was the guilty trespass of a Peeping Tom. Unable to fuse the artistic and erotic into a single creative epiphany, he burned and blanched with shame.

Not a bad interpretation, Charlie thought, even as tears hatched in his eyes. If he whom the muses love is happy, Charlie was at that moment most unhappy, most unloved. Crying like a kid, he recited the single line of his short story: "Had I been flawless, the whole thing would have been impossible." Sleep reluctantly staunched his tears, but his dreams were all of deserts and salt water.

Friday morning he woke feverish and pale. The sky was blank gray. He had slept fitfully, heard distant chords of the Sirens' voices; two or three times that night he had flipped on the lights in an irrational fit, swearing he sensed the Automatic Writer at work, quiet, sinister. Then he had collected the scattered leaves of "Misfortunes" and burned them, one by one, with Motel 6 matches. Though all hard evidence of the machine was gone, something was still awry with Charlie: an inner entropy disheveled his nerves. Armed with only his single sentence and a smoldering Camel Straight, Charlie headed for class. Maybe he wasn't a great artist, but he suffered like one.

"Would anyone like to read your story out loud?"

The students huddled around the long desk with the seriousness of diplomats at a U.N. assembly. They were all awfully grave: shy, somber guys with beards and berets, touchy women with marked-up copies of Doris Lessing novels in their Guatemalan backpacks, and the crusty, perverse, sci-fi nerds who wrote ultraviolent yarns about alien worlds. In front of each of them was a neatly-stapled tome, the weekly chronicle of their inner lives. Charlie was the exception, of course, blushing over his feeble sentence. Luckily, a brave student volunteered to read a few paragraphs about her old dog Chipper, who had died. Charlie found it all extremely touching, and nearly wept. After she finished, the class resumed its monastic silence.

"I'll read," said Jeremy Blower. Jeremy Blower read aloud for at least five minutes every class period. He was an absurdly handsome freshman, with long, silky, blond hair and a close-clipped goatee. ENVIRONMENTALIST, SONNETEER, PLAYBOY is probably how his resumé would read. Charlie always imagined him in a tux, with a starlet on each arm, saying: "Better to reign in Hell than to serve in Heaven." Every heterosexual female in the class locked her eyes on Jeremy with subtle reverence.

"My latest piece is called 'The Misfortunes of Eric Lundgren, Part II,'" he stated, with the inflection of a smooth-jazz DJ. Charlie shuddered to hear that abominable name. Jeremy read:

> Eric Lundgren was an egotist.
> And Eric Lundgren secretly wanted to be a black woman.

Charlie lost control. He erupted from his chair and lunged across the desk, his hands converging on Jeremy Blower's pale throat. There were screams and gasps, though the professor looked amused, and did not intervene.

"What the *fuck* have you done with the Automatic Writer?" screamed Charlie, strangling the incredulous yuppie, whose locks were getting seriously tousled. "Answer me, you well-groomed asshole, come on. Have you been messing around with Calliope?"

Jeremy Blower had never been so scared in his life, not even the time he had mistakenly driven out of the suburbs two years before. When Charlie jerked him from his chair by the arm and out of the room, Jeremy did not resist. The girls watched their

Byronic hero exit with open mouths.

Charlie shoved Blower to the wall, feeling like a bona fide thug.

"Take it easy, man," said Blower, trembling in his cashmere. "I was throwing out the trash last night, and I saw this shiny thing, and..."

"I'm a pacifist," said Charlie, relishing the moment, "but to be absolutely frank, I really ought to beat you. I won't. I won't, though I'd love to."

"Hey, man, I apologize. I really appreciate how cool you're taking all of—"

"Shut the fuck up, Blower. Where's that blasted machine?"

With the Automatic Writer under his arm, Charlie found Calliope leaning back in her desk chair. She was reading this month's *Playboy*.

"Chuck!" she cried, sloughing off the magazine discreetly and adjusting her dress. "I wasn't expecting visitors, you know. How are you?"

Charlie's pallor did not lift. She neared him, stroking his cheek with her delicate hand. Somehow, the acrimonious speech he had composed on his way dissolved at her touch.

"You're dissatisfied," she said. "Don't take it personally, Chuck."

"Don't take my subconscious *personally?*"

"It's really pretty simple, Chuck. Let me try to explain." She looked ruminative for a moment, lighting a cigarette and picking up a loose sheet of paper. "I've always been a sexual fantasy, even for the Greeks; you won't catch me denying it. But in the old days, when Joes still wrote epic poetry, the sex was distilled with a healthy dose of worship. Now, God's out of the picture. And what do you have? Sex. Sex, sex, sex, and your ego. It wasn't that way for Milton, though he surely got his kicks poeticizing about Eve's naked arse in The Garden. The point is, you write for the woman in me, not the goddess, and that's something you'll have to live with. I don't hold you responsible for the Decline of the West, Chuck. You shouldn't, either. Kiss me."

Before Charlie could respond she sunk her tongue deep into his mouth. Was it the same ambrosia that Psyche sipped on Olympus? Whatever it was, the kiss felt like a baptism to Charlie.

"You know, Chuck, I was trying to teach you a lesson."

"What was that?"

"Humility, you moron. 'Humility comes from meeting the Gods.' Who said that? Hmm. Guess it was me."

She balled up the piece of paper she had been waving and tossed it into the wastebasket.

"I was writing you a sonnet, but I've always been a lousy poet. Come back soon, will you?"

"Sure," said Charlie, and waded out of the room.

As he crossed the boulevard, the afternoon sun washed over him in auburn waves. His blood thrashed and hummed through him; his lips quivered with an electric charge. The sky seemed to open like a flower, cloudless and bright. *To live, to err, to fail, to create life out of life!* he thought, and the wind passed through him like a ghost as he walked the edges of the city, alone, blissful, cursed, with Calliope's lipstick still wet on his mouth... [*The Manuscript Ends Here*]

A PROPOS OF "THE AUTOMATIC WRITER"

So, are we to believe that Charlie Dick, after this lascivious encounter with the Muse-figure, is released, like Stephen Daedalus from his endless merry-go-round of sexual repression? Is his virility buoyed by his creative work, or *vice versa?* These and other fascinating queries are posed by the unfinished text, which I myself have undertaken to edit and submit for this month's issue of *Fetish.* While organizing this amazingly disorganized little work, I was intrigued and saddened by the squirmings of Mr. Lundgren's imagination in the muck of his libido. Feminists and others will perhaps object to Calliope as a sex-toy, a fantasy given flesh and tongue. May I urge such critical readers to explore this text as a psychosomatic study with complex and troubling implications. My organization, and occasional corrective touch, has at last made publishable a rare specimen of a diseased creative mind. I say "diseased" to express my shock upon learning that the author, my former student, died in a masturbatory accident last summer. Experimenting with the autoerotic qualities of asphyxiation, Mr. Lundgren's death came at the end of a black leather belt. With the wisdom of aftersight, we can already see in the pointed reference to William S. Burroughs on page 3, the germ of his wayward behavior. Though it must pain any professor to see a young man's talent strangled in the crib, so to speak, my editorial work on this piece is more than an act of mere fondness. The trials of young Charlie Dick may be a springboard for discussion on the convergence of literature and sexuality, a topic I have considered at great length in my new book, *Metaphor and Masochism: The Muse as Dominatrix,* available from Cambridge University Press. Though one must be wary of a direct equation of Lundgren with Dick, we can assume that Dr. Freud's notion of literature as fore- and aft-pleasure, that is to say wish fulfillment, was much on the author's mind. Lundgren's relationship to Joyce, whether or not it be viewed as a Bloomian "family romance" among Poetic Father, Muse, and ephebe, superbly demonstrates the castration anxiety of a young man who kept playing that game of "fort—da!" right until the end. The author's work, infantile as it often is, deserves lively scholarly debate, and I am assured that the intelligent readers of *Fetish* will provide this. This psychological specimen brings to mind a frequent refrain of my beloved mentor, Dr. Fredrich Willhelm von Sternberg: "Ze vorld outside of ze vomb iss a colt place indeed."

DR. HANS D. FURCHTBAR
Associate Professor of Psychology
Reed College

Scott Snyder
Brown University

Tattooed

I am supposed to give a lecture in the Crystal Room, but the whole thing goes to shit. My notes are typed clearly, my charts rolled into bundles and ribbon-tied. I've practiced my gestures—easy on the fist-pounding, don't blink too much or they'll think you've got an optical disorder. All I have to do is clap off my lights and hang the 'Service Please' sign on the doorknob. I am all set. I am ready to go. That's when Castorelli calls.

"Give this lecture and you'll be pushing up daisies," he says.

"Threaten me all you want," I say, "my days with the freak show are through."

There's a knock at my door and I let in the maid, who is carrying a milk crate loaded with miniature soap. She is short and foreign, and she doesn't understand that tattoos are, in fact, deliberate acts (though mine were forced upon me), that they are artwork grafted to the body and not stains. She brings me these soaps so I'll have enough to clean off the images mapped across my person. Before I can shoo her off, she's in the bathroom arranging the soap in a pyramid by the shower stall.

Castorelli laughs. "So, you think that there are careers aplenty for tattoo boys like yourself?" he says, his voice tight with mocking. "Go ahead, fly the coop, try to make your own way. I could count the number of jobs out there for the likes of you on one hand. No, not even a hand, a claw or perhaps a hoof."

"I can lecture," I say defiantly, "I'm good at speaking about issues, and important ones at that. In fact, I have an appointment at the Crystal Room this very afternoon. While I talk from a podium they are going to serve wheels of cheese and seedless grapes and whole Georgia watermelons, juicy to the rind."

"I heard, I heard," he says. "And you didn't even invite me, your old ring master? The man who chose you like one does a small, shivering fish from a barrel of many."

"I owe you nothing, Castorelli," I say, the phone trembling in my hand. Meanwhile, the maid is sprinkling bittersweet chocolates on my pillow.

"Believe what you will," Castorelli says with a slight chuckle, "but even if you don't owe *me* anything, you certainly owe Sidney Elenor Clatz a small fortune."

"Who?" I ask.

"Why, the tattoo artist, of course," he says.

Funny, despite the dizzying amount of work the old goat's done on me, I've never known him as anything but Castorelli's Tattoo Artist. "I thought you paid him for everything," I say.

Castorelli gives a terrible laugh and I picture him at the other end of the line in his ring master's outfit of buttoned velvet, with his head thrown back, the lollipop spiral pinned to the brim of his top hat spinning away with abandon.

"I never gave him one red cent!" he says. "He's been running a bill on you ever since you got that first tattoo of my flying otter done on the small of your back. Look at yourself. You're his retirement plan and change. But I should let him tell you himself. He's on his way to collect right now," he says. "He's probably rolling down the hallway to your hotel room as we speak!"

He starts laughing again, and I drop the phone on the bed, fling open the door and look down the corridor. Sure enough, there he is, barreling towards my room in his motorized wheelchair. Not just any chair though. Old Clatz's seat is built for speed, complete with racing stripes and fins and a flap with an eight ball silk-screened on, that flaps out behind him like a paper cape as he guns towards me. The tires are huge and treaded, and leave singed teeth marks smoking in the carpet. His hair is bone white, and shoots out from his head in pointed shocks, and though he's blind, he's got a mad look in his milky eyes, Clatz does. Even through the fog in his peepers I can see those tiny pupils fixed on me with a rabid intent I've never seen in another living being. Not even Castorelli's monkey girl, despite all that practice behind her triptych mirror, ever achieved such a look of unhinged wildness.

"Me money," he cackles. "Hand over me green!"

I slam the door and break for the window, nearly knocking over the maid. Clatz batters down the door just as I'm climbing through the frame. He sniffs the air for me as I scramble down the ladder. I hear him give a horrible howl, like a starving prairie dog, and then go to work on the maid with his tattooing stencil. She's screaming in foreign, his needle is buzzing, and before I know it I'm down the ladder and out of there.

When I get across town to her hotel room, Bessie's got her suitcases packed and arranged on the water bed, and she says that she's going to hop freights out to the West Coast. Bessie was the bearded lady in Castorelli's freak show with me. Though she still has her facial mane, neither she nor I work for that bastard anymore. We escaped last month and high-tailed it to the big city in hopes of starting a family. Not that it was hard to get away. We were only kept supine in cages for performances. For the greater part of the day we walked around upright like everybody else. We wore loafers and jeans and, believe you me, if she didn't have whiskers and I wasn't covered in tattoos, you wouldn't be able to tell us from Adam.

But the life got tiring. Sure, the cages had wall to wall straw and water bowls made from Taiwanese porcelain, but there was no air-conditioning or central heating in those things, and so really it came down to an issue of comfort. A man's got to feel at home after all, and neither I nor my Bessie did with Castorelli running the show. So one night, while the rest of the gang was out at a bar filled with tanks of piranha you could feed canaries for a nickel, Bessie and I collected our valuables and took a cab to the train. Strangely, as soon as we hit the urban sprawl, I was offered this opportunity to lecture at the Crystal Room by a small man in suspenders made to look like orange tape measures. So I took a place for myself near the engagement and rented this one for Bessie on the bad side of town where I assumed Castorelli wouldn't snoop about. It was hell separating, but (little did I know) I figured this to be safer for the both of us.

"How can you walk out on me?" I say to her now, and pull her close so that her beard tickles my collar. "What about our hopes, our dreams, our plans for the future?"

She turns away. "I got an offer from the Plastic Room in Seattle to teach courses on the important issues to retarded children. It's what I've always wanted."

"But we're a team," I say, "and there's no 'I' in team."

"There's also no 'u' in team," she says, and before I know it, she's through the door and out of my life for good.

I stand there, alone, and listen to some kids on the corner below dislodge a hydrant with an elephant gun. I start thinking about my life then, the few ups and the many downs, and I grow blue. I wonder why solitude is always my lot. Sure, I had friends in the show: me and Candice the Brain the Jar had some good laughs. And there were many heart to hearts with Bartholomew the Pretzel Man, but really, I've never been too attached to anyone. You might think that this is because I'm stitched head to toe with tattoos, but this isn't true. My loneliness came first. Even as a child I was a failure at making friends. Castorelli went to the same elementary school as me, and he was even in the same class until he got bumped up a year for inventing an electric chair for frogs. Yet, I still remember that first day of kindergarten with him, just two little boys each with a shiny apple for the teacher. Unfortunately, just before we handed them over, Castorelli managed to switch my apple with his, which was bruised slightly on its bottom. After examining by monocle all the apples lining his desk like shrunken heads, the teacher pulled me out in front of the class and said, "Children, some homerooms have guinea pigs for pets, others have goldfish. But we're lucky," he said and patted me on the head, "we have our very own moron!" He went on to explain that, being a moron, I could only communicate via a series of grunts and tongue clicks.

It wasn't so bad though, one girl built a giant wheel out of pipe cleaners for me to run around in, and the other children were always sociable. Often during recess they'd hurry over to my corner of the yard all rosy and out of breath and say, "Hey Moron, can we bury you in broken glass?" Well, I'd grunt-click, "Of course you can!" and they'd tear off my clothes and heap on the bottle shards, and we'd all laugh and laugh until the siren went off, and we had to rush inside before the draw-bridge was raised.

Most days I'd play by myself in a deserted corner of the Recreation Pen, drawing pictures on the asphalt with nubs of colored chalk until my knees were red and bumpy from the gravel. Always, I'd draw the things that I saw around me, what were to me life's signposts; I'd sketch portraits of the boy living next door to me, looking plucked and bloodless from influenza, or the man across the street who'd lost his hand in a factory accident, and was often out on the corner with a "Will Work For Food" sign made from a window shade taped to his chest. Carefully, I'd plot out the lines of his face, hard and angled, and always I was cautious to avoid the grid of the hopscotch court.

A year before I graduated, Castorelli came back to visit wearing a shark skin suit, and sporting a mustache that looked like two enormous black teardrops about to collide beneath his nose. He found me in the Pen and said, "Well, well, you must get tired of those doodles washing away with every drizzle. How'd you like to have them made permanent?"

Before you condemn me for accepting his offer, here is what I did not know: Castorelli had no intention of stenciling me with my own images. Instead, as soon as I agreed to join the show, my body became his to illustrate, to transform into his own easel, private property on which I would not be allowed to trespass. I didn't realize that soon my skin would be sutured to ads for the show, sketches of leopards and beehives of cotton candy and pinwheeling billboards lettered with Old West script. Clatz would sew it all on beneath a high power lamp that pinned me to the waxy paper like a butterfly to a cork board. That's what I didn't see, and so I clicked my tongue twice for yes and the rest is history.

All that's left of Bessie now are her beard hairs, scattered over the pillow. I sweep them into cupped hand, and clutch them to my chest, sobbing. I decide that it's too painful to stick around, so I go out for a walk. I'm passing by some teens luring a cat-size alligator from a sewer grate with a ferret on a string when I spy the Trout sisters, Gert and Deluth, coming towards me. The Trouts are big-boned women attached at the head, and when Bessie and I left, they were still part of Castorelli's rabble. I've always liked them, these two. They've got charisma with a capital 'C' and one hell of a pretty smile.

"Gert! Del!" I call and run towards them.

They're overjoyed to see me and we all embrace, but they're linked at the back of the skull so the only way to hug them both at once is to put them in a kind of double headlock, which I do.

"You gals look fantastic," I say. "Did you pick a law school yet, Gert? And Deluth, how's that trapeze act coming? Don't swing too close to those lights, ha ha."

"No, that's all over and done," Gert says. "We're doing documentaries about the issues now."

Oh," says I, "I was supposed to give a lecture on them this afternoon."

"What a coincidink," says Deluth. "We've got a screening in the Styrofoam Room at five."

"What happened to your lecture?" Gert asks.

"Castorelli," I say.

"The fiend!" they say in stereo. "We left just after you and Bess did. You started a veritable exodus, you know."

I ask what they mean and they tell me that after we fled, Bea the Fat Woman hired a midnight crane to help her on her way; Cornelius the Sword Swallower stuffed his rapiers down his throat and split; and even Brian Z. the Lion-Faced-Boy stuck out his paw and hit the highway.

"Only Pete stayed behind," Gert says. "So, Castorelli thinks that if he can get you and Bess in check, we'll all follow suit."

I feel a rush of fear then, because I finally understand why Castorelli's been so ardent about hounding me. Yet, at the same time, I begin to get excited (not for the Trouts, though any red-blooded, American man would be hard pressed to turn down these fillies), but because I realize that I've come to be a symbol of freedom to these people, a beacon of hope. I'm so proud, I can feel the colors sewn into my skin growing brighter; the red, the green, the turquoise, they're turning rich and vibrant, and I can sense them pulsing all over my body in a kaleidoscopic frenzy, arranging themselves in new formations, bleeding into one another in strange, frightening equations.

I'm about to thank the Trouts for the news, but just then Gert finds the "kick me" sign crazy glued to her fanny.

"You're dead meat, Deluth!" she screams. Gert lunges for her sister, but winds up spinning them both in a circle.

They're twirling around like two halves of a propeller, and Gert shoots me an apologetic look and says, "Sometimes I'm embarrassed to tell people we're related." I can see that they're busy, so I blow them a kiss and sneak back to Bessie's hotel room, drunk with hope.

Back at the room, I decide to call Castorelli and let him have it once and for all. I dial the freak show, expecting him to answer, but instead I get Pete and I slap my forehead in frustration. I've always hated Pete. He thinks he's so great because he can hammer house nails up his nostrils all the way, while whistling old, honky-tonk tunes, but in reality, he's just an asshole. Plus he's got this permanent cow-lick, not just like a small tuft of hair out of place, it actually looks like a cow snuck up on him, and slurped at the back of his head. Go to a party with him, and you'll be mingling and enjoying yourself when all of a sudden you hear this "clink-clink," "clink-clink," and what do you know, all eyes will be on Pete, whistling "Dixie," with these iron spokes in his nose. Meanwhile, his hair is giving you a "thumbs up" sign and any chance you had of being the life of the party is in the crapper for sure.

"Traitor," he hisses at me through the receiver.

"I didn't call to talk to the likes of you, Pete. Give me Castorelli."

"He isn't here," Pete says, and then I hear him rustling around in some kind of tool box.

"Where is he?" I ask.

"He's with Clatz. The two of them are on their way to that room you rented for Bessie right now. They're hot on her trail so you might as well raise the white flag."

"Never," I say. But now I'm thinking about my Bessie. If she finds out that they're really after her, maybe she'll come running back to me. With those two tracking her, she probably turned on her heel, and is on her way down the hall at this very moment.

"Hey, guess what," Pete says, "I've moved up to railroad stakes. Listen to this."

He's hammering up a storm and doing something vaguely musical, but just then there's a knock at the door. *Bessie!* I think, and I hang up on Pete and rush to the door. I swing it open and see a hunchback in a plaid suit standing there with a large steel suitcase. He stares up at me for a moment, and then he reaches into his breast pocket and pulls out a handful of dirt, which he tosses onto the carpet. Then he pulls up his pant leg to reveal a shiny white cleat on one foot, which he uses to grind the dirt into the rug. "What are you going to do about that?" he asks.

"I'll show you what you're going to do about that!" he says

and pushes past me into the room. He throws the suitcase on to the water bed, undoes the heavy clasps with two snaps that sound like small necks being broken, and from the parts inside, begins assembling a vacuum. "The model four is the most powerful unit to date," he says and fits a long nozzle to a cylindrical chrome canister. "There's no stain in existence that can withstand the steam jets of this purchase." He finishes putting the vacuum together, and it stands tall and immaculate like an giant chess piece in the middle of the carpet.

"Watch this," the hunchback says, and flicks the switch at the machine's back. Sure enough, it roars to life, and the tubes braided along its handle fill with scalding water. The hunchback steps on to the hood, and rides it over the dirty patch in the rug like a child on a carousel pony. I watch, amazed as the dark spot vanishes beneath the vacuum's blast. He sees that I'm impressed and says, "Truly, love, there's no stain so deep that it can't be removed."

I'm about to say something to this man, but just then the door crashes inward and there's Clatz in the threshold, his eyes filmy and iridescent like the insides of twin oyster shells. He sniffs the air for me. I try to tell the hunchback to run, but he's quoting figures, and before I know it, Clatz is on him like white on rice, stenciling terrible things all over him that would make a bathroom wall blush. I race over and tug at Clatz, but he knocks me backwards against the bed so hard that the mattress pops. Water shoots out and floods the place. As soon as it hits Clatz's chair, the motor explodes in a sparkling series of bursts and wheezes, and suddenly he's out of control, hydroplaning around the loop of the room like a harnessed comet. "Me money!" he cries, but he's speeding up now, and the centrifugal force is causing a whirlpool, so I hand the hunchback some bills, and tuck the vacuum beneath my arm and dive through the window. The wind from inside shoves at my back, and I bounce off the fire escape, and land on the street.

When I look up, I see Castorelli leering over me like a carnivorous plant. Behind him I find my Bessie, tied at the wrists and ankles inside a large cage on spidery wagon wheels. Mechanical animal heads fixed to the top of the cart move up and down to organ grinder's music: giraffes, zebras, gazelles, bobbing and bobbing as though in a perpetual attempt at agreement. Castorelli is done up just like I remember him, velvet to the nines, the spiral spinning away at the base of his top hat.

"You can't win," he says and snaps his fingers. At once Pete drops into Bessie's cage from a compartment in the roof. He grabs her, takes an electric razor from his pocket, and holds it close to her beard.

"No!" I scream. "Leave her alone! She's got nothing to do with this."

"Come back to the show or he'll do it," Castorelli sneers. "He'll shave her clean."

Pete snorts a laugh and clicks on the razor. It buzzes away, inches from her beard.

"This is between you and me, Castorelli," I say. "Leave her out of it."

Castorelli narrows his eyes. "It's over, you've lost. There's nothing for you to do but return to the show. Not that it's ever been otherwise."

A molten anger rises in my throat. "I can do other things!" I yell, my fists clenched. "I teach people about the issues!"

He grins and the ends of his mustache curl like a second smile. "Don't you see?" he says. "Thanks to me, when you go out in public you are always already the issue at hand."

I open my mouth to retort, but the design on his hat starts to spin and I'm lulled to silence.

"You are pure entertainment," he says. "Your body is delightfully spectacular, and though the ones who pay you to talk and talk and talk until your tongue dries up like a pepper might pretend that they've brought you to this or that room to discuss the issues, they are, in truth, mere copies of me. And poor ones at that."

I try to say something, to tell him that this is a far throw from true, but his voice is so soothing, it envelops me like a mist. And the spiral pinned to the sash on his hat is spinning away like a miniature cyclone. I feel myself growing so tired suddenly, so drowsy, weakening at the joints. I look through the haze of my dizziness at Bessie, struggling against Pete's grasp, and I try to apologize to her but the words won't come. I know that I'm being sucked in then, that soon, my knees will buckle and my body will fall against the concrete with a thud, and I'll lie there like a boneless chicken.

Suddenly there's a horrible shriek from above. With my last bit of strength, I glance over my shoulder and see Clatz crashing through the hotel window. Glass showers us, and then he's soaring through the air in his wheelchair, eyes wide open and pearled, his hair flowing behind him like the ivory flame of a blowtorch. The chair looks like a war zone, all pops and electric flashes, and as it passes over my head it leaves behind a bow of blue smoke.

The chair slams into Castorelli, and in one great motion, Clatz snatches him up and unzips his velvet tuxedo. "Me loot!" he cries and then goes to work, stenciling away like no tomorrow. I watch them careen down a long avenue, Clatz stabbing tattoos along the dotted line of Castorelli's back, and then I hurry over to my Bessie.

Pete has already taken the steel bolts out of the cage and pounded them up his nose, so really it's no trouble getting Bessie out of there.

"Oh my love!" she says, rubbing her beard all over me. "I'll never leave you again. I'll find work regarding the issues on this coast."

I pull her to me and say, "Let's go finance a home."

"Wait," she says, and pulls one of the spikes from Pete's nose. She puts my hand on it and then, carefully, together we cut a small heart into my chest, over the fading designs left by Clatz. "Bessie and Me," we write inside the outline, and all at once I feel a surge of love high and mighty as a tsunami. Bessie gives the bolt back to Pete and grips my wrist. "Now, get to your lecture!" she says.

My appointment at the Crystal Room comes back to me. I make to leave, but then remember Castorelli's words and hesitate.

"Go!" Bessie cries. "Onward, press onward and educate!"

"You think they've rescheduled?" I ask.

"Get packing, superstar," she says.

I kiss her long and hard and switch on the vacuum. The bag fills up like a sail. With tears in my eyes, I step on to the hood and wave good-bye before setting off, leaving in my wake a clean, wet line.

And so now I'm here. I've made it. I've arrived. And we can finally get down to business, you and I, and start talking about the issues.

Donna Svatik
UNIVERSITY OF WASHINGTON

Pediatrics

Frank and I have been rearranging our one-bedroom apartment. *See, now,* we'll tell our visitors, *look how nice it is to have the living room couch right by the stove.* Now I can watch t.v. while I do the dishes, and all of the guests can sit on the sofa and watch me or watch t.v. or just smoke cigarettes.

It took us a while to get the breakfast table to fit through the kitchen doorway and into the living room, which we redesigned to be a place for projects and crafts and my sewing machine. Although I'm not manic, not high, not bi-polar—I'm still pattering around the house. I have no excuse for staying up this late, redecorating and lifting refrigerators, and talking to Frank loud over the classical station.

I'm still awake. Frank has been hypo-manic for at least two weeks. He curbs this energy with four a.m. projects, and I do the directing. I reshape our tiny rooms into new walkways, and sneeze up the dust that I unsettle.

Frank has heavy arms and a sweet-set face. When he walks by himself, people say that he must be in a hurry, or else angry. Something about the way he walks will smear that face when you see him. He goes so fast you can't focus. He always has his head forward and strides past anyone—even if you're his good best friend—without tipping his chin or shaking a wrist hello.

It would be strange for you to see him, halfway galloping along in black knickers, knee socks and a white blouse. You'd wonder where did that nice boy go, how come his eyes drop—like the part of Frank you met indoors sank into his waist once he started walking. You'd think that a good-looking boy like that would smile at lamps, or even hydrants. You'd think that he'd be a real waver. A real hand in the air.

Instead, there he is, chasing down blocks. He'll hum quieter than you can hear, along to the whirr of everything else that clicks through his mind. If you could put your ear up to his neck just then, maybe you'd hear a few notes of him singing inside himself.

When I see Frank outside of the house, stomping down concrete like a worn-out flute, I chase him down. "Hi, sweetie," I say as I slip my hand through his arm and feel the pull as he crawls up to the top of his spine. Frank will climb out of his very own eyes. That's when we match up like two beans from the very same can. If Frank smiles, I'll smile right back to him. I'll be the lake he can walk around, and look into. Anyway he bends to see me, I'll just be Frank. Smiling back over and over again.

I'd kiss him on the cheek more than I do, but I wouldn't want to smudge him. I'd give him more hugs, but I know he doesn't like being wrapped up all the time. So I make dinner, or start reorganizing the bathroom shelves.

Frank could tell that I was sick before I could. While we're searching for the Windex under the bathroom sink, he notices that I've arranged all of the shampoo bottles like they were a window display for a store-front. I took a toothbrush and scrubbed the faucet handles on the sink until I could see my nose big in their reflection, and then I'd pull my head back further until my eyes bobbed up on the faucet, two black creases under my eyebrows. I like looking at myself that way.

When he's manic he'll start reading books, and highlighting them, and taking notes in a white notebook that nobody's allowed to look at. The latest book was *Healthy Habits* (something my aunt sent to me) and Frank took forty-three pages of notes about vitamins, eating, symptoms of weakness.

He doesn't tell me. He doesn't let me know that I'm not right, because Frank isn't one to voice his observations. Sometimes he'll finish my sentences for me, but mostly I think he starts them. Frank gets an idea and that's where I go, talking and yapping like a puppy by an ice cream truck, chasing his idea around like my tail with some loud jingling backdrop.

The apartment is completely reorganized and he finds me, still intact, but crouching low on the floor of the bathroom with a scrub brush in one shaky hand.

"Why are you all curled up like this?" Frank's asking.

"I'm just trying to figure out what I'm supposed to do—"

"—Now that you've done everything?"

"Uh-huh." I am tilting back and forth on my feet. He hands the Yellow Pages over and says, "It's time someone looks at your head."

Here's my morning, sun finally up and all the floors dry. Frank and I. Not sleeping. The phone somewhere between us on the breakfast table. There's something so terrible about finding yourself out. Suddenly your fingers are unable to separate the thin pages of the phone book and you start calling numbers under Psychiatry whenever you see a woman's name. I spin my finger around the Yellow Pages. After calling around a few places I finally land on Betsy, a therapist with room for me tomorrow afternoon, her secretary says. "Betsy is a very friendly, very easy person to talk to. You should have no problem talking with her. She's very nice."

The secretary forgot to give me directions to the clinic. I call back and talk to some other secretary. This one's a guy. He's got all of the highways figured out clear. He knows where to stop, where to merge and when to swerve into the parking garage. He's friendly, so I'm nice right back, saying "please," and words like that. I write everything down.

"Do you get teary sometimes?" he asks, and instantly I am in tears.

"Sometimes, yes," I say and he says, "That's okay, I don't mean to make you teary right now," and I say, "It's not your fault," and he's telling me other information about Betsy. I don't remember what he says even as he says it.

"—And remember to bring three dollars in quarters for parking," he says. Then it just seems like the phone closes down on itself. I pull on a sweater and make Spaghetti-O's in the pink kitchen, in my socks. The kitchen is pink because I wanted it to look like Pepto-Bismol. I wanted it to look like a thousand bridesmaids had thrown up rose-coloured wedding cake.

Frank says the goddamn paint has to go. I watch him fly back and forth through the kitchen, feeling the pink slide under his skin. Frank doesn't look so good in those semi-gloss, Dutch Boy, pink shock eyes. I can tell he's having problems with his ups and downs, like his head won't make up its mind in that kitchen. He's on pause.

I do good, though. I say, "We'll find a nice blue and paint it over."

"This weekend?"

"Oh, yes."

At this point, Frank nods vigorously, and I know that he knows that I know. We are laughing, making plans for our new shades of blue.

Frank is here, stuck in my head on the day I first go to see Betsy. He helps me search the apartment for quarters. We come up with two dollars and fifty cents. I take a dollar downstairs to the fruity neighbors and they give me some quarters. Then I'm off, keys in hand, making my way to the parking lot.

Someone must have stuffed Kleenex in my head because I feel like the tires are off the ground. Emergency brake hills and cars all piled up around me. I turn up the radio louder, Brazil coming across in violin jazz, and try to drown the surroundings.

I sing "Sadness" with my clarinet tongue. The Juniper exit comes almost too fast, heading south, where the sun bounces on skyscrapers, and the windows all reflect out. Astrud Gilberto sings the Portugese song, "Tristeza." I am not really singing, but I hum alongside her. I am driving also. I am shifting and using the signal.

The parking garage is right there, just like the boy secretary said. I make an easy turn in, and Astrud just about finishes off her song. My seat belt is off and the door light flashes open. Now look, those quarters have to fit into space thirty-four, and I can't push them in too fast 'cause then they'd get stuck. The man in the garage booth giving me smiles while I lose all of those sad quarters down the slot. They must've listened to "Tristeza" too, through my pocket.

Into the building and *Can you find the elevator? Psychiatric? That's floor ten, you'll find it just fine.* Good. Good.

See me there? I am the doe by the elevator rail wondering how many buttons everyone else will push. Wondering how the air will taste on floor ten.

You should know, I'm practically twenty-three years old. You should find this strange because the secretary at the front desk sends me to wait in the Pediatric-Psychiatry lobby. The seats are shaped like crayons, and the receptionist watches everybody like she was your baby-sitter.

Now, you'd think I'd get mad about this or cry maybe, since people who are falling apart do stuff like that in lobbies. Maybe I'll say, "I don't want to sit in those dumb, baby-ass chairs," and turn myself right back out the door. But I'm trying. I'm trying to fit my arms into the Periwinkle Blue chair. I'll let this go. I'll flip through this fine edition of *Ranger Rick,* and I'll smile until Betsy comes to find me.

Nobody else is yelling in the office. They are all quiet behind their doors. I won't make a peep.

I'm sunk into blue with my knees jutting towards my chin. The way-too-small chairs make my legs fit wrong. The receptionist answers the phone, and smiles at her computer screen, adjusting dates and rearranging appointments. She seems very competent at what she is doing. Clicking keys and clearing the desk with her elbows to reach—she doesn't seem to have any problems there, oh no.

Also, she can wear eyeliner and not worry about losing it in a public rest room, face cracked and dripping all over the sink. She wouldn't paw at her eyes on escalators at the mall and smudge it all away. She has her eyes set right there for display, No Crying Please, it'll ruin her make-up. Her face staying dry like a new paper boat.

Now there's a burgundy and teal green pattern all over the arms of a sweater that walks through the lobby with a smiling lady face. "Hi, Margaret!" the sweater and the lady inside say to my receptionist. "How are you?" Margaret gives the lady a thin smile.

"Oh, all right. Dan and I are still working with the mortgage brokers and Angie still has whooping cough, and I cut one of the dog's toenails too short this morning and it was bleeding—" Margaret is really letting it all go, but the undersized lady in her oversized sweater just smiles and makes little "uh-huh" sounds as she looks for a file or something.

I think how strange it is that Margaret had a morning. That she was anywhere else but at this desk, making me wait, all folded up here, for Betsy. Now I hear my name.

Betsy behind me, in a denim skirt and sequined blue t-shirt, holding out her arms to me, and calling my name just to check which one I am, out of all those empty scats. I look up to her, and toss the *Ranger* onto the waiting room table. I give her my best teeth. A smile that fits so far across my face you'd think I was doing just fine, wouldn't you? So I stare at her, grinning like an open can.

"It's so great to see you!" Betsy chirps, and suddenly this small woman is hugging me, like we've met a hundred times before. I am a little confused here, wondering if maybe Betsy is a little confused too, only she doesn't seem aware of that. The Yellow Pages didn't say anything about how nice ladies would embrace you upon entrance to therapy.

I follow Betsy into her office. She has a view that doesn't look anywhere but at the windows of the matching tower across the way. There is a desk, two chairs and a round coffee table. One chair faces a bookcase and the other chair faces the window. How ordinary this office is. No special blue paint to relax me. Just three strategically placed Kleenex boxes so I can cry if I want to, no matter where I choose to sit.

I sit in the chair that faces the bookcase and Betsy tucks herself into her desk while she skims its surface with her glasses bent low, looking for my file. "When was the last time you came in?" Betsy asks me, eyes finally landing on the envelope with my name written at the edge.

"This is my first time," I explain and she turns reddish beige, a shade of embarrassment that highlights the yards of denim which flow from her hips. "Oh, I'm so sorry!" says Betsy, taking off her glasses and wiping her eyes. "I'm still getting over a twenty-four hour flu I caught this weekend."

I'm okay with this, this so-far glitch that the crayon chairs started and Betsy picked up with her walk to come find me. I jump right in anyhow, to spill myself at Betsy.

Betsy and I talk back and forth. Summarize my family, my job. I tell her about my wonderful friend Frank, my homosexual soul, paint her a good couple of postcards (me and Frank baking muffins together, me and Frank doing arts and crafts on a Sunday) and wipe my hands across the lap of my slacks.

Half of me describes this, smiling to Betsy with my hands in my lap, another piece of me looks at the window. *When Betsy drives by on the highway, does she search the outside of this building to find her window? Has she ever tried? Does she look for the tip of the geranium peeking out from the flower pot on her windowsill? I won't ask.* Betsy listens, smiling at me with her hands in her lap. She wants to hear about who I've had sex with and whether I've got any junky tattoos. She wants to know if I'm a drinker. She takes notes so I can't see them.

The rest of our time should be dedicated to talking about the way I look. Betsy is sure of this. "Why do you think," she asks "that you make yourself look, well, what most people might call different?"

"How do you mean?" I ask. Although I am bending very sweetly for her, going along with these questions, she has to do more than cough up vague whys in order to steer conversation. I've decided on that.

"When I look at you, with your sweater full of patches and extra stitches, I can't help feeling that you've set out to make yourself look different. It's almost as if you're trying to appear poor," Betsy asserts now, sure that I'll respond somehow. Sure that I'll find that I'm hurt and angry about something concrete. I tell Betsy the story of my sweater, about how my mother donated it to The Green Window Thrift Store years ago and then I bought it back, purely by accident, for a dollar fifty. I think that's a remarkable enough reason to wear a sweater until it needs more stitches. I can put this sweater on and almost feel like my mother at nineteen. I can sip glass bottles of Coca-Cola and sing her old favorites in my head.

"There's something else, though. . ." Betsy starts with a look on her face as she searches the room for whatever that something else may be. Her search ends by accident when her gaze is snagged by the clock. "Tell you what,"—she is wrapping now, wrapping me up so I'll float softly to the parking garage in my worn-out sweater—"set up another appointment with me for a week from now, and we'll talk about a plan to see one another on a regular basis."

I thank Betsy for her time, careful to slip out the door before she can get another hug in edgewise, and make my way towards the receptionist desk. I tell Margaret "I'd like to arrange—"

"—An appointment?" Margaret fills in the blanks. "Who are you seeing, again?" Margaret asks me.

Turns out Betsy doesn't have any appointments next week. She doesn't have any in two weeks, either. *How'd they get me in to see her so fast, then?* My appointment card says I'll see Betsy next month.

There are new things to organize. I'll have to buy a change purse now. I should probably start saving quarters, put them all in there so I've got enough for my next day with Betsy.

At home the door's closed and dead bolted. None of the kitchen lights are on and Frank has moved the t.v. I walk to the bedroom and see him through the doorway, filing his nails in bed, watching something on the Discovery Channel about tigers.

"How was your appointment?" Frank asks me. Sometimes he's really good at remembering to ask me about things like that right away. I tell him it went so-so but he says, "You know, that's how it usually is, you have to give it time." I go on about it, the windows and my sweater, but he has stopped hearing me. Frank's had more doctors, therapists and psychiatrists than anyone I've met. Frank is good at remembering, but I am better at listening. I join him watching tigers and we both sleep. All through the night like old babies.

Me and three weeks until my appointment. I skip through them the way I do through everything, with my feet hanging off at the ankles. I don't mind if I can't find the floor. Frank and I've only taken to daytime mania now and I've been scrubbing up all of the lint stuck in the edges of our floor vents. I dust every single piece of Frank's tea cup collection and arrange them from widest to slim, and by color. I skate the hours into rings, only piling up on the floor a few times.

I'll wear something good and ordinary to Betsy's next time. Frank helps me out. We dig though my closet to find whatever has the least stitches. I shouldn't wear the old sweater. Wouldn't want to distract her.

This time I'm easier with the garage, my quarters held together in the green change purse Frank found under a couch. Bang, bang, bang. I choke the slot. Quarters flying through like smoke out of my nose. Three dollars and the man who smiles isn't even there.

Floor ten again, please. I make it there, not noticing anything about the elevator this time. I'm too busy adjusting my jacket. Checking my sleeves for discoloration. Shaking the poor out.

I head straight for Pediatrics. Otherwise, what if Betsy can't find me? I'd like to see her soon, because my head's too full with all the things I've remembered to tell her over the past weeks. I've decided already to talk about Frank a lot more. Frank is an easy metaphor. I always feel the same as Frank. He fits in with everything else.

Margaret doesn't recognize me. I check in like I've never been in that lobby before. As if I'm confused how to do it, almost. She directs me to the crayon seats.

I don't make it there because Betsy is sliding down the hallway, file in hand, looking for me. "Ah, there you are!" she says. She doesn't hug me but she touches my arm, as if to steer me blind into her office. "How have you been?" she asks.

Why, I wonder, *would you ever ask a mental patient how they were before you got to the office and the door was shut? Is it so they can say "Oh, fine, fine—" and feel like an ass in front of Margaret and anyone else waiting. Everybody knows you're not fine.*

Inside, I start off with a good breath about being glad to have finally reached my appointment. "Oh, sorry about that," Betsy says "I should've warned you that there can be scheduling problems."

"Well, now I know," I say.

We are talking about my silly little life. You probably wonder, oh yes, what is her job? Who are her other friends? Where are her parents? Maybe you are jealous if I don't tell, if this conversation is just me and Betsy. Well, here she is talking and here I am talking and you are wondering, why can't I see? It's nothing really, just me and Betsy bantering back and forth about how I am basically a nice person and so why do I have these troubles anyhow? And then I say "I was just asking Frank the same question all week and we were trying to figure it out, what it was, and we didn't know—"

I start to talk about the blues we've been looking at for new kitchen paint, about how Frank and I get sick together, how we feel happy and sad at the same moments, and about how we make dried-flower bookmarks sometimes.

"Now, tell me," Betsy starts, "have you slept with him yet?"

Surely this could not be happening. Betsy took notes last time. She knows Frank's gay. Surely. I won't give her all the cake on one clean fork. Let her sift through her notes. I'll ignore that little slip.

"Frank is very intelligent, he says I'm obsessive-compulsive, well, so is he, but yes, I think I am." Why do I have to figure it out and guess at it for myself, can't she just tell by looking at me? What does she listen for?

Betsy might be hissing. I don't know what that sound is out of her mouth. She's mad that I skipped her, "Well, we'll look into that. But I want to know, are you two sexually involved?"

"Oh, sure," I say, now joking with her "but we never have sex." I am making no sense. If she's allowed to forget who Frank is, I can forget what sex is, too. I can forget her name and where the Kleenex boxes are and how many minutes there are left. I can forget anything, and Betsy can too. Betsy thinks I've really gone off the chair, that I've got carpeting stuck in my ears. I can't hear.

"There are some issues here that you're avoiding, and I'd like you to think about that. We'll move on, and talk about something else, and then I want you to get back to my question," Betsy asserts.

The rest of the time we talk about clothes. And my hair. I try to answer her questions, but can't finish my own thoughts. By the time I remember where my jacket is from, and how I liked the doorway of the shop where I found it, I've forgotten Betsy's original question. The doorway was shaped like an oval at the top, with a curlicue handle. It was painted green and lighter green, chipping along the edges.

And then our time is up. "Do you have another appointment set up?" Betsy asks me, as I reach for my purse and stand up. She is smiling very hard at me.

This is where my mind starts clicking. Look at this Betsy with her sad, little, mouse-brown hair and her dry blue eyes, smiling at me and making her own special difference in the world. Look at this silly woman who can't remember one patient from the next.

If I'm looking for a shampoo bottle, and I need to know which one is for dry to oily, and I'm wondering where did I put that shampoo bottle, I know that I will find it in its carefully arranged place among the products in the bathroom. If Betsy has a patient and she needs to remember, where was that patient the last time I left him? Truly, Betsy will not remember, she has no organization. She is underly-obsessive compulsive, and this I realize just by looking at her.

"Next week," I say. "Next week I have an appointment." I give her a wink and a smash-up hug. My eyes and my nose and my new bright sweater all saying *I just love you*! to Betsy, almost. She seems touched. I don't want her to ever know how silly I know she is, to forget and keep smiling is fine for Betsy. She'd feel hurt otherwise, you see.

Out the door. Down the hall. Me gliding, skipping under my walk, past Margaret and her keyboard fingernails. I go too fast, grabbing for the door *Out*, swinging my shoulder bag around corners.

"Oh, Miss! You dropped something—" Margaret's voice follows me. She laughs into the phone as she stands up to look over the desk. Probably her sister or Dan on the phone.

The green change purse. The one for the quarters. It's empty. Fell out of my bag. I leave it behind. It'll find a new couch to get lost under, probably, and Frank will find it again in a strange circumstance. *How funny*, we'll say, *How funny you found my old Betsy purse.* And then we'll toss it out the window.

Nobody else is in the elevator and it takes me down all ten floors without stopping. I get down to the garage, and unlock the car door. It's three o'clock in the afternoon and Frank should be home, sewing knickers or playing with the hot glue gun.

I will organize everything but this time not because I am afraid. I will do it for the sheer beauty of organization, and I will love every minute.

Beep beep! I give the garage attendant a good smile. I roll out of the parking garage, and he's waving, waving to me until I'm all the way gone.

Paul Graham
ST. LAWRENCE UNIVERSITY

Strength

That afternoon William's brother, Marty, showed up uninvited in an old Ford pickup that grumbled like a tank. The bed of the truck was loaded down with what looked like ten thousand pounds of York-brand barbells, dumbbells and a bench. When Marty stepped out of the cab, it looked to William like he was carrying ten thousand pounds too—of solid muscle. The last time William had seen his brother was Christmas when Marty had the same barrel-chested build, but was flabbier. Marty was living at home then and driving their parents nuts because he'd dropped out of college but refused to move from the t.v. Now, he was ripped. He looked confident and strong, like a conqueror.

"Marty," William said with a mixture of surprise and annoyance in his voice. He felt sure that Marty had come to check on him, since, much like his ex-girlfriend, William had gone AWOL as soon as things got rough.

"Willy," Marty said as he came up the walkway. He was carrying himself like all big men, with that strange combination of daintiness and pride, as if he feared accidently destroying something with his huge upper body but was satisfied to know that it could indeed be done. His chest and arms seemed ready to explode out of his plain white t-shirt and his skin was a rich copper color. He had peroxided and spiked his hair. As he drew closer, William also noticed that his arms and legs were curiously absent of hair. Marty had always been a hairy guy. "How's it going, man?" he asked. Then he smiled, and William thought that even his teeth looked whiter.

"Not bad, not bad," William said, because he had nothing else to say. He stuffed his hands into his pockets and took refuge in the fact that he didn't have to say anything to Marty. It wasn't expected. It had been forever since they'd really had a conversation, and growing up they never were close. William had been the over-achiever, unintentionally grounding Marty into the turf by being president of his class, valedictorian, going off to Princeton, the whole bit. Marty, for his part, had been well-known by the county police. It was he who shot the water tower behind the high school with a twelve-gauge one November night, giving them a week off; and it was he who was pulled over for drag racing down the long straight strip of county highway in front of the school. Once, when they were very young, William had convinced Marty that he was adopted. He'd done it only to be cruel, but growing up he often thought that it didn't seem totally impossible.

"What brings you down here?"

"Passing through," Marty said. "On my way to Virginia."

William didn't ask him why. He was too intrigued and troubled by his brother's display of purpose. Purpose was something he couldn't remember Marty ever having. He couldn't decide whether the confidence came from Marty's massive strength and was nothing more than a puffed-up chest, or if something real was going on. "Come inside for a beer," he offered.

Marty sat down awkwardly at the kitchen table. "So," he said, "I'm trying to become one of the World's Strongest Men."

"Like those brutes on ESPN?"

"Yeah. I've even changed my name. What do you think of Mar-*ten* Hammerskjold?"

William shook his head. The fool. "What the hell is that supposed to be, Finnish? Swedish?"

"Something like that." Marty made a waving gesture with his hand and took a sip of his beer. He had never cared that much about geography or anything else academic, for that matter. William could imagine him taking chunks of names from the weight lifters on t.v., and piecing them together until he came up with something that looked and sounded foreign, powerful, and original. Marty was like that—whatever worked.

"It's all show business, of course," Marty continued, leaning back in his chair; it creaked with strain. "Kind of like the Terminator haircut. I don't think it's me, but it works."

"You're competing?"

"And winning money. Got some rope? Want to see me pull my truck up the driveway *sitting down*?" He flexed the muscles in his forearms then—big, beefy muscles all tied up with bulging veins. William tried not to look and placed his own arms under the table on his lap. Pale, thin-boned, long-muscled like a ballet dancer, and endowed with the metabolism of a thirteen-year-old boy, he had never been able to break 155 or do more than twenty push-ups at once. But lately he'd gotten even thinner. He hadn't eaten much since Veronica left; and since he dropped out of his graduate program, he'd stopped playing squash in the athletic center. What little physical countenance he had, had disintegrated. He felt especially weak in Marty's presence. And mean.

"You're just a carnival sideshow until you're on ESPN," he said.

Marty either didn't hear the insult, or didn't care. "You have to pay your dues. You have to start local, then go regional." He smiled. "Someday I'll meet that Lars Magnusson on t.v. And I'll beat him. It's a process. Kind of like college, right?"

It surprised William that Marty would willingly mention college. A few months ago, when it became clear that it would take him twenty years to finish college, if ever, Marty had withdrawn and returned home. He jumped from plan to plan: from flying Sea Kings for the Coast Guard to fixing Mercedes at the dealership in town, never giving any of them enough attention to allow himself an honest chance at succeeding. There had been grim predictions from their parents about how his life would play out: janitor, road crew worker, nothing at all. William had agreed. Marty, apparently, had not. It was pretty clear that he was doing all right for himself. Better than all right. He had found a way to succeed by using his body, not his head, and he was proud of it. He was beaming. William felt an uncomfortable mixture of envy and happiness for his brother.

"Well, you look good," he said, hoping that Marty would take it as a sign to drain his beer and leave. "I'm happy for you, Marty."

"Thanks," Marty said. He sat forward in the chair and swirled his beer in the bottle. It was still about half full. "So. How about yourself?"

"Fine," William said. Then he sat silent for a few moments. He grabbed the salt shaker on the table, poured some out onto the table, and tried to do the trick of balancing the shaker on its edge. Every time it tipped and fell, spilling more salt onto the table. "Fine," he repeated without looking up. He thought of stupid, insignificant things they could talk about until Marty finished his beer and left: baseball, his plans to sell his car, the bands that were coming to town. He sat quiet for too long though, making it impossible to skillfully change the topic.

"Still in grad school?"

"All the time."

"Still the physicist?"

"Working on it."

"You must be close to done."

"Getting there."

"Still thinking about working for NASA?"

William just nodded.

"NASA. Wow. You know, Willy, I've always been proud of you. I'll bet you always thought I was jealous, since I was such a bad kid growing up and a screw-off in college, but now I can admit that I never once hated you for it. You always worked hard for what you got, were always on the ball. Sharp up here. Had all your mental ducks in a row. And if you bust out into this world making two hundred grand a year because you're as famous as Einstein for putting men on Mars and shit, well, all I can do is sit back and smile and say to my friends, 'Hey, man, that's my brother talking to Barbara Walters on the t.v.' That, and maybe hope you give me a ride in your Porsche sometime. Willy? You feeling all right, buddy?"

William had slumped back in his chair. He sick. He wanted to throw Marty out of the house, but he couldn't do that, not on his own, not without a catapult. "I'm fine," he said. "Getting over a little stomach virus. And I think this beer is skunked."

"Skunked? Ha! It's better than what I drink. You're a lightweight and you don't want to admit it, Willy. That's okay. You don't have to talk about it. Willy?"

He was staring off at the shadows in the other room, thinking about what he must not let come to light: his ex-girlfriend, Veronica. Marty didn't know about her. Nobody in his family knew about her, about how he had first gotten her pregnant, and then a few nights later in a bar with some friends gotten tanked and proposed to her in front of the whole dining room on a dare. Veronica had been sober, but it was too loud for her to hear the dare that came before the proposal. The next morning, when she woke up and saw another girl's ruby ring still on her finger—one of their friends had loaned it to William for the sake of authenticity—she thought it was for real. When William tried to explain that marriage and kids were the furthest things from his mind, Veronica took off. Poof. Gone. She was missing for ten days. The police came to his apartment and questioned him. The local newspapers made him famous. He was a suspect in her disappearance until she came back to visit the police, and told them everything. Then she vanished again. The people in the physics department where they had met and worked together, and the people in the neighborhood where they had lived together, however, weren't convinced. William knew what they were thinking: that there were all kinds of killers out there who can lie like it's their job, set up scams, bury bones in the backyard beneath the marigolds. People got suspicious with him, nasty. He withdrew from his master's program and picked up work pulling espresso at a pretentious coffee bar in the next town over, while he tried to get his head straight, which was turning out to be harder than he'd thought.

In his moment of greatest weakness, William had sought the counsel of a minister from a local reformed Baptist church where he dropped in every Easter. The minister seemed slightly put off by his audacity to call him with such a request, but he must have recognized his duty to all of God's people, even the hopeless ones. He invited William into his parish after last week's Sunday service. William did not go to the service; he showed up during the coffee-and-crumb-cake social afterwards, and scanned the room carefully for compliments about the sermon that he could repeat if asked. The minister was a prim man who sat with his legs crossed tightly, and talked like an actor who had played the part of Dimmesdale in a movie version of *The Scarlet Letter* that William had been forced to suffer through as an undergrad. William talked about Marty for half an hour. He told the minister about how Marty was never really good at anything, how he'd almost been arrested twice, been suspended from high school countless times, and had most recently bombed out of college and returned home to watch daytime t.v. and eat Ring-Dings. Then he talked about himself for half an hour, telling the minister about his time at Princeton, and his research at Penn State, and the recruiter from NASA. He did not mention the proposal or the pregnancy. "Now I'm working in a coffee bar for five bucks an hour, plus tips," William explained. "I used to work with propulsion. *Propulsion.* I'm worried that I'm turning into my brother." He knew that by leaving out the most critical parts of the story he was making no sense, but he sat back anyway, waiting for the minister to say whatever soothing things ministers said.

"Judge not, lest ye be judged," the minister quoted with a shrug.

William had left in a hurry. Since then he'd ventured out of his house only to go to work, avoiding contact with people. And he'd been getting by, until Marty, of all people, showed up out of nowhere, ten times bigger than he used to be, and talking with a candor and admiration that William had never known him to have. God was punishing him, he was sure of it.

"Hey, man," Marty was saying now. "You don't look so hot. Why don't you lie down for awhile?"

"Yes," William said.

"As in, on the couch."

"Sure." William looked at his brother and realized that if he passed out right here, Marty could pick him up and carry him to the couch. Carry. Not drag. William couldn't think of one man he knew of whom he could lift. Veronica often asked to be carried from the couch to the bedroom, and he'd managed it, but always just barely, reaching the bedroom just as his muscles were about to give out and his heart was pounding in his chest. He stood up and walked into the living room.

"There you go," Marty said. "Mind if I hang around for a while? Mind if I stay the night? The headlights in my truck don't work too good, so it's dangerous to drive at night."

"Stay as long as you like."

As he lay on the couch, William had to struggle to keep from blurting it out. The kid. His kid. *His* kid that he hadn't wanted, but had created nonetheless. The way the shame and guilt of it weighed him down, *he* might as well have been carrying it, not Veronica, and it might as well have been a full-grown man as big as Marty. Veronica had left a message for him with the police, saying that she had taken care of things, and that she didn't want to hear from him ever again. What exactly was that supposed to mean, *taken care of things?* That she'd aborted the pregnancy, that she'd quickly found someone else to take his place, or that she was going to try to hack it herself? Whatever she meant, nothing could cut through his shame, his disgrace; it sat on his chest and shoulders like a thousand pounds.

He became aware of a steady clanging behind him which lasted for a few moments and then stopped briefly before resuming again. When he looked through the doorway he saw that Marty was bringing in his weights. On this trip he had two eighty-pound dumbbells, one in each hand.

"Don't want anyone to steal them, you know?" Marty said as he walked by. "You don't mind? I'll just put them in the back room."

William shook his head. His brother was carrying 160 pounds—more than he himself weighed. Unless, of course, you added in the ghost of his kid and possibly the ghost of Veronica, who'd once taken Prozac but stopped and might have checked out because of all of this. How much did a human life weigh? It defied measurement, even though he'd spent nearly six years learning how to weigh the intangible.

Marty made one more trip with the weights before he crashed down in the chair opposite the couch. "Feeling better?" he asked.

William nodded.

"Good. Then it's time to lift some steel."

"I still don't feel so hot."

"That's your body wimping out. Ask it, and it will always say it doesn't feel so hot." Marty stood up then, and William looked up at him. His brother loomed in the half-lit room, blotted out the light.

"I don't think so," he said. "I'm not that strong. I never was."

"We all have to start somewhere." Marty motioned for him to stand up. "A hundred pounds on the bench. Just give it a try."

William shrugged and stood up. It would be easier to lift weights than to speak. He followed Marty into the small bedroom in the back where he kept his computer and books from school. Marty had all his weights spread out on the floor in order according to weight; they ran from five pounds to one hundred. In the corner he had set up a collapsible bench like the ones William used to see in the athletic center. No wonder Marty was so huge, he owned his own private branch of Gold's.

"Watch me first," Marty said. He pulled off his t-shirt and put on another with the sleeves cut away. William watched him stretch, load the bar with two hundred pounds, and lay back on the bench, where he effortlessly rattled off ten presses.

"Shit," William said when he was done. He would kill himself if he tried to bench press two hundred pounds.

Marty was flushed and breathless. His arms and chest were swelled up and even bigger than they were before the workout. "Your turn."

William didn't move. He was thinking about something he'd heard in a high school gym class once—that muscle deteriorates at the rate of thirty percent a week once you stop working it. Was the same true, he wondered, of the rest of the body, the heart, the soul, the mind? Lately he'd felt like he'd been wasting away. "I need more than ten pounds of muscle, Marty," he said.

"C'mon."

"I don't think so."

"Come here and lay your candy ass *down*, chicken shit." Marty was smiling at him. It was a mischievous, boyish smile, one that immediately brought to mind pictures their mother kept in a collage of the days when they were very young, seven and ten, say. They were living in northern New Jersey on what had once been a thirty-acre farm, and the only friends they had were one another. He recalled a photo of the two of them with their arms around each other, smiling and dripping wet after fishing golf balls out of the nearby country club's pond. They used to sell those golf balls back to the golfers three-for-a-dollar and then use the money to stock a tree house with a battery-powered radio, flashlights, posters of Dwight Gooden and Darryl Strawberry, water pistols, and stashes of candy and Cherry Coke. In the summers they spent every clear night perched high above the ground, laying side by side and breathing in the smell of damp plywood as they silently listened to broadcasts of the 1986 miracles at Shea Stadium: the stellar pitching performances, the two-out, bottom-of-the-ninth game-winning bombs. When the games ended they turned the radio off and talked each other to sleep over the chugging of the cicadas. Someday they would play on the same pro baseball team, maybe the Mets. Marty would be the catcher, and William, a pitcher. The sports world would be stunned at how they communicated without signs; no index finger for a fastball, no two fingers for a curve. After years of playing together, William would simply know when Marty would call a fastball, a curve, or a slider, and down the batter would go. Looking back, William knew the exact moment when that ease about being together, that sameness between them, had begun to break down. He would like to think it happened when the Mets began to lose, but in truth it began when he entered junior high, and left Marty behind. But now William had the feeling that he and Marty once again stood on level ground, that things had come to a state of equilibrium.

"Marty," he said. "Things have been—"

His brother raised his hands to stop him and then gripped the bar. "I know, man. I know all about it."

Something flooded through William's body—either panic or relief, he couldn't tell which. "How?"

"A guy I know lives around here. He sent me a newspaper clipping." Marty looked down and shook his head. He was smiling. "What an asshole. We never got along."

"Did Mom and Dad—"

"Nobody knows. I don't even know that much. I don't want to. All I knew was that things were probably a mess down here, and judging by the way you look, I was right." Marty shook the bar. "I don't want to hear about any of it, man. That's not why I'm here. Now lift."

William wanted to search his brother's face, but Marty turned away and began checking the clamps that held the weights in place, a sign that they would not talk about this anymore. There was nothing to do but lay back on the bench and struggle with the weights while Marty spotted him, slowly counting upward from zero.

Dan Mancilla
WESTERN ILLINOIS UNIVERSITY

Vatos Locos

Paris fell somewhere beyond the EL tracks and before the Dog Star. Stretching out on the last row of the bus, as if he were riding the CTA instead of a Greyhound, Jimmy Shines calculated the distance in city blocks instead of miles. The city betrayed him and now Judas led on through suburbs to rural scenes. And without compass points like Tuesday *Novenas*, or the Lincoln Avenue bus, or Chano, Jimmy Shines was lost.

The Greyhound passed over crumbling superhighways, arteries spilling blood from wounds the same way red paint ran from Christ's hands on the statue at St. Al's. Outside, cornfields rolled by, rewinding Jimmy's mind like a hypnotist's swinging watch. He and Chano were ten again, running down rows of pews at church, racing to see who would collect the most song books, as if that could somehow swing the rusty gates of Heaven enough for one of them to slip through. Jimmy's mind returned to the bus, and biting his fingernails down past the soft pink underside, Jimmy Shines could feel something calcify inside himself.

Chano.

It was Chano's face that Jimmy Shines saw now, reflecting back to him in the tinted safety glass of the bus. It was a face that filled his mind with memories of home: an amalgamation of apartments, babies, plastic couch covers, and pork hoof stew. Through a stolen childhood that spanned most of grade school and part of high school, Chano shared a bedroom with Jimmy Shines. Chano was Jimmy's cousin by way of Mexico. Chano, *El Magnifico,* who could kill pigeons from twenty yards with a sling shot and jump the third rail of the EL tracks with his shoes tied.

Chano was the same age as Jimmy, but kids grew up faster in Mexico. *Cervezas* were stolen at a younger age, and *chicas* discovered sooner. These were all things that commanded Jimmy's respect. It seemed to be the same kind of respect that the Marys at Catholic school now had for Jimmy. He would walk his grandma to *Novena* on Tuesday afternoons where she would pray to find her extra set of dentures or for world peace while Jimmy sold Winstons and Salems and sometimes weed to the Catholic school boys who Chano always used to call "Marys."

A girl ran down the aisle of the bus with her arms outstretched, an airplane taxiing down a runway; like Chano, a gassed up plane without a real runway. The priests used to tell the boys that service to God was the highest sacrament, but forgot to tell them that God was a selective employer.

"MARYS," Jimmy wrote on the window of the bus, using the hot breath that spilled from his mouth like candy from a beaten *piñata.* He wrote the letters backwards so any Catholic schoolboys could see them. The highway was leading through a work zone, a conglomeration of asphalt, gravel, and tar. The road looked like crushed glass glued onto black construction paper, the same kind of paper Jimmy and Chano would make battle ships and nun's habits out of at catechism. They always called it *cataclysm.*

Jimmy tugged on a patchy sixteen-year-old beard that looked out of place on his twenty-four-year-old chin. Chano would laugh at the instructors at cataclysm. Jimmy's family didn't have enough money to send the boys to Catholic school, so they received the condensed version every Wednesday for eight years. In class, Chano would bet the white boy, lay-person teacher that he got laid more. Chano always told Jimmy how the *chicas* down south put out more.

Chano stopped going to cataclysm in the sixth grade because he never got to be an altar boy. Father Constantine said that he was too much of a risk, but Chano knew it was because he wasn't one of the real Catholic school kids. Jimmy thought that was Chano's problem, nothing real ever permeated through the construction paper to his life.

After Chano gave up on becoming an altar boy, he and his dad began fighting about church. Jimmy Shines remembered how Uncle Nacho and Chano would fight; Jimmy heard them argue in English, so they wouldn't upset Grandma.

"Come on, Chano, we're going."

"Not me man, if you want religion, why don't you just go outside and kiss the sky, Pops, cause we the 'People of the Sun.'" He told his dad and anyone else who would listen that they were all being put down by *The Man*. "The Aztecs didn't worship statues of the Blessed Virgin, Pop. They forced that shit on us when Columbus came here."

"The Aztecs sacrificed virgins and cut the heads off children. Is that the kind of religion you want, *mi'jo*?" Jimmy's uncle would ask. Jimmy always knew that deep down Chano was an Aztec warrior. Chano would gather slain pigeons in the EL tunnel, hold them by the necks and reverently carry them the same way that the *abuelitas* carried their Rosary beads to Mass.

When Chano moved into Jimmy's room there were two beds, a dresser, and a bookcase with no books. Chano had a model of the Eiffel Tower, and Jimmy let him keep it on the empty bookcase. Sometimes, Jimmy Shines felt sick when he saw the model. It was a crazy thing to look at. Chano didn't use instructions, and there were parts missing, but it wasn't the piecemeal appearance that bothered Jimmy, it was the glue. Chano had used super glue to put the thing together, and it warped and distorted the shape of the tower the same way buildings in the movies bubbled and stewed in the wake of Godzilla's firey breath.

"Someday, homes," Chano would say in the middle of the night, "someday, I'm gonna boogie on over there. To France. Then I'll see what color it really is."

Jimmy would laugh when Chano dreamed of Paris; he knew that no amount of paint could hide the twisted metal of Chano's tower.

"You could come with me, man," Chano would tell Jimmy in the darkness of their room.

"Stupid, you don't even know where Paris is," Jimmy would answer his cousin before throwing a pillow and pouncing on him in the dark.

On the days they ditched class, Jimmy and Chano would go on rat and pigeon hunts in the darkness of the Ravenswood EL tunnel. For Chano the hunts became a ritual, just like yelling "HOW MUCH?" to the *putas* standing on the corner or the weekly polishings of his tower. Days before the hunts, Chano would make slingshots out of wire coat hangers and patches. They usually lost the slingshots in the tunnels, but even if they brought them back, Chano made new ones. It was something he was good at. For each hunt, Chano's slingshots became more and more elaborate: a paper clip sight, a double stone shot, or extra strong rubber bands for the added pressure to take on rats and winos. Jimmy knew, even if Chano didn't, that there were only so many ways to make a coat hanger into a killing machine, and there weren't any CTA busses that ran to Paris.

During the day when the trains ran slow, they forgot about the rest of the world. "Watch that third rail, James," Chano always said, like he was reciting a Hail Mary, mostly to comfort himself because Jimmy knew better than to get close to the third rail. Chano ended the warnings with a deep, guttural spit in the direction of the electrified steel. With contact, the rail would hiss and the saliva crackle. To Jimmy it was as if the track were an amped up vampire, and Chano's spit the Holy Water taming it.

They would sit just inside the shadows of the tunnel, their

backs propped against each other, so they could keep a look out for pigeons. That was what they told each other, but Jimmy liked sitting back to back to keep a lookout for trains and winos. Chano would always face the darkness without any complaints. Jimmy knew that Chano could tell he was scared by the way his skin would shiver and tense. Chano never asked Jimmy if he was scared though, instead he would hold his hand. "Keep my shootin' hand warm, bro," Chano would say.

The bus ground to a halt. The road had been narrowed to one lane. He and Chano had wasted hours on the bus dreaming. They would take the Lincoln Avenue bus to school, always sitting in the back. Jimmy would sit normal and keep his space, but Chano liked to sprawl. He would contort his pipe cleaner body around an entire row of seats while humming some half-made-up tune in his head. Those were the times of inspiration for Chano, when things got going in his head and spun him around like beer caps dancing on a bar. "I got it all planned out, man," Chano would say to Jimmy over the diesel groan of the bus. "France is gonna be the shit."

"What do you know about France, man?"

"Well . . . it's all French and shit. And besides my tower they got that Notre Dame Cathedral . . .church is *goin' on* at that palace, man."

"I thought you was through with church."

"Yeah, but check it out, James. Notre Dame's the place that hooked up that hunchback and a whole bunch of other outlaws, you know, 'sanctuary' and all that. Over there they ain't down with the Pope like they are at St. Al's."

"That's just movies, Chano."

"And unlike punk-ass Father Constantine, I know they'll let me help serve Mass there."

"How you gonna get there, puto?"

"I got my ways, man."

"Whatchew mean you got ways?" Jimmy wanted to believe in Chano. He needed to.

"I got it covered, man, when the time's right."

But the time never got to be "right" for Chano. After a while, when Chano had given up on school and moments of inspiration, Jimmy rode the bus solo. And even without Chano, Jimmy never did sprawl across the back of the bus.

On winter Tuesdays, when Jimmy escorted his grandma to *Novena*, and it was too cold for the Marys to come across the street, Jimmy Shines would finish business early and hang out in the vestibule of the church waiting for his grandma.

Rows of candles lined the vestibule's walls, piling black smoke on the vaulted ceiling as they burned for sons in wars and mothers afflicted with cancer. They were the same candles that Chano told Jimmy he lit for him to get laid some day.

Jimmy felt safe with those candles in the shadows of the church. The same way, he thought, that Chano felt safe dreaming he was in Paris, sketching his Eiffel Tower and serving Mass at Notre Dame. And when business was slow for Jimmy Shines, he would pitch in a quarter and light a candle. Although he never had a prayer attached to any of those twenty-five cent salvation flames, he would smile and think of his cousin. The flames would dance in unison, until he moved his arm across the banks of fire, and they lost time and fell out of step with one another.

"You know how I'm gonna do it, man?" Chano would ask Jimmy while staring at the model on the empty book case.

"How? Hijack a plane?"

"Not a plane, homes. You know how you always hearin' about them Arab cats gettin' caught and gettin' their brains shot out by the Delta Force and Chuck Norris and shit? Well ain't none of them *locos* tried a bus. Nobody ever heard of a Greyhound gettin' jacked. And if I got me a bus I'd use a hatchet or somethin', cause they ask you now if you got any guns or bombs in your luggage, and then I'd be lying and have to go to confession, and I hate *The Church* cause you know that they's the ones who killed Montezuma and Geronimo, and Pancho Villa, man."

Jimmy spent his school days in the basement, and there were

a lot of things he never could get, like algebra or Shakespeare, but he liked history and the stories teachers told about the past. He remembered a teacher telling everyone about alchemy, on the day they spent studying knights and kings. Jimmy saw Chano as an alchemist in a way, always trying to produce gold from nothing, like his plan to get to France, or the sling shots, or the *Eighteenth Street Killa Gatos*, the crew he ran with.

When Chano first found the *Gatos*, not much had changed. But eventually like streaks on a mirror, he began to fade. At first, Chano would be gone a night or two, but after a while it would be weeks at a time. On a Sunday, while the rest of the family was at church, and Jimmy Shines had come down with poison oak, or scarlet fever, or anything that kept him in front of cartoons instead of the altar, Chano came through the door with some of his homeboys.

"Aye, *cabron*," Chano said to Jimmy, trying his hardest to sound cool in front of his crew. "Whatchew doin' round here, man?" Jimmy asked the same way the blacks questioned him if he ever cut across the projects on Diversey. Chano chicken scratched something to his homeboys in Spanish and they laughed. Jimmy hated Chano when he talked like that, like a cockroach hauling ass under a sudden light. He felt betrayed because Chano knew Jimmy's Spanish was CTA slow.

Chano looked at Jimmy through sunglasses that were too dark for the blind. "I told 'em that we was some foxes in the chicken coop, but it sounds better in Spanish, man."

"Yeah, well Grandma and them gonna be back from church soon, you better go. Your pops don't like talkin' about you. He put your pictures in a box, and he tried to throw out your Eiffel Tower, but I kept it."

"Yeah? Well that's cool . . . hey, *carnal*, maybe some day we could go pigeon hunting like we used to."

"We ain't got no slingshots, Chano."

"Don't need no slingshots, man, got somethin' better." Chano opened up his jacket. In the waistline Jimmy could see the handle of a pistol.

"Maybe some other time, man," Jimmy told Chano.

A few months later, the family found out that Chano had been shot in the back of the head. They talked about it in English, so Grandma wouldn't get upset.

The bus was back on track again, at a good clip, just under seventy-five. Jimmy Shines walked slow, emerging out of the shadows and the smell of diesel and shit. As he walked to the front of the bus, Jimmy looked out on the road ahead. He could see the Eiffel Tower just past the corn fields, the sun flipping across its top like red vestibule candles.

Jeannette Darcy
University of Houston

The Wrong Number

"Hey Kyle, have you seen Ernie?" Kyle, a senior computer analyst at GigaSoft, looked up from his desk and, while listening to his phone mail, shook his head no. Everyone at GigaSoft was racing to get the newly advertised software put together before the release date that had been imposed by an overly ambitious marketing department. Kyle and Ernie, another senior analyst, each headed a group of twelve programmers. Together their groups formed the heart of the company and, as such, felt the worst heat. Software glitches, appropriately named bugs, were crawling out of the woodwork like a late night nest of roaches discovered by a kitchen light. Ernie was nowhere to be found and Kyle was completely inundated with phone calls.

The big boss, Mr. Wedgeworth, had just left a phone message saying he needed Kyle to do another dog-n-pony show this afternoon: present a demo of their software to possible clients. "These guys are really big players!" Mr. Wedgeworth had forewarned in his message. Kyle knew what this meant; if GigaSoft could land contracts with these companies, it'd be fat city for everyone: raises, bonuses, awards, new employees, larger budgets and bigger egos. At the moment however, the dogs and the ponies were running wild in every direction, his phone was ringing again and Kyle had exactly forty-five minutes to throw together a knock-em-dead presentation.

The whole day whirled on in a frenzy, each fire of a crisis being put out in semi-panic fashion, and it continued on into the night until finally, at midnight no amount of caffeine could unblur Kyle's fuzzy brain. Looking up at the clock in the computer lab, he announced to no one in particular, "To hell with it, I'm going home." One or two of the programmers looked up at him, but most did not.

The lab was full, all twenty-four programmers were at their terminals but each was so fiercely concentrating on his or her own software code that they were, for the most part, oblivious to any external sounds in the room. *Why is it,* Kyle wondered, *that the later it gets, the harder they work? Such a crazy bunch of kids,* he laughed to himself. No life, just computers. When they started to get older and marry, if they married, you couldn't expect them to work long hours like this. A few might end up like him, unfit for anything except computers, but most would find a mate. Some of the mates would even be normal. But now, while his group of college hires were still young and bold, they derived pleasure and pride in scaling the seemingly impossible software mountains.

When each programmer's code was finally working, they'd join the twenty-four programs and hold their collective breath to see if it would all work together. It wouldn't, of course. But then a miracle would occur. Someone would notice some vagrant little code hiding in a corner, correct the seemingly insignificant error with a few clicks of the terminal, and the whole monstrosity of collected pieces of code would work exactly as expected. There would be shouts of joy from the extroverts, smiles of pride from the introverts and days spent by everyone basking in the afterglow. The male programmers would gloat over their own cleverness, reveling with their proud co-warriors over the defeated bug-dragons. The female programmers would recount to each other, in excruciating detail, the tortuous path they had taken in order to solve their riddles, and with thinly disguised maternal joy, release their babies to the wide world of software distribution.

Kyle's shoulders sank as he walked out into the dark parking lot and headed for home. His metallic black Camaro, which he had always regarded as the ultimate sex machine, sat alone in the executive parking lot. *Just like me*, Kyle thought, *alone at night*. Work was usually a relief to Kyle. The cold impersonality of the office relieved him of any need to make excuses for the emptiness of his life. It was only at the end of the day that he would sigh in resignation.

In his kitchen for the evening ritual—a glass of Scotch on ice—he noticed that the answering machine on the counter was blinking. As the first gulp brought a wave of relaxation, he hit the replay button and heard Ernie's voice; it sounded fearful and urgent. Ernie said he was in some sort of trouble and left a number for Kyle to call, imploring him to call as soon as he got the message.

Ernie and Kyle had started work on the same day, twelve years ago when the company was just forming. They had become good friends over the years, sharing their joy of computers, their love of high-tech gadgets and their complete lack of social skills.

Kyle dialed the number, but he must have misdialed because after one ring a recorded sales pitch began. He replaced the phone on the hook, listened to Ernie's message again to double check the number. Sure enough, he had dialed wrong. In picking up the phone, he started to dial again, but he didn't have a dial tone. The line had not been disconnected from the previous attempt. Sometimes that happens if you do things too quickly, but a few minutes had elapsed between the first call and this one. He slammed the phone down, huffed in anger, waited an impatient second, and picked up the phone again. Still no dial tone and that idiot sales pitch recording was still going. "Stupid phone," he said, annoyed, and smashed the receiver down again. All the small disappointments, all the big disappointments, *I'll call tomorrow morning*, he thought, as he collapsed across his bed.

The next week was a blur. Ernie showed up without any explanation for his absence or the mysterious call, and Kyle was too busy to think about it anyway, he figured he'd hear about it later, maybe over a few beers.

The software made it through its initial debut, the big companies agreed to sign and the programmers were jovially sharing their war stories. He went home early, around 7:00 p.m. Since it was Monday night a game would be on t.v., and the only thing to do was order a pizza from Cosmo's and run down to the Quick Stop for a six pack of beer. He picked up the kitchen phone but there was no dial tone, a recorded voice was speaking. He replaced the phone on the hook, looked blank for a moment, then remembered the incident with Ernie's call last week. With a frown, he picked the phone up again; the recorded voice was still going. With angry, colorful cursing he slammed it down again and got his cell phone out of his briefcase. He called Cosmo's, ordered a large veggie supreme and switched on ESPN.

How bizarre, he thought. *A line that won't disconnect. I'll have to call the phone company tomorrow.* He went to the tiny kitchen where the black phone lay on the counter near the fridge amidst a disorderly pile of half-read mail, half-read newspapers, unpaid bills, junk mail and, somewhere under all that, a calendar with nothing penciled in on any date. Ever the scientist trying to solve the riddle, he thought he'd listen to the message to see what company had so ridiculously attached itself to his phone line—maybe he could play a prank on them with his computer. He and the programmers often played hacker-style pranks on each other and whoever it was that was tying up his phone line now certainly deserved to be pranked.

"...You may have already won! Yes, millions of dollars in the Texas State Lottery may already be yours! Just play these lucky numbers: 13-26-39-52-65-78, and millions of dollars may already be yours. Yes, that's right! The winning numbers for Monday's lotto..."

Kyle listened to the recorded message and when it repeated the second time he wondered, *what are they selling?* The overly happy male voice repeated the same message a third and fourth time. Disturbing the pile of papers on the counter, he found a pen and wrote down the numbers. He stood transfixed while it repeated itself a fifth time. *How very bizarre,* he scratched his chin thoughtfully as it repeated again a sixth time. Over and over again, the same numbers.

Feeling a slight thrill of adventure, Kyle bought a lottery ticket at the Quick Stop when he got his beer. He normally didn't play the lottery; everyone at the office called it the "stupidity tax." Besides, he had never been lucky in anything. Not in romance, not in sports, not even in his career, which had been the focal point of his life since college. After twelve years he was still in the same position and wasn't making nearly as much as other people similarly qualified. But this jerk sales guy on the phone was something he couldn't figure out. Could it be?

Exactly what he could dare to believe, Kyle had no idea as his mouth hung open that night. With one hand on the remote, pointed at the screen, he had flipped over to the news channel to see the winning numbers: 13-26-39-52-65-78! The same numbers on his very own ticket! *I am way too drunk,* he thought. Was this really happening? A shock of adrenaline jolted him into sitting upright. *Don't get too excited,* he thought apprehensively. He looked at the screen. He looked at his ticket. He looked back and forth, suddenly very sober and lucid. He blinked. It was still there. He sat back and laughed, the momentary panic subsiding. Yes, he'll get a good laugh out of this in the morning. He'd be sure to tell Ernie, and blame him royally for leaving that insidious message in the first place. They'd get a good laugh at how screwed up things look when you're drunk. And with that, he swigged down the last of his six pack.

At lunch the next day he stopped off at the Quick Stop where he had bought the lottery ticket the night before. He picked up a stale sandwich, a giant Coke and one of the lottery hand outs on the check out counter. These handouts displayed the winning numbers for those who hadn't seen them on t.v. Derek, behind the counter, gave his standard mantra, "Maybe you won this time." The corner of Kyle's lip went up in polite acknowledgment.

It was 6:30 in the evening before he had time to think of it again, because he had had to hit the ground running when he returned from lunch. And now, sitting amidst the piles of papers strewn helter-skelter across his desk, he crammed down another nutritionless meal from the vending machine. His heart skipped a beat when he thought of the Lotto. Like a thief, he looked left and right, making sure no one was around, then he pulled the ticket and the handout from his wallet. The same numbers! So it was true!

"Damn!" he said and sat straight up, every cell in his body instantly energized. Holding his breath, he blinked and carefully, one by one, backwards and forwards, checked the numbers again. "Damn!" he repeated. His face flushed, he grew hot all over and his head started to swim. He replaced both the ticket and the handout in his wallet with hands shaking and heart racing. He checked that they were safe in the wallet, then checked two more times before carefully sliding the wallet into his back pocket. *Well,* he thought, *if I've won millions of dollars, do I still need to work here? Can I just quit?*

His head was still reeling a few days later when his winnings had been confirmed, and the papers had all been filled out, and it was really going to happen. A sizzling $13 million in cash! Like a man blown over by a blast of wind, he lay spread-eagle and naked on the bed, completely stunned. Clearly, the only things left to do were to get drunk and masturbate.

He had never notified the phone company about the phone. He had never asked Ernie what had happened on the night of the call. As he watched the blades rotate on the ceiling fan, he wondered out loud if the line was still connected.

In the kitchen he popped open another beer, and picked up his mysterious phone. The recorded voice could be heard talking even before the handset reached his ear. *Maybe he'll tell me more numbers!* A chill of excitement shimmied down his naked spine.

"...A SMALL BOY WALKING DOWN PONDEROSA LANE AFTER SCHOOL WOULD JUST LOVE TO BE WEARING THESE COWBOY BOOTS. MADE OF PURE ALLIGATOR HIDE, THESE BOOTS WILL MAKE A MAN OUT OF EVEN THE NERDIEST KID AT WALLACE ELEMENTARY..."

At first Kyle couldn't make out what he was hearing, it was the same happy, recorded voice as before but now it was saying something different. Then the wheels in his brain engaged. *He* had been the nerdiest kid at Wallace Elementary and *he* had walked alone down Ponderosa Lane, back and forth from school, wishing his parents could afford to buy him alligator boots like the popular athlete, Johnny Meinhart, had worn to school in second grade.

"...YES, YOU HEARD THAT RIGHT, ANY LITTLE CHILD WOULD LOVE TO BE BIG AND STRONG AND THE CAPTAIN OF THE FOOTBALL TEAM, STRONGER AND TALLER THAN THAT MEAN OLD BILL KRUEHOFF..."

Blinking his eyes and trying to comprehend how this computer recording could be saying anything so personal, Kyle thought of Bill Kruehoff—the big class bully— who delighted in humiliating Kyle all those years in PE class. Was this some kind of joke? Who would know this about him?

"...BUT THOSE BOOTS WERE MADE FOR WALKING, AND THAT'S JUST WHAT LITTLE SISSY BOYS DO UNTIL THEY'RE OLD ENOUGH TO GET AWAY FROM HOME AND GET THEIR COMPUTER SCIENCE DEGREE AT THE UNIVERSITY OF TEXAS. YES, AND THEN THEY'RE READY FOR A SEXY, BLACK CAMARO. THE ONLY CAR A REAL PLAYBOY EVER NEEDS..."

He hung up. Should he keep listening? This was obviously some really elaborate joke. Who on earth could pull this off? Ernie was capable of some hilarious pranks, like the time Kyle's computer screen was eaten up, row by row, by the little lawn mower man until everything was gone, or the time he turned Mr. Wedgeworth's screen saver into a big clown face. *But tying up the phone line like this would be impossible,* Kyle thought, *and besides he had misdialed that night, hadn't he?* Why would this prankster give him the winning lottery numbers? He picked up the phone again.

"...MANDY, MANDY GOOD AS CANDY! WOULDN'T YOU LIKE TO TASTE A WOMAN THAT COULD DRIVE YOU WILD WITH EXCITEMENT? SHE WANTS YOU BIG BOY! SHE'S HUNGRY FOR YOU..."

Slam! How many times had he fantasized about Mandy? It'd be impossible to count. She was the pretty (married) secretary at work who was never anything more than courteous to him. It never ceased to amaze him that such a petite body as hers could be so shapely. Of course, she flaunted it by always dressing in soft, revealing tops, dinky little skirts and dangerous looking heels. Her long, thick, blond hair framed a pixie face that made him think of Disney fairies gone nymphomaniac. When he watched her breasts bounce as she walked down the hall, he felt pleasant waves of erotic desire all the way to his bones. He couldn't help but believe that she liked for men to look at her. His unrequited lust for Mandy demanded that he pick up the phone again. Maybe this would turn into an obscene phone call. That would be OK.

"...NOW, FOR A LIMITED TIME ONLY, THIS OFFER APPLIES TO YOU. YOU MAY HAVE ALREADY WON! YES FOLKS, THIS IS A ONE-TIME ONLY OFFER FOR ONE GLORIOUS NIGHT OF UNCENSORED, UNCONTROLLED, UNABASHED, NO-HOLDS-BARRED WILD, WILD SEX WITH THE ONE AND ONLY MANDY STINGER, GODDESS OF WOMANHOOD, GIVER OF PLEASURE. YES! YOU MAY HAVE ALREADY WON THIS ONE-TIME ONLY DEAL! JUST REPEAT THE FOLLOWING PHRASE THREE TIMES IN A ROW. REPEAT IT THREE TIMES A DAY FOR THREE DAYS. IT'S THAT EASY! YOU MAY HAVE ALREADY WON! AND HERE'S YOUR LUCKY PHRASE: 'KO ENOS HERMES.' YES, IT'S REALLY THAT EASY! JUST REPEAT 'KO ENOS HERMES' THREE TIMES IN A ROW, THREE TIMES A DAY, FOR THREE DAYS. NO MORE AND NO LESS! THIS WONDERFUL PRIZE CAN BE YOURS, BIG BOY..."

The message was repeated in its entirety, but it changed a little each time around—the descriptions of Mandy got more graphic. The lucky phrase stayed the same though. "Ko Enos Hermes" was a phrase he was already familiar with, "a theft taken together." The idea of stealing Mandy for one night was perfect. Clearing the piles of newspapers off the couch, he sat down and said the lucky phrase three times in a row, with all the earnestness of Dorothy in the Wizard of Oz telling herself there was "no place like home."

During the next two days, Kyle quit his job, talked to the bankers and carefully repeated his lucky phrase in the privacy of his home exactly as he remembered the instructions.

After the third day he surveyed his sloppy apartment, and realized it was no place to enact his Mandy fantasy, which by now had become a fixed certainty in his mind. *Should I hire someone to clean this place up? And let them discover the phone? No way! Where could he take her for their wild night?*

His first stop was the Ritz-Carlton. He liked the name. And it was the first one he saw as he drove around the high class Galleria neighborhood of Houston, where all the well-to-do shop for their Nieman Marcus must-haves. Putting on the Ritz. Yessir, that's what he was going to do.

When he asked to see their finest suite, a middle-aged, uniformed man politely led him up to the twelfth floor. It was magnificent. Kyle's untrained eye surveyed the crystal lamps, crystal ash trays, original paintings on the walls, authentic Chinese vases, the expansive living room with antique, cherry furniture in the Queen Anne style, the large armoire in the corner holding the t.v. and stereo, the marble bathroom and the Jacuzzi. He had no idea of the furniture's value but he knew this was style! A mere six hundred and fifty dollars a night? What did he care? The clerk at the front desk smiled deferentially when Kyle asked for the name of the finest restaurant in town. *Respect, that's what money will get you,* he thought smugly.

On his way out, he thought he had better stop off at the bathroom before he got back in his car. In the hallway to the restrooms, several people were standing and talking. Just before stepping through the bathroom door, one of the women turned around. He looked down and Mandy looked up, and smiled.

"Hi, Kyle! How nice to see you! What are you doing here?"

Time stopped. His heart raced, his mind went blank, his palms sweat, he tried to stammer out a few words, but before he could put together a cohesive sentence, she took him by the arm and started walking toward the parking lot, talking and laughing all the way as if they were the best of friends.

"I'm crazy about you," she confided as they stood together at the Camaro, his back leaning against the car because the force of her confession made his legs weak. "I've been crazy about you ever since that first day you walked into the office." She went on about how she couldn't leave her husband and kids (but they were out of town this weekend), and about the lucky coincidence that she was here at the Ritz to attend a prosperity seminar. When she saw him in the hallway she knew it was her one and only chance to satisfy her passion. She wanted to go for it.

She was wearing his favorite outfit, a low-cut, slinky, black and red, floral dress with little, red, flower-shaped buttons running down the front and red high heels. The dress hugged her curves tightly all the way down to the top of her thighs, where it ended abruptly. The bottom two buttons were already undone.

She wanted to have sex, he was aching for it, what else mattered? "Let's *really* do it Kyle," she said as she fixed her dark gaze directly into his soul, while her manicured fingers rubbed his chest. "Let's get totally wild together for one night. When it's over, you go back to your life and I'll go back to mine and it'll just be our little secret, OK?" He reached out, hugged her close and nestled his nose into her golden hair. "Oh Mandy!" he whispered, "Mandy at last!"

Dinner came first, complete with waiters whose only job was to whisk the crumbs off the table in between the courses of elaborately decorated plates of food. Mandy's toes played with his leg under the table, just like in the movies! When they were finally alone in the room, with the lights down low, the scene that Kyle had imagined a million times was actually happening. Mandy took control. After kissing him and undressing him, she undressed herself, unbuttoning each and every little, red button with an exquisite smile. She led him to the bed. To his amazement, his love-making prowess took Mandy to heights of ecstasy that she probably had never experienced before. She screamed and moaned in wild abandon. The rest of the night they fondled each other in the Jacuzzi, laughed often, watched HBO, found the X-rated channel and had sex several more times.

The next morning after breakfast in bed, while Mandy dressed, she said, "Last night was wonderful, it meant so much more to me than that prosperity seminar that I missed." But the *way* she said it rang false. Something unsaid was hanging in the air, and she was standing there as if she were waiting for something. Suddenly, it hit him. It was the money. She had done all this for money, not because she really wanted him. How could he have been so stupid? With a sting of hurt pride, he pulled out a thick wad of hundred dollar bills from his wallet and handed it to her. She didn't protest, but she didn't smile either. Feeling like a complete fool, he watched her leave in silence.

At home again, he sought solace from the black phone.

"...NOWHERE IN THE WORLD CAN YOU EXPERIENCE ANYTHING LIKE THIS. AND NOW, FOR A LIMITED TIME ONLY, WHILE SUPPLIES LAST, YOUR OWN PERSONAL GENIE WILL BE IN CHARGE OF YOUR LIFE..."

A Personal Genie? Yeah right. Although that did sort of describe the wild events of the past week. But of course this was all so ridiculous, he was a free man now, no one would ever be his master again.

"...YES! YOU HEARD THAT RIGHT FOLKS. IT'S COMPLETELY OUT OF YOUR

HANDS. SIT BACK AND ENJOY THE RIDE WHILE YOUR PERSONAL GENIE DECIDES WHAT WILL HAPPEN NEXT. YOU'RE IN GOOD HANDS NOW SO…RELAAAAAX …"

He slammed it down and shivered. The voice was sounding increasingly more sinister. *Maybe he just needed a vacation*, he thought with a sigh. Maybe he could find someone to vacation with now that he was Mr. Moneybags. In any case, it was definitely time to get the phone disconnected. He had everything he needed now.

Nighttime found Kyle slumped on the couch in a drunken stupor, remote control aimed at the t.v., swiftly changing channels. The euphoria from his windfall had worn off sooner than he had expected. Where once he felt an insulated core of numbness inside, a red hot torment had erupted and taken over. As if having mad conversations with an inanimate object like his phone wasn't bad enough, visions of a bleak future danced in his head. In his mind he could see an endless gluttony of empty hedonistic pleasures, extravagant purchases that would mean nothing to him, women who would prostitute themselves for a chance at his money, and fair-weather friends who would measure his worth in dollars and cents. The frantic pace of his life had kept him conveniently shielded from the fact that now blazed flagrantly in front of him: he was utterly alone.

In the middle of the night he woke in a sweat. He could almost remember hearing the phone ring, but wasn't quite sure. From where he had passed out on the couch, he could see the ominous, black phone on the kitchen counter. Yes, it was ringing!

"Who the hell are you?" he demanded into the phone.

The recorded message droned on. "…IT'S NOT *NICE* TO DISCONNECT THE PERSONAL GENIE. THIS ONE TIME ONLY OFFER REQUIRES STRICT OBEDIENCE!"

"WHO THE HELL ARE YOU?" he yelled now.

Suddenly, there was silence. The recording stopped. And then it began again, this time with a mocking tone:

"…*TOO* BAD. THE PERSONAL GENIE DOESN'T LIKE YOU ANYMORE. SO NOW, FOR A LIMITED TIME ONLY, APPEARING IN A NEIGHBORHOOD NEAR YOU, THE UZZ 109 THAT KILLS YOU DEAD…"

Slam!

No, he thought. *This is too bizarre. I'm dreaming this. I'm getting that damn thing disconnected tomorrow. Maybe this whole thing is some drunken hallucination. He'd been under too much stress lately, hadn't he? UZZ 109? Was that some kind of a Uzzi machine gun? Maybe he had better call the police. Or better yet, call Ernie. This whole thing was Ernie's fault anyway with that blasted message he'd left.* On his cell phone he nervously dialed Ernie's beeper number, hung up and waited.

Tomorrow he could take a taxi to the airport and never come back to Houston again. Then what? Maybe he'd go to Hawaii and learn to surf and amuse himself by screwing the scantily clad babes. With enough money even a clumsy blob like himself could become cool, couldn't he? With a sting he thought of Mandy's dark eyes; she must have despised him.

It was the middle of the night and he didn't have a lick of food in the house. *No problem for a smart guy like me*, he thought. He called the 24-hour grocery store on his cell phone and had them deliver all his favorite comfort foods. He tipped the young, pimply-faced driver with a hundred dollar bill and the boy's face completely lit up. *Fool*, Kyle thought. *People are fools. They think money will solve anything.*

He had started to fix his breakfast when the phone rang. The black phone. Should he answer it? Maybe it was Ernie! His hand reached out for the phone. But then again, maybe it wasn't Ernie. The recorded voice couldn't scare him if he didn't listen to it. *No, I won't answer it*, he thought.

But it rang and rang. How long can you listen to a phone ring? He checked the answering machine; it should be picking up by now but it wasn't. He tried turning the ringer down, still it rang just as loud. He pulled the plug out of the wall, still it rang.

He felt nauseous and his head floated. Kyle ran to the living room closet, pulled out a hammer and smashed the black phone with a vengeance. The ringing stopped. And then, from somewhere among the broken pieces on the counter or on the floor, the ringing started again. Kyle screamed, "Leave me alone! Leave me ALONE!" as he flailed the hammer on the phone again.

There was silence. But not for long. The recorded voice snarled from the broken pieces, "...THE PERSONAL GENIE IS GONNA GET YOU, YOU THANKLESS PIG! YES, YOU HEARD THAT RIGHT..."

Whamm! Whamm! He hammered the pieces again and again, but he couldn't silence the phone. And now it was laughing at him. From where? From all over, all the little pieces were laughing at him. Kyle began to plead, "Please, let me go. Look, I don't need the money. I'll give it back!"

Still it was laughing, only now it was laughing harder and louder and in stereo. The pounding of Kyle's rapid heartbeat filled his senses as he teetered on the edge of his sanity. And then the laughing stopped. Kyle dropped the hammer onto the floor. He'd leave right now and catch the next flight at the airport wherever it was going.

The smell of burning oil broke the spell. Twirling around, he saw the pan that he'd left on the stove, smoke was billowing out of it. As he pulled it off the stove, its contents went POOF into flames! In shock, Kyle dropped the pan, and it landed on the counter amidst the papers and before he could think, the piles of paper caught fire, and the flames leapt up into the cabinets over the counter. From cabinet to cabinet, from curtains to rugs, the ceiling fans stoked the blaze and spread it quickly. The smoke alarm was wailing, and Kyle looked around for something to put out the blaze, but was too stunned and confused to actually do anything. He grabbed his cell phone to call 911, but when he turned it on he heard the recorded voice.

"...SOME RESTRICTIONS DO APPLY, YOU *IDIOT...*"

He opened the front door, threw the cell phone out as hard as he could and then ran down the hall to a neighbor. He pounded on their door, but there was no answer. He pounded on another door until he finally woke them up. They called the fire department and joined him in waking the rest of the neighbors.

In five minutes, the flames consumed his apartment. In ten minutes, other apartments were on fire. Within fifteen minutes, the flames engulfed the entire wood-frame building and turned it into a bonfire. People were streaming out of the nearby apartment buildings, some screaming, others crying.

Now a huge, blazing inferno, fanned by a strong north wind, the fire had leapt to the trees and to other buildings. Wherever he ran, it seemed the smoke followed him; billowing black clouds obscured everything around him. His lungs hurt, his face was scorched black and he didn't know where to stand in the confusion of people and cars going everywhere.

In the distance the wail of the fire engine sirens signaled rescue. He found a patch of grass that looked safe, and went down on his knees, coughing and wheezing in pain from the smoke which still seemed to be following and engulfing him. When he raised his head he heard the loud siren and saw the tail lights of the fire truck backing up toward him. *Why was it coming toward him?* He looked around and saw he was kneeling near a fire hydrant. He was in between the truck and the hydrant! He stumbled up to get out of the truck's path, but tripped over his own clumsy feet. His legs wrapped around each other, he fell flat to the ground, and wrenched his back while hitting his head. The truck driver never saw him in the thick smoke. In the those final seconds, as the huge wheels rolled over Kyle and crushed his body, the last thing Kyle ever saw was the license plate of the truck: Texas UZZ 109.

Daniel K. Lewis
SOUTHERN ILLINOIS UNIVERSITY

Stealing Rope

There have been times in my life when I considered myself so learned as to believe I was near genius, and other times when I've been just as sure I knew nothing at all. But one thing I will always know: everything of significance in my life I've learned from women. From my mother I learned honesty and valor, and from all the women who were my grade school teachers I learned telephone etiquette and the multiplication tables. But it was from Debbie Ponder that I learned the most fantastic lesson ever: how to spend two dollars and seventy cents with absolutely nothing to show for it except the desperate desire to do it a second time.

I was fourteen that hot, June day in the summer of 1964, with no responsibility in sight except my paper route that lasted through September. Roy, myself and Jimmy were huddled in our clubhouse, or what was once known as our clubhouse, for we were by then much too grown up and sophisticated to still call it a clubhouse. It was a slat board affair, about eight feet by eight feet square and stood on stilts, tucked into the upper, back corner of an old garage building at the back of the abandoned lot next to my house. The garage faced an alley, and the only way into the clubhouse was to climb a two-inch-thick, knotted rope we'd stolen from the ramparts of Lock and Dam 27 on the mighty Mississippi. We hadn't actually stolen the rope; it had washed up on the pilings near the lock gates where some barge hand had lost it overboard, but there's little excitement in saying you found something. The only way the tale of the magnificent rope was ever worth telling was if the rope had been stolen, and so that's how we always told it.

My cousin Roy was two years older than my best friend, Jimmy, and Jimmy was half a year younger than me.

As Roy spoke, we stared into his face as though he'd come from the future to tell us we were going to be astronauts when we grew up. But that wasn't what he was talking about, and I'm not sure we'd have been more spellbound if he had. He was talking about himself and the previous night with Debbie Ponder, and "the truths" of the ages.

Debbie Ponder was fourteen, like me, and her family was poor, like mine, but that's where the resemblance ended. She was almost two inches taller than me and while I'd talk to anyone who would talk to me first, Debbie Ponder wouldn't. If you said hello to her in the hallway at school she might say hello back, but then she might not. She had something about her that fourteen-year-old kids didn't have a name for back then, so she was just cool. Well, that isn't really precise; if you were another fourteen-year-old girl, then Debbie was a bitch, so I came to understand, but if you were a fourteen-year-old boy and she had in any way acknowledged your earthly existence (especially in front of someone else), she was cool.

I had seen her many times in the school hallway as we advanced through the crowd toward study hall, where she sat four seats ahead and two rows to the right of me, in the perfect position for either admiration or assassination. As it was, I had decided she was much too shapely to assassinate, and so I had stared at the back of her head, or the back of her skirt, for the entirety of that semester.

She belonged to a very special club, the Stared-at-by-Me Club, though she didn't know it. There were about five or so select members at any given time, all with the minimum prerequisites: legs, brown eyes, long hair, and two breasts (the last being absolute with no negotiation). It wasn't until Roy had told us "the truths" that I even remotely considered amassing the gumption to call to order a meeting with any one of the members. I would ask her for a date.

Boys were luckier in 1964; a ninth grade date didn't have the same connotation it apparently has today. For us, thankfully, dating meant only frayed nerves and sweaty palms during a ride to the skating rink in the back seat of an un-air-conditioned, Chevrolet station wagon, with one's mother at the wheel yammering about seeing someone else's mother at a yard sale or squealing repeatedly, "Oh how pretty your date looks!" These days I sometimes find myself waiting at a stoplight next to a chauffeured limousine with two adolescents, a boy and his smiling date, in the roomy, leathered rear seat, with a food tray filled with such treats as caviar on crackers and stemware brimming with bubbly. She laughs and waves at me with two passes to Disney World, but the boy does not laugh; as the light turns green and the limo races ahead, he stares hauntingly at me through the window, as though it were a disappearing porthole on the Titanic.

A date with Debbie Ponder, according to Roy and the rumors, required little more than a towel and a Tarzan yell, but I came to learn that there was more to it than that. It cost three night's sleep, payable in advance, simply to ask her out. I did though, ask her out, by way of a mile and a half detour on my bike to a run-down house in the woods during my paper route.

My knock interrupted a midday meal evidently, for she joined me on her front porch and accepted my proposal, barefoot in frayed, denim shorts and a sleeveless shirt open almost to her navel, with little more than a disinterested "okay," while gnawing suggestively on a pork chop bone. I didn't finish my paper route; I rode out to the river instead, and threw the rest of my papers one by one onto barge tugs as they passed, and did cart wheels and sang rock n' roll love songs at the top of my lungs, and practiced my Tarzan yell.

Had I been slightly more cognizant, I would have realized that if I threw all of my newspapers onto barge tugs, I didn't get to collect as much money as when I actually sold them to customers. Instead of my usual seven dollars and fifty cents gross profit, I found myself late Friday afternoon with two dollars and seventy cents, and about twenty-three hours until my date. I had considered (before the barge tug blunder) to hire a taxi and take us both to a movie show, but now a romantic, evening stroll along the river in the moonlight seemed perfectly in order…and in case one or both of us decided to recline and look up at the stars, I would bring a large towel. When I rode out to Debbie's house that afternoon, and told her about my plan, she looked at me for a long minute then said, "You don't have any money, do you?"

"Two dollars and seventy cents," I bragged.

"Bring cigarettes," she said, "…and rubbers."

"No problem," I said as though my lungs were filled with helium.

That was that.

Roy didn't believe me. I rode to his house on my way home, because I knew I could buy cigarettes at the confectionery down by the school, but I had no idea how to obtain rubbers.

Jimmy and I knew about rubbers because Roy was always flashing a fogged cellophane wrapper that he'd wave through the air real fast and then jam into his pocket while telling us wild stories about whoever he was "doin,'" as he called it. I'd never really thought about where he got them, but in the back of my mind, I had the notion that there must be a dad store somewhere, where you just walked in and bought rubbers. They'd be hanging on a rack right next to the Bermuda-shorts-and-wingtip-shoe ensembles, already-wrapped anniversary presents, over-sized barbecue brushes, cigars, shotguns and fedoras.

"You're kidding, right?" Roy asked as he stepped out through his screen door and joined me on the porch.

"No, really, Roy. You gotta help me," I pleaded.

"Really," he said. "You got a date with Debbie Ponder...and she told you to bring rubbers." He said it not like a question, but more like he'd just been told his entire family had died in a fiery car crash and was repeating it in shock.

"Yeah," I said. "What am I going to do?"

"Shit, man, you better get some rubbers, I guess," he said, scratching his head. "She told you that? For real. Said to bring some rubbers?"

I just looked at him, and he grinned real big and cuffed me on the shoulder.

"You got any money?" he asked.

I held out both dollar bills and the seventy cents, and he grabbed a dollar and stuffed it into the pocket of his jeans. "Okay, here's what you do," he said, "go down to Smiley's Garage. Got it? He'll fix you up." He cuffed me again, a good one on the chin this time, then closed the front door behind him. I went home, ate supper, and made the final payment of another sleepless night.

Saturday afternoon I went down to the confectionery by the school and peered over the counter at the massive cigarette racks on the wall. Debbie hadn't said what kind of cigarettes to bring, and I had never paid attention to how many different kinds, sizes, and styles there were. I picked out two kinds, one frilly and one with a cowboy on the display over the rack. I paid the lady behind the counter, and told her how much my mom and dad loved these two separate kinds of cigarettes, that these two kinds were their favorites of all the kinds that were there on the racks. She looked at me a moment, then grabbed the cowboy cigarettes out of my hand and showed me that a flip-top box opened differently than a regular soft pack, so I would get it right and look like I knew what I was doing before someone beat me up. Outside on the walk I pulled up my jeans at the ankle, shoved a pack into each sock, then headed for Smiley's.

Smiley's garage was an old, run-down gas station at the edge of town, on the way to Debbie's house, that had been affiliated with just about every major brand of motor fuel at one time or another; the windows across the back were covered over with some of their old, tin signs. The brown, tar board siding, the kind that was pressed to look like bricks, was frayed and broken and coming off around the bottom of the walls where the weeds grew. He had an air hose out by the pumps where we all aired up our bike tires. And Smiley's was the place to stop if Halloween fell on a weekend, because old man Smiley was usually pretty liquored up by sundown Saturday night, and you might come away with a box of valve stems, or front wheel bearings, or a five-dollar bill, or even a '59 El Camino generator if your trick-or-treat bag was strong enough to catch it when he dropped it in.

It was getting late in the afternoon, and old man Smiley was slump-shouldered from the heat on a stool behind the counter when I walked in. His eyes had a glassy look to them. Behind him on its own stool was a half empty, grease-smudged bottle of Seagram's, and no drinking glass in sight.

"How you doing, Smiley?" I asked like a regular customer. I scanned the back wall shelves and the top of the desk in the corner and even the dusty cardboard candy display on the glass counter, but saw nothing resembling the fogged cellophane wrappers that Roy was always waving around. I had the money and I had the date and I figured I was close enough in age, so, clearing my throat, I swallowed hard, then dropped the last of my money on the counter and said it out loud. "Smiley, my cousin Roy sent me down here to get him some rubbers."

Smiley laughed, then reaffirmed their relationship, "Roy who?"

The temperature in the place shot up another forty degrees, but old Smiley didn't seem to notice.

"Come on, Smiley," I squeaked out, "you know Roy. Me and him was in here a week ago. You fixed a flat on his bike."

"That little shit? He wouldn't know what to do with a rubber if you slapped it on him and shoved his ass back an' forth by the back of his belt!" He laughed again, like he'd just thought about it some more, then leaned back and grabbed the whiskey bottle and upended it. His Adam's apple throttled up and down a couple times like an old well pump, then he lowered the bottle and set it back on the stool behind him. I stood there like my shoes were nailed to the floor, and the old man leaned closer and grinned. "You got you a sweetie?" he asked with a drunken, yellow smile.

"No sir," I stammered, then decided to come clean. "Actually, it's Roy's dad that needs them. Yeah, my Uncle Hank, you see, actually, he told Roy to have me come down here and get some rubbers for him. My Uncle Hank, that is, yes. Roy was supposed to send me 'cause Uncle Hank, he needs some rubbers, I mean."

I was thinking, just then, that maybe I should have practiced that speech a little before I got there, when he chuckled.

"I seen your aunt, boy. Hank don't need rubbers…he needs this," he said, and shook the Seagram's bottle, then took another swig.

I stood a moment longer, looking at him while he looked at me. He lived in the back of the place, alone and had forever it seemed. His hands were dark and stained, with cracked and blackened fingernails from working on too many old cars. His clothes were crumpled and filthy, and his hair was thin and gray and tossed. His face was wrinkled and covered with gray stubble, and I worried for a world where those like him had rubbers and those like me did not. Then it struck me, as I stood there, that our lives were mirrored; I was staring into my future, I was sure, and would never have a meaningful relationship as far as I could see. Finally I turned to go, and took a couple steps toward the door when he mumbled something. I paused and looked back, and in his eyes I saw a mirrored thought, and he flipped into the air a fogged cellophane packet, which I caught and pocketed with a smile.

I didn't meet Debbie at her house, but had agreed to meet her about dark, up on the river where Hubert Creek poured in. I was running late, and running hard along the levee, when I saw her. She stood near the water in the light from a rising moon, like Venus, the goddess of love, descending to aid the ignorant. Her shirt was completely unbuttoned and fluttering in the sultry night breeze like silvery wings at her back. The skin of her flat tummy was taut and white and shadowy under small breasts which, in my young mind, made anything Michelangelo ever did look like a mud brick.

"Did you get the cigarettes?" she asked, as I skidded to a stop in the grass.

I was trying to control my breathing but not having much luck. "Yeah," I wheezed, and knelt down to retrieve them from each sock. I held them and the rubber out, and she giggled as she took them from my shaking hands. The soft pack she slid down the back pocket of her short, cut-off jeans along with the rubber. The other pack, the flip-top box, she opened, then pulled one free, lit it with a match from another pocket, and took a long drag. She breathed in deeply, then pulled it from her lips, offered it toward me, but I hadn't noticed. She leaned down slightly to catch my gaze. "Relax, it's no big deal," she said as she took my hand.

We walked, hand in hand, along the river, and time ceased to move as she held my hand and talked about her somedays: the someday when she would leave this place, and the someday she was going to be somebody, and so many other somedays that I lost track, and noticed only the scent of her skin, and a barge far to the north, and the feel of her hand in mine. Somewhere in that time she took my hands and held them to her breasts in the moonlight, and then was silent and soft and relenting as the barge whispered past us late in the night. A moment later it was miles downstream and rounding the bend out of sight. And later still, long after she had kissed my lips and whispered things I never wanted to forget, I understood that although many often speak of things that never happened and never will, some never speak of the things that did.

Lisa D. Gerlits
Lewis & Clark College

Maggots

They stared down at the dead animal, a squirrel they thought, though the absence of a tail made it difficult to tell. It lay on the brick sidewalk in front of the UC, curled over on itself like a fetus, bald and red. A soothing oak spread its shroud to shield them from the harsh sun. Having seen the carcass two or three days ago, Jeff figured it had been around all weekend. Tess guessed five days dead.

Jeff said four, arguing, "I've had much more experience with dead animals than you."

She tried to raise one eyebrow, but both went up. "Oh really? What kind of *experience?*"

He shrugged and looked down at the squirrel.

"Uh-huh," she said, "I thought so."

They continued to stare, she with the push broom and he with the shovel, unmotivated. The sun rode high in the sky, and the air hung still and thick. It was 4:30, so they had time to kill before heading back to the shop. Neither felt like working.

Behind them stood a group of people—a man with a pink face, two women and a toddler in a red jumpsuit. The adults stood over in the sun but close enough for Tess to see droplets of sweat on their foreheads and noses. The toddler bobbed around the adults, tangling his way in and out of long legs and skirts, tripping over swollen feet until he discovered a patch of shade a few feet away. Smiling, he plopped down. *He's the smart one*, she thought, turning back to the squirrel.

Flies swarmed around the carcass, swerving to avoid collisions. She looked over at Jeff's face, searching his eyes, watching the perspiration quivering on his upper lip, noticing the stray chin hairs he'd missed when shaving. She wondered what he thought of her. They had been working together all summer but had only recently begun the brutal process of getting to know one other.

Tess' stepfather had moved the whole family out here midway through her senior year of high school. Until just a few months ago, Tess had kept only one tie from home—David. The thought of their prom picture framed on her mother's dresser made her shudder. Everyone expected them to get married—even Tess. So when she moved, nobody thought they'd have problems withstanding the perils of a long distance relationship. But then he flew out to visit for spring break. Even though they spent a pleasant week together, Tess sometimes felt herself putting on a smile. When he left, Tess waved good-bye but didn't stay to watch him board the plane.

A week later Tess called to say that she couldn't be in a relationship right then. She just needed space or time or something else.

David didn't understand. "You're half-fucking-way across the country! How much more space do you need?"

"It's not that kind of space," Tess tried to explain. "It's not distance-space, it's me-space. David, you know where you're going, but I'm not so sure I want the same things that I used to."

"You want someone else?"

"David…no." Tess stopped, holding her breath. "I just can't, okay?" Through the silence that belongs to telephones alone, she listened to David's slow and controlled exhale.

"Well, don't expect to ever come back," he said.

"I won't," she said and laid the phone gently in its cradle.

They hadn't spoken since.

Now Tess was free, though she didn't really feel it. Instead of heading off to college like everybody else, she was working manual labor to try to make enough money to go to Europe. She wanted to travel, to see the world on her own before getting stuck in a career or marriage. She felt that if she could just get away, then she could really get on with her life. But saving money was taking longer than she'd expected.

Meanwhile, Tess had Saturday evenings filled with travel brochures and historical romance novels that she would deny reading if anyone ever asked. She also had Jeff. Well, she didn't really have him. But she knew him, and that was something at least. He was a year older and had worked at the university the previous summer. He showed her the ropes of the job, which meant that he showed her how to slack off without getting caught. Jeff introduced her to extended bathroom breaks, lying down behind the rhodies to pull weeds, and strolls around the perimeter of campus just to get a new washer for the hose. Of course, these activities always required at least two people.

One time, they spent the whole afternoon lounging on a strip of weak lawn behind the economics building. Under the guise of pulling weeds, they wished on dandelion seeds.

"Maybe we shouldn't be blowing these all over the place. They'll just come up as weeds and we'll have to pull them," Tess said.

"Aw c'mon, you know nobody ever comes back here," Jeff said, rolling onto his stomach and reaching for the last two dandelions. He plucked them and handed the fuller one to Tess, then rolled onto his back. He poised the dandelion inches from his nose, closing his eyes. "I wish for every one of these seeds and every other dandelion seed in the entire world to fall on concrete or unfertile soil so that Tess won't have to deal with them," Jeff said, opening his eyes to wink at Tess, "and so that this dandelion will mark her very last wish."

He sucked in a lungfull of air and blew, rising up to a sitting position, as his face turned red with the attempt to dislodge that last clinging seed. It finally parted, reluctantly, and Tess watched it bob through the air and disappear. She held up her own dandelion and blew with a short, quick breath before realizing that she hadn't made a wish. Watching her dandelion seeds float on the breeze, Tess felt she had somehow missed her chance. She wanted to recall each of those seeds as if they were her children, to send them away with her blessing, each one a promise of fulfillment. But it was too late, and Tess wasn't sure what she would wish for anyway.

Usually Tess and Jeff only saw each other at work. But last week when it got up into the hundreds Jeff had invited her over to his apartment after work for a swim. Following the swim they hung out with his roommate, Kyle. Kyle also worked grounds and was even more of a slacker than Jeff. He had dangerously white skin and perpetually chapped lips.

Tess could tell they had an all-male household as soon as she walked in. The hallway smelled of dried sweat and leftover fast food. Against the wall in the living room stood an old video arcade game—Joust. They tried to get Tess to play, but she only laughed at the flying turkeys or camels or whatever they were.

After Joust, Jeff and Kyle decided to break out the darts. They didn't have a dart board, so they threw the darts at their other roommate's couch, his bulletin board, his wooden box of CDs. When they tired of that, Kyle removed a Mountain Dew can from the shrine surrounding the t.v., which boasted over two hundred cans and set it on the carpet in the middle of the room. Tess watched them laugh and throw darts until the can folded over on itself.

"Woo-hoo!" the boys yelled.

"Yeah, all right!"

Kyle took another can from the shrine and filled it with water. This time, as the darts punctured the can, water spurted out, browning the cream-colored carpet. Tess watched from the couch wondering what the hell she was doing with her life. Three cans later, they graduated to a two-liter bottle. It stood up longer but expelled more, and soon the stain on the carpet grew to human size. It looked as if someone had taken a hose to the carpet. Tess hoped it wouldn't soak through the floor and drip on the people downstairs. When Kyle and Jeff brought out the milk jug, Tess got up to leave.

"Thanks for the swim."

"Yeah," they said without turning to face her, "see ya tomorrow."

"Yeah," she said and walked out thinking that David would have loved these guys.

Now, as she looked down at the shriveled squirrel carcass, she thought of David and wondered if she had done the right thing. She couldn't tell what made her happy anymore.

"Guess we better get to it," she said.

Jeff squinted up at the sky. "Yeah, I guess." He looked back to the group of people behind them. The toddler had pulled a handful of grass out by the roots and brought it up to his mouth. His mother noticed and swept him up to totter on her hip.

Tess ignored the swarm of flies and held the push broom against the squirrel's head, while Jeff positioned the shovel where the tail should have been. She began to slide the squirrel onto the shovel, but as soon as she moved it, a thin membrane gave way and an avalanche of maggots spilled from the belly. She dropped the push broom, squealed and backed into the oak tree. Jeff set the shovel down and leaned in for a closer look. The top half of the squirrel rested on the shovel, but the bottom half hung over the edge, suspended inches from the ground. Every so often a maggot dropped from the carcass. Tess wasn't usually squeamish about dead things, but those maggots sent shivers through her whole body.

"Hey, check it out," Jeff beckoned.

She inched forward. The maggots squirmed in and out, under and over one another. Magnified, they would have looked like the stilted special effects from a low-budget, horror flick:

"Isn't that disgusting?"

"Yuck," she replied.

"Here." He lowered the shovel. "Scoop the rest on."

She started to brush the maggots toward the shovel, but couldn't stop squirming. She suddenly felt cool, even in the sun. "I can't. I can't. You do it." She dropped the push broom, and the wood handle struck the brick with a loud and hollow clap.

"Geez," Jeff said.

Self-conscious, she looked around. The noise had attracted the attention of the pink-faced man, who now approached them. His shoulders looked unusually high and his arms were too big for his sleeves. He seemed to bulge everywhere. His stomach bulged over his belt. His eyes bulged out of his head. With open mouth and upper lip raised to make way for bulging gums, the man squinted and bent over the squirrel.

"Is that a dead animal? Is that a squirrel? Are those maggots?" Even his voice bulged as it escalated. "Cool!" The word sounded unnatural coming from him. The man straightened up and turned to the women. "See that?"

They nodded and smiled with closed mouths.

The man turned back to Jeff and Tess. "See that?" he said, pointing at the carcass and gesturing wildly. "That is your life! That is what happens after you die! That's your life! That's all it's worth. Here, hon, come look at this."

"I don't want to," she said, setting the toddler down and holding him against her legs.

"But that's your life!" His face reddened even more, voice cracking at the end of each sentence. "That's your death! Your life. Look at it! Take a good look! That's you!"

He looked at Jeff and Tess expectantly, then swung his head around to the two women now standing in the shade. They smiled at Tess in apology. The man turned frantically back to Tess, who couldn't meet the wild look in his eyes. She looked down, her gaze accidentally falling on the pile of writhing maggots, helpless in the sun. She felt her stomach begin to turn, so she looked at Jeff. His hairline was wet with perspiration.

"Geez, that's an awfully depressing thought," he said.

The man sucked in his breath and began to move toward Jeff.

"Stop it, Harold." His wife spoke up. "That's enough now."

"But that's your life," he said weakly.

"I know. Now let's go."

The three of them retreated, toddler in tow. Jeff and Tess watched in silence. They could hear the women's skirts swishing and their heels clicking on the brick sidewalk until they were nearly a block away and had dissolved into the heat mirage.

"Yikes," Tess said after a long silence, "that was strange."

"Yeah."

They finally managed to scoop the carcass onto the shovel, leaving the maggots to fend for themselves. Half of the flies accompanied them to the dumpster, while the other half stayed behind with the maggots. After disposing of the carcass, Jeff and Tess headed back to the shop. Passing the oak tree, Tess tried to avert her eyes from the maggots that still squirmed on the bricks, blindly searching for their lost carcass.

"I wonder where maggots come from?" she asked as they sauntered along dragging the shovel and push broom behind them. "I mean, do they just suddenly appear when an animal dies? Do they smell it from miles away? I mean, how do they know?"

Jeff looked at her and raised an eyebrow. "They come from flies."

"Oh, that's right. I knew that. I just forgot." Tess knew she had sounded stupid. She really did know about flies and maggots, somewhere in the back of her mind.

They walked on in silence except for the sound of the shovel scraping and the push broom pulling against the sidewalk.

As they neared the shop, Tess slowed and stopped in a patch

of shade. She didn't want them to reach the shop and join the rest of the crew.

Jeff leaned on the handle of his shovel and said, "Geez, it sure is hot out here. Bet it's almost a hundred."

Tess suddenly wanted to tell him about herself. She wanted to tell him of her plans to go to Europe and her dreams of wandering the streets of Paris in the rain. She wanted to confess her breakup with David, that she thought Mountain Dew tasted like piss in a can, that she read travel brochures and historical romance novels on Saturday nights and that she didn't have many friends. She wanted to tell him she was lonely.

"Yeah," she said, "it's hot."

George Fountas
GEORGE WASHINGTON UNIVERSITY

Performances

Phineas is my lover and he is a beautiful spectacle twenty feet up. The blue and yellow big top tent serves as his backdrop. The lights bounce off his silver lamé costume and reflect like rainbows. He is a prism of light slowly moving across the thin wire. He calculates each movement; he has told me that before he lifts his foot or moves his arms he carefully considers how it will alter his center of gravity. Each step brings potential disaster. One wobble, one slip and he will fall. Each night, following my family's performance, I watch Phineas execute his high wire routine and wait to escort him back to his trailer. I stand silently in amazement. It is not his performance that impresses me—I walk a high wire through my life—what amazes me is the way he holds his ass so tightly as he walks, holding all of his fear right there; mine is in my stomach.

"Honey, Oscar's tummy is acting up again. I told him he could skip practice this morning." I hear my mother say this from outside my trailer.

"Olga, he's gonna have to get over that. If he keeps missing practice I'll kick him out of the show. I can't have him screwing up my act," my father says. "That boy needs to stop acting like such a pansy and be a man. If only you'd stop babying him. I'm gonna have a talk with him after breakfast. Oh, have you mended my leotard yet?" His voice fades.

The circus is my father's; he inherited it from his father. My involvement was never an option. Our trapeze act consists of my mother and father, sister, Ophelia, brother, Oswald, and his wife, Eleni. Eleni is beautiful and so my father loves her. When Oswald first married her it was a scandal because her name didn't begin with an 'O.' This name game was all a part of my father's sense of perfection. We had to be the perfect act—"The O. Wows." Our last name is really Wozirski.

There are some days that I just cannot perform. I have been lying in bed for three hours. The pain in my stomach has subsided. I stand to venture out of my trailer but fall back down, dizzy. I try again, slowly this time. I need to eat something to give myself some strength. I pull on a pair of cut-off denim shorts, slip my feet into sandals and walk outside towards the make-shift cafeteria.

The breakfast table is still out with Granny Smith apples, a banana with a few bruised spots and a half bagel remaining. The coffee pot is empty. A trail of ants moves towards some spilled honey. I choose the banana and go back out to sit in the sun. I find a patch of grass in view of Phineas' practice wire. I love watching when he doesn't know I am there. He is rehearsing an addition to his act where he does a pirouette in the center of the wire. Unable to maintain his balance, he falls on the cushion. He hears my gasp when he falls and glances over his shoulder.

"Shouldn't you be practicing?" he asks.

"Um, I wasn't feeling well. I'm resting."

"Well, perhaps you could rest where you wouldn't disturb me."

He climbs back on the wire and continues his practice. I walk back to my trailer to put on my practice leotard, so I can join my family for the final practice before the four o'clock show. In my quiet, cool space, as I pull off my shorts, I hear a noise outside and then a voice.

"Oscar?" It's Phineas.

"Hold on, I'm changing," I answer.

Despite this he walks in and I quickly pull the black leotard up to my waist.

"I've already seen you naked." He pauses, stares, and kisses my lips. "I just wanted to apologize for snapping at you."

"That's okay. I shouldn't have been bothering you."

"I wasn't mad at you. It upset me that I fell. That stunt has to be flawless by tonight."

"I don't understand why you're so worried; your act is fabulous already."

"Well, your father demands perfection, and I have to keep him happy. I'm not his son, remember, he doesn't *have* to keep me in the show."

"Are you implying that the only reason he keeps me is because I am?"

"You have to admit that job security isn't really an issue when your father is the boss."

"Yeah, well, knowing my life rests in his hands isn't the greatest comfort either. What happens when he finds out I'm a faggot?"

"I hate it when you use that word. And so what if your father finds out. He knows I'm gay and he still keeps me on."

"It's different. You don't serve as a personal embarrassment to him. He would take my homosexuality as a direct insult."

"Well, if things turn bad, you know I'm here for you. We can run off and start our own show," he says this sweetly. "I love you, Oscar."

This is the first time he's said that to me. I cannot help but smile.

"Go on to practice now before you really anger your father. I'll see you later, sexy." With this my face turns red. I am still not comfortable with all this; boys are not supposed to fall in love with each other. I pull the straps of my leotard over my shoulders and run over to the big tent.

"Nice of you to join us, sir. I hope we didn't disturb your rest!" my father shouts from the platform.

"Are you feeling better, hon?" my mother asks.

"Yes."

"Get up here. You need to practice your part, especially when you and Oswald switch places on the 'peze. You stuttered a little last night. It's all in the timing—when I let go of your brother you need to release the bar and catch my arms. Let's go!" my father orders.

I powder my hands, step up on the platform and grip the trapeze. I fill my lungs through my nose and then release through my mouth before leaping forward. As I swing through the air I wish I were really flying. I would release my hands and soar through the air, fly over my father and wave good-bye.

I miss my father's arms the first time. Each time after, I come close enough to touch them but pull my body away at the last minute. My mind is cluttered. I have thoughts of running away, being anywhere but here. I cannot concentrate. I keep falling, my father cannot catch me. I drop into the net and my mother helps me to get back up.

"Honey, what's wrong?" she asks.

I think *everything* but instead say, "nothing."

"Well then do this for your father."

"What about what I want?" I mutter.

"Well, what do you want, dear?" she asks, full of concern.

"To stop performing, I'm tired of this act."

"Well, why don't you try something new? Have you given any thought to the high wire? I'm sure Phineas could teach you a lot."

"Yeah, I'll think about it," I say and smile to myself.

"Now Oscar!" my father screams.

This is the last time, I think.

I reclimb the rope ladder that leads to the platform. It sways as I move up.

"Focus, goddamn it! You miss it this time and you're out. We've been practicing all morning and we're tired. We can't wait for you to get it right."

It's humorous to watch my father yell while he hangs by his legs. His face is red from the blood that gathers there, making his head look as if it might burst.

I take the trapeze in my hands and swing way out over the net and back, and forward again. My father gives me the signal and I release. This time I catch his arms. When I care, I can give an excellent performance.

"There, that's what I'm talking about. Now don't screw up tonight." My father knows he cannot go on without me.

We stop at two o'clock to wash up and rest before the first performance. My family always takes an hour nap, but since I slept all morning I decide to go for a walk instead. I slip a magazine out of my trunk and wrap it in my shirt.

In the woods that surround the circus site I can hear moving water, so I venture in further to find the river. I sit on a rock and take the magazine out of my shirt. Across the top it says "Freshman" in red letters, and a rather unattractive, oiled-up man poses on the cover. Inside offers more men in various positions, in various states of undress. Phineas had shown it to me a few weeks back, and I had asked to borrow it. It served its purpose, replacing the *Playboy* my father had given me last year for my sixteenth birthday, telling me to hide it from my mother.

Although sometimes I wish I could attain the expectations he has for me—to marry my own Eleni and give birth to more trapeze artists—it would never be *my* wife and kids, it would be my father's, my father's dream. My dream is of Phineas.

Phineas joined our troupe three months ago. My father had seen him perform one day while spying on the competition. He promised him higher pay and a longer winter vacation if he signed on with us. He was eighteen and had few other prospects besides the circus. After his first performance with us I had gone to his trailer to congratulate him. He sat on his bed wearing only a robe. It separated at the top and fell to one side.

"Your act is amazing," I told him, feeling lust and confusion as I spoke to him.

"Thank you, my mother taught me everything I know."

"Where is she now?"

"Dead."

"I'm sorry."

"She fell during a practice. Just put her foot in the wrong place and down she went. She broke her neck. I couldn't bear to stay with that troupe, too many memories of her. I'm very grateful to your father for this chance."

"Where is your father?"

"I never knew him."

The whole time he spoke I had been staring at his chest. The exposed nipple was a perfect circle, about the size of a quarter, and was a beautiful golden brown. A small patch of hair surrounded it, but other than that his skin was smooth and well tanned. I felt ridiculous—lusting after him when he was confiding in me.

"Do you miss your mom?" I asked. As soon as the words escaped my mouth I regretted asking. Of course he would.

"She was all that I had. She was my best friend. Yes, I miss her, but it is almost too simple to say 'miss,' it's more like I ache because of the emptiness she has left in me."

I saw a tear form in the corner of his eye and then slowly trickle down the side of his nose where it paused for a moment before falling off his face and on to his robe. I moved closer and put my arm on his shoulder to console him. He rested his head on my shoulder and I rubbed his arm as I held him. When the tears stopped he turned his face towards me. His eyes were red and puffy and his skin was kind of blotchy.

"I must look like shit now," he said.

"No, you're beautiful," I said.

He turned his face a little more, moved his lips closer to mine and kissed me. It was a kiss that radiated through my entire body. It filled me with warmth and desire. I knew it was taboo to be kissing a boy and yet I wanted more.

Now it's more than I'm capable of coping with, but nothing I'm willing to give up. My emotions are in flux. My sexuality is no longer a mystery to me, but I'm not sure it's a secret I am ready to reveal. Phineas came out early; he told his mother when he was eleven, and she loved him. I know it will be different for me.

I arrive back at my trailer to find my mother in a panic.

"Where have you been? Go change. We're wearing the purple outfits. With the silver sequins."

"Mom, I need to tell you something first."

"Quickly."

"I think I need a break."

"Well, we'll be taking a month off in ten weeks."

"But I can't wait that long. I'm not happy. I want to leave."

"Don't be silly. You're just upset with your father. Just ignore him when he gets like that."

"It's more than that. There's a lot more I need to tell you."

"Well, now is not the time. I laid your costume out on your bed. Your father is with the others greeting the audience. Please, hurry up before he gets upset."

In the trailer I throw my clothes and the magazine onto my bed and slowly pull on my outfit. *So close to telling her*, I think. She didn't want to hear me. I tie my silver cape around my neck which feels tighter than usual.

Outside the tent everyone is in costume and mingling with the crowd. Walter and Vera, our star clowns, are performing with their trained poodles. They try to get the dogs to jump through hoops but they will not. Vera tries to demonstrate and gets the hoop stuck around her overstuffed ass. I wasn't sure it was funny the first time I saw it either.

I look all around for Phineas and finally locate him standing off to the side of the crowd, in the center of a group of swooning teenage girls. He is signing autographs. Not wanting to bother him, I go inside to find my father and siblings.

The show begins with a parade. There is a frenzy of colorful confetti, bright lights and costumes of every gaudy color, in silk, sequin and feathers. The audience is consumed by all the activity, unable to concentrate on any one act for fear of missing another. It all bores me and when the parade is over I sneak out to return to my trailer; there is an hour before we go on. I grab Phineas as I sail past.

At my trailer we peek into all the corners to assure we are alone. Just a precaution because I know my family is watching the show, it *never* bores them. We sit on my bed and Phineaus picks up the magazine I left out.

"You should be more careful with this. Your father might find it."

"Here, let me put it back in my trunk."

"No, I think I'm going to take it back. I get lonely at night," he teases.

"Sorry, you gave it to me," I say.

I try to grab it from him but miss and fall on the bed. He pounces and then kisses me. I struggle at first, but he holds my arms down. I lift my head up and kiss his Adam's apple. He slowly releases my arms and rolls off of me. We lie face to face. His large, brown eyes take in my face and I stare back in wonder. He nibbles at my lips and then down my neck. Suddenly there's a bang on the trailer door.

"Oscar! Are you in there? We're on in ten. Stop wasting time and get the hell out here!" It's my father.

"Uhhh, I'm coming, hold on." I push Phineas off of me and stand up to adjust my purple lycra.

"Wait for us to leave and then come out, so he doesn't see you," I whisper to Phineas.

He gives me another kiss and I run out.

"Let's go," my father says through clenched teeth. He walks away, a few feet ahead of me.

I stop behind him.

"What are you doing? I said let's go," he hisses.

"I feel sick, I don't think I should go out there."

"I don't care what you think. It's not up to you. Now get in there before I get mad." He gives me a shove towards the tent opening.

I stand on the platform listening to the introductions of my family by the ringmaster. The crowd cheers for each one of us. When I hear my own name I am startled for a moment. I have heard it announced millions of times, but this time it doesn't sound like it belongs. I glance behind me to the ground, Phineas is standing there and I smile at him. I suddenly feel a sense of relief.

I take the trapeze into my hands and swing way out over the net. The wind I create feels cool against my body. I take one more swing and release my grip. My body tumbles through the air, but like in practice, I miss my father. I hear the gasp of the crowd as my limp body hits the net. I bounce several times, and when my motion is controlled I look up to see the disappointment on the faces of my family. I stand and begin to move toward the rope ladder, but instead of climbing up, I climb down to the ground. I walk over to Phineas and take his hand.

"Will you come with me?" I ask.

"Anywhere," he says.

"Where the hell are you going?" my father yells.

The crowd stops cheering as they realize this is not part of the show. I turn back one last time to see my family standing in bewilderment. I share a kiss with Phineas and walk away from the show. Trying to regain the show's composure, the ring master calls attention to the center ring. A tiger growls as we pass its cage. I tighten my grip on Phineas' hand and look back one last time. In the background I hear the crowd, mixed sounds of screams and laughter. The calliope begins to play. The show must go on, but not for me; I must escape this circus.

Jennifer Vickers
East Carolina University

Waiting for Lucky

I light a match and suck on the yellow butt of an old cigarette that I've scrounged from an ashtray outside of Piggly Wiggly Supermarket. Sitting on a charcoal-colored curb, underneath the beginning of a blackening sky, I sip on my Private Stock Finest Malt Liquor—oh, it goes down as smooth as light slipping underneath a dark sky. The warm malt liquor and the stale taste of the cigarette fill my mouth as I watch two cardinals in Ailanthus trees, imagining they were dancing like Indonesia's Birds of Paradise. The parking lot's grey cement contrasts with the glorious pink of the sky.

I'm waiting for Lucky.

I like the ambiance of Piggly Wiggly at sunset. This Piggly Wiggly in particular, on the other side of town, closes at six o'clock in the winter and seven o'clock in the summer. Wearing my pale yellow toreador pants, I sit on the curb (sometimes I lean my back against the Coke machines) between the dirty, glass doors that lead into the dusty, rotten smelling, "Ultra Savings and More" Supermarket. Lucky's Pool Hall, the only official pool "hall" in town, is right next to me. A neon sign reads "Lucky's," and has an outline of an overflowing beer, with the foam flashing. I watch my shiny leather boots reflect the green, red, orange of the lights. On the other side of town they have big polyangular pool clubs, some of them with memberships and shiny oak bars. The supermarkets that kick people like me out of their parking lots are open twenty-four hours, smell good, and have new lighting and sneaky cameras. Their customers aren't afraid after dark.

I sit anachronistically in a part of town where nothing seems to change except ages and seasons. The *enfant terribles* rage and rule like the dark shadows of city streets.

I don't think that anyone knows his real name, but people know that the owner, Lucky, is not a man to be reckoned with. I doubt that anyone even knows what he looks like, but from the collection of tales I hear from the homeless men whose butts fill the cracked, wooden stools of Lucky's, he is a handsome, witty, infamous man. From their stories I've created an image of a man that would have the answer to it all. He is said to be a healer, who has traveled across the world by foot, relentless in his pursuit of discovering the intricacies of life and of death. He is said to have died and come back to life. Someone once said that he drives a Harley. They say he dresses in black leather from head to toe and has long, slick, black hair to match. He is supposed to have eyes the color of water and if you get a chance to look into them you can see your future. I am here every Sunday of every week, normally with a different man on the curb beside me each time, waiting for Lucky and his Harley.

I don't know how it happened—a girl with a college degree, aspirations, a family who pushed and pushed for her to be something someday, and a boyfriend who stuck by after one emotional break down to the next—sitting in front of a pool room waiting for a man who may never show up.

One of the derelicts, who I scarcely recognize because of his gaudy pink slippers and garish, orange make-up, comes stumbling out and stares at me as if I were a lost relative, a beautiful whore, or nothing at all.

He sits down next to me, or rather next to my forty, with glaring eyes adjusting themselves to the glow of my shoes.

He looks up at the sky, so empty tonight, and says to me, "Can I have a cigarette?" I reach into the Kool, sand ashtray and toss the biggest butt I can find up in the air.

His wrinkled fingers move slowly, like in those dreams where no matter how hard you try to move your body it won't. And I just can't believe it! He misses, and it falls to the ground in a puddle, rolls into the drain pipe and is gone.

I hear the slush-slush of the sewer and then notice the smell of urine. I imagine the thousands of people sitting on their toilets right now, thinking, flushing. And here it all is. And there it all goes, right back into the system.

"I'm sorry about that," I say, staring at the stream of sewage rushing by below the metal grate.

"That's all right, hon. Got some change you can spare?" His voice sounds muffled and his cheeks sag like Droopy's. His ears wiggle when he hears the sounds of silver and nickel in pockets. My hand is in front of him, full of dimes, nickels and quarters; I don't know exactly how much.

He reaches out and closes my hand. His nails are painted white. "I can't go in there," he says. "Can you?"

"Why not?" I ask. "You got some phobia for supermarkets?"

He laughs and says, "No, only Piggly Wiggly."

"Yeah, well then I have a phobia for Harris Teeter. What's up with these supermarket names anyway?"

"I don't know." He laughs again and says the words "Piggly" and "Wiggly" really slowly and then "Harris Teeter" in the same way. I laugh too. "Man!" he says. "I'm banned from both those places." He takes his white fingernails off of my hand. "'Bout a week ago I was caught sleepin' in the warehouse behind the store. Since they already caught me in the women's bathroom, they told me to stay clear from Alfred for awhile. He's the mean 'ol, white store manager. I could've sworn he had a crush on me though…" He continues talking as I get up and walk away.

Inside the store it is cool, but stinky. Food stamp week is almost over. As my shiny boots cross over the yellowish-brown floor towards the beer aisle I imagine running into Lucky near the packaged meat aisle, which is practically empty and now lined with pools of coagulated blood. I would stand in the stench of it all and glimpse into the water to discover what I need to know. I'd tell him that I am confused; I'd ask for the right way to go; I'd tell him that if he could tell me what to do and that everything will be fine, then I will be fine too. See, I have been told that the world is free, but I've been taught irresponsibility. I can't be responsible for this freedom of choice, because what if I choose the wrong thing?

In the beer aisle I pick up another couple forties of Private Stock Finest Malt Liquor and then make my way back out to the curb.

I manage to salvage another butt after a big-breasted woman tossed one, still burning, into the Kool ashtray, and say, "Here you go." I feel him looking in my eyes, as if trying to tell me something just with his expression.

"Ya live around here?" he asks, picking up the bottle very slowly and taking a sip.

"I live uptown," I reply, looking out at the parking lot. A slight breeze whispers in the trees.

"Are ya a student?"

"I just graduated a few months ago."

"Got any big plans?" Several children are behind us, banging on the Coke machine, jumping up and down in a frenzy, and wailing over and over, "Mamma, Coke! Mamma, Coke! Mamma, Coke! Mamma, Coke..."

"I had plans. Lots of plans, but now I really don't know what to do."

The woman is standing, legs straddled over a greasy puddle, in front of a cart heaping full of packaged red meat. I can't believe how much meat is in her cart! There must be sirloins, shredded meat, canned meat, sausage, steak...and she isn't budging for one second!

"A pretty girl like you, with a college degree, and ya don't know what to do?" he says, pulling out make-up from his bag and powdering his nose. The kids behind me are driving me crazy. I find solace in my malt liquor and grab another butt.

"No." I take a sip. He looks over at me with that same expression and then looks me in the eyes. It's strange because his eyes look so familiar.

"I'm at this point where I just don't know. It's not like I want answers for everything, because life isn't worth living if you can't experiment, make mistakes, and learn, but my mind is just overwhelmed with questions. And at night, when I dream, the questions just become a whirlwind, and I am stuck in them."

"What kind of questions do you have?"

"Oh, just silly ones. Like, whether I want to have children or not. Or what kind of job I want. Do I want to continue to go to school? What's going to happen to my sister, who is a single mother with two children. Who is my boyfriend, and does he really love me? Will he leave me someday? Will the years just pass me by so quickly that I end up growing old alone, dying alone? Will I get to travel the world, or will I be like my mother, stuck with a husband I'm unsure I love, two children who are insecure and distant, in a small town with no friends and nothing to do but cook and clean and wonder what if..."

"O.K. Settle down, little girl. Those are some pretty tough questions, but ya need to slow down. No one can give you the answers. Everything in life happens for a reason. There's a reason why you're sitting here on this curb right now, drinking malt liquor and smokin' old cigarettes. There are unfathomable reasons for everything. There's a reason why your mother is here; she gave birth to you. And believe me, that is something wonderful in itself. There's a reason why those children are screaming behind us. That woman there, has seven children, no husband, and is on welfare. She married an alcoholic who used to abuse her and them kids day after day."

"What happened to him?"

"He died in some mysterious way. Doctors did an extensive

autopsy and still couldn't come up for a reason for his death. But the way I see it, the mysterious ways of life helped her out. She may be poor as hell right now, but she ain't got no drunk husband beating her up and molestin' her children no more."

The children scream louder and louder. He finishes his beer and stands up very slowly, and then walks towards the door to Lucky's. When it opens, the inside of Lucky's gushes out. Blondie's voice is heard from the jukebox, singing "Living in the Real World," beer is being drunk, and balls are cracking. I think about going in, but I've become a *habitué* of the outside world and don't like to wander too far in.

I hear a whimpering in the distant night and a series of gunshots paralyze the air. Piggly Wiggly is getting quiet; all of the shoppers are on their way toward Douglas Street to buy drugs, or to go home, or to feed the crying children on their porches. I wonder where Lucky is.

A few gun shots later, I hear the rumble of a motorcycle. Two people pull in on the bike. A bony girl with flaxen hair and artificially tanned skin gets off the bike. The man is wearing black leather and a silver helmet with the words "Jesus Loves You" and underneath that "But I Don't Give A Fuck About You." Strands of wind-blown, black hair fall upon his shoulders. I am looking him up and down as his legs unstraddle the bike and stand before me. I feel like a derelict smoking these old butts and sipping on warm, cheap, but fine, malt liquor, waiting for this man, who has never even seen me before. To try to attract his attention, I cross my legs this way and that way, puff my lips out as I suck on the last few drags of this cigarette, lean back and jut out my left shoulder, and look as desperate as I possibly can. As he walks past me to the Coke machine he ashes on my head. The heels of the woman following close behind him go click-click.

"Hey, sexy momma, let me spend some silver on ya." His voice doesn't sound smooth like this malt liquor, but harsh and raspy. A cigarette hangs from his mouth.

He places one of his hands into black leather pants. I hear

the jingle-jingle of change.

"Sure thing," she says.

"I know how much ya like cherries," he says, handing her a Cherry Coke and then reaching both hands around her and grabbing a handful of her ass. She giggles and then the soda can goes "phsstclck" when she opens it up. I try not to stare, but if I could only see those clear eyes underneath the sunglasses he wears. He laughs like a hyena and then kisses the flaxen-haired girl.

They begin to make-out, right here. He looks like Lucky, but doesn't act like Lucky. Who is this girl? I decide to say something.

"Excuse me," I say to them, standing up.

"I ain't got no more change if that's what you want," he says. The girl whispers something into his ear and they both laugh at me.

"No, I was wondering if..."

"You just leave me and my girl alone, you hear me?" he says opprobriously, taking off his sunglasses. "I don't want my girl to be bothered by no freak. Now, get outta here!"

I look into his eyes, but I don't see the color of water. They are dark, practically black. I can't believe this. I don't know what to say. I manage to mumble "Lucky" as I walk away.

"That's right you're lucky," he yells. "Lucky for me not beating your ass!"

I disappear into the dark neighborhood. All of the houses are run-down, with chipped paint, crooked front porches, and missing street lamps. I sit down on an empty swing in the middle of an empty playground. After swinging back and forth, feeling the rush of the night air and listening to the sounds of life—birds chirping overhead, children laughing or crying, a television mumbling someone into a trance—I run home to my apartment and sit in the darkness for hours. Without realizing where my conscious thoughts cease and my subconscious ones emerge, I dream of floating in clear water.

Cleôn McLean
University of Southern California

Voodoo

<u>Chorus Canticle [A]</u>
. . . Let her be some Sabrina fresh from stream,
Lucent as shallows slowed by wading sun,
Bedded on fern, the flowers' cynosure:
That she is airy earth, the trees, undone,
Must ape her languor natural and pure.

She sits at the window watching the evening invade the beaten, sickle-shape road that sleeps beyond. Beside this road, the Dutch Oak trees stand like towering cathedrals, their limbs saluting a deity. Slowly, the sound of a flute begins to pierce the silent air with six sharp *flutes*, flooding Nana-Ama's ears, and forcing her to clutch the patched, hand-me-down, red, cotton dress on her lap, in response. Turning from the window, Nana-Ama faces the dark room that holds her. The half-burnt out *flambeaux* fillings can't sufficiently supply *lumière* to overtake the thick blackness that defines this room tonight. Yet, Nana-Ama manages to feel her way to the bed, put on her red dress, wrap a cloth into a turban on her head, and lave her brown body with coconut oil. The sound of the flute stops. A cool night air swims into the room, engulfing and caressing Nana-Ama's frail body. The breeze attempts to unwind the tenseness of her body, but to no avail. Instead of feeling relaxed, Nana-Ama fears the punishment she will receive for her rendezvous. *Wha' wou'd masa Charnel do if 'im catch mé? Mé sure 'im wil hang mé o' chap aff mé han'. Gad! Mé jus wan' fa know whe' mé chil' de.*

The flute begins to sound its six sharp *flûtés* again, reminding Nana-Ama to prepare for her meeting.

Chorus Canticle [B]
Shall I compare thee to a summer's day?
Thou art lovelier and more temperate:
Rough winds do shake the darling buds of May...
By chance, or nature's changing course untrimm'd;
But thy eternal summer shall not fade...

Twice, five years passed since Nana-Ama first called this home. She, the fairest of all the plantation slaves, was the only slave granted the privilege of retaining her true name: the name that marries her to mother Africa. Yet still, she is but simple property on Monsieur Rudoyer Charnel's sugar plantation in Essequibo: that place known to the Spanish and then the French as, El Dorado:

El Dorado, la ciudad de oro
El Dorado, el sueño trágico
El Dorado, las lágrimas del paraíso

The French came to this southern world in search of the city of gold. And when they found none, they cursed the bloody savages and their ridiculous myth before they settled on sugar as a profitable commodity.

But Nana-Ama is no myth.

Her body, "...with Phoebus' amorous pinches black," a gleam in the sun, rendering her tricklings of perspiration beads as that quality most desirous to man: thick droplets of gold. Of course, masa Charnel saw this in his investment. His nightly sojourns to her slave-quarters began as soon as masa Charnel registered Nana-Ama under his assests and they continued as often as the Essequibo River tides.

Chorus Canticle [C]
...Thou child of my right hand, and joy;
My sin was too much hope of thee, love boy,
[Six] years thou wert lent to me, and I thee pay,
Exacted by thy fate, on this just day ...
To have so soon 'scaped world's, and flesh's rage,
And if no other misery, yet age!...

Night after night, Nana-Ama lay on sugar sacks like a peacock on display, performing an occasional *fellatio* or provocatively attractive flipped up *fouetté* when need be, while masa Charnel wore her innocence away.

He did this even after Nana-Ama married Jacques, a field slave affectionately known on the plantation as "the great pretender." Jacques was an English slave who fled that British land—Jamaica— in hopes that this French one might be a safe haven for him. But this was not to be, for within that same year he entered this country, he was stocked on Monsieur Charnel's plantation and within a year's passing, he was hanged for attacking the plantation Over-Seer. Bless his Christian soul. For this, Nana-Ama raged inside for several full moons, like a trapped and wounded Juliettá. After this, she resolved to find Jacques' love and tender spirit in Barrow, their son.

One week ago, Barrow was stolen from his sugar-sack while Nana-Ama lay nearby, exhausted. The following days, Nana-Ama searched the plantation like a buccaneer on a captured Spanish merchant ship looking for treasure, but found nothing. Nana-Ama searched more frantically these past few days, and each time that her search was unsuccessful she cursed masa Charnel for tiring her of her guard. And she vowed that when she gained knowledge about the thief who stole her Barrow, she would seek revenge.

Late this afternoon, Nana-Ama ventured out of her quarters, meandered through the thick vegetation on the western-side of the plantation, crawled through the abandoned poultry pens, glided over the muddy earth, and stole away into the boiling house: a place she should not be. No woman should be. It is Pluto's own avernus, as defined by the dominant colors that lick the iron walls: red and black. Black also are the men who feed the boiling gourds the pulp of ground sugarcane. This is the house in which strength and endurance pays for a slave to retain the extensions of his body from the sharp teeth of the grinders or the red-hot bellies of the boilers. In this house, Nana-Ama searched through thick bundles of sugarcane that left their marks in her skin. She poked around in the boilers, hoping to find nothing. Then, she took a nearby poker and began poking around in the six molasses barrels that were left open to cool. While doing this, the Over-Seer came into the house. He, without any cleverty or art, quickly caught and bound Nana-Ama, like Ixion was, on a post amid the house. Here, the Over-Seer ripped the garments from Nana-Ama's bony body and licked her six, then six, then six more strokes of his cowhide. Each lash ignited a wave of wild rage inside Nana-Ama, whose shrilling howl shattered the silence of the ripened afternoon.

Chorus Canticle [D]
Threshed out by beaters, the long rushes break
In a white dust of ibises whose crises
Have wheeled since civilization's dawn
From the parched river or beast-teeming plain.
The violence of beast on beast is read
As natural law, but upright man

After the Over-Seer released and ordered her back to her quarters, Nana-Ama knew that there was only one thing left for her to do—seek the help of Vieille Dame Carabosse, the voodoo mistress.

Upon her return to her quarters, Nana-Ama received word from ol' man Sage that masa Charnel ordered her presence at his *maison de plantation* at once! Nana-Ama slipped on her patched, hand-me-down, red, cotton dress and requested of ol' man Sage for word to reach Vieille Dame Carabosse of her intended visit. This, ol' man Sage agreed to do. He had his ways. Vieille Dame Carabosse would get word.

On her way to Charnel's *maison*, Nana-Ama is perplexed as to why masa Charnel would desire to see her while his wife, Dame Mary Antoinivelle Charnel, is visiting from France. To any end, Nana-Ama doesn't find her presence at the *maison de plantation* befitting. Especially since Dame Mary is an unpleasant woman who doesn't particularly fancy her. Often she beckons other house slaves to "punish Nana-Ama" while she, Dame Mary, drinks bourbon and writes secret letters to her relations in Austria and Prussia, as she swings aloft in her imperial hammock.

When Nana-Ama gets to the *maison*, she sees Rudoyer Charnel vesseling down a bottle of madiera. She timidly approaches him and quickly scans the room for any sight of the visiting prude; she isn't there. "Ne t'en fais pas mon amour. Mary s'est déjà couchée. Maintenant, pourquoi ne me couches-tu pas?" Nana-Ama doesn't quite understand what masa Charnel is saying, but somehow she knows it means that she is to be a layer between him and his bed.

Her presumption is right. Within minutes, Rudoyer Charnel lays his thick, heavy-hair body upon her. His wife sleeps three rooms down the hall. He doesn't even question Nana-Ama about why her skin is so bruised, or why her eyes are like burnt dumplings. Perhaps he feels that his drivels and perspiration that rain on her wounds and swellings are better illustration of interest in her welfare than words. True, Rudoyer commands Nana-Ama's physical self into his vassalage, but her soul, her spirit and her love are far-removed from any chance that his display of *savior faire* or *savior vivre* would profit him access to. Nana-Ama is nauseated. The smell of digested madiera, the taste of sweat, the pinching pain, and thoughts of her son, muster in her a violent gyre that can only be released if she screams and smashes Rudoyer Charnel's head in like a pumpkin.

He's done. Before Nana-Ama could've climaxed her frustration and hurt, he rolls off of her. Within seconds he is out the door, and perhaps now suckling under the nurture of his milky wife. Nana-Ama gets up from the bed, picks up her red dress, and walks over to the window to watch the evening invade her world.

Nana-Ama calms her thoughts and seconds later she breezes out of masa Rudoyer's *maison*, limping slightly, and steals away from the plantation. She runs until she is safely tucked away in the dense forest nearby a less trodden path.

<u>Chorus Canticle [E]</u>
...If this
Be but a vain belief, yet, oh! How oft—
In darkness and amid the many shapes
Of joyless daylight; when the fretful stir
Unprofitable, and the fever of the world,
Have hung upon the beatings of my heart—
O sylvan Whye! Thou wanderer thro' the woods,
How often has my spirit turned to thee!
And now, with gleams of half-extinguished thoughts,
With many recognitions dim and faint,
And somewhat of a sad perplexity,
The picture of the mind revives again...

Nana-Ama darts through the thick, bossy trunks of coconut trees, slipping through the wild masses of towering vegetation and wild *feijoa*, hopping the mossy roots of bamboo trees, and sidetracking several times to avoid manhole traps set for runaway slaves. She knows the forest quite well, after trying many times in the past to escape. The pitch darkness of the night is Nana-Ama's only fear. She claws and rips the thick, juicy banana tree trunks that bend awkwardly because of their giant branches and weighty fruits. The thick, stagnant, moist air of the forest, along with vicious mosquito attacks, taunt Nana-Ama's sanity.

Nana-Ama hears the six sharp *flûtés* again. This abrupt awareness causes Nana-Ama to slip on a rotten coconut shell and fall face-up to the heavens. The wet threads of her patched, red dress rips in consequence.

No sooner does she fall, than it begins to rain in thick, long drops. Nana-Ama lies still. Raindrops dance a ritual of healing on her legs, while thick, wild *eddoe* leaves bow and curl around her thighs, covering them from raindrops like a coconut shell its core. Meanwhile, rain and earth soon rise between the arch formed by the angle of Nana-Ama's legs, as though Cybele is inviting her, Nana-Ama, to become one with her. Soon, this heaven and earth mustering seems to find a tender reservoir within the warmth of Nana-Ama. She feels her blood calming after hours of its rushing like the wild Sargasso Seas. Her heart takes leave of its woodpecker's rhythm, and recomposes from trepidation. Thick droplets soak Nana-Ama's lips with the sweetest of the sweetest, while softening her skin and babying her wounds and bruises. Dry leaves falling from coconut trees flip and twist in the air before finally lashing, gently, across Nana-Ama's eyes and mouth. This Nana-Ama doesn't mind because whatever she desired to say, masa Charnel always silenced her, and who she wants to see, she can't find. Besides, nature wants her this way; the leaves atop her eyes, mouth, and thighs, and the mud between her legs, all do their service, as their creator does charge them.

Within an hour's passing the rain eases to a drizzle and Nana-Ama tenderly releases herself from nature's hold. And slowly, she begins to amplify her pace in continuing her journey to Dame

Carabosse's house, which she knows to be only two deer pauses away.

Arriving at Dame Carabosse's house, she is breathless, in pain, and tired. It's pitch dark and Nana-Ama can only make out the silhouette in front of the door, framed by the illumination of a kerosene lamp in the background. Within seconds Vieille Dame Carabosse is greeting her saying, "Ah mé chil', mé hear wha' happen to ya pickney. Mé gwan help ya fin' 'im...na worri." Then, Dame Carabosse takes Nana-Ama by her waist and leads her into the forsaken plantation Great House. Inside the house, Dame Carabosse, gives Nana-Ama zeb-grass mixed with what smells to be cerecy bush made into a *julep* tea. This tea induces a late *siesta* into Nana-Ama's fatigued body; one so potent, Nana-Ama falls into the company of Morpheus and dreams of a different time.

Chorus Canticle [F]
Ere on my bed my limbs I lay,
It hath not been my use to pray
With moving lips or bended knees;
But silently, by slow degrees,
My spirit I to Love compose,
With reverential resignation,
No wish conceived, no thought exprest,
Only a sense of supplication;
A sense o'er all my soul imprest,
That I am weak, yet not unblest,
Since in me, round me, everywhere
Eternal Strength and Wisdom are.

O' what mysteries and awe the spirit fancies drama, when all watches on except consciousness, who takes leave of his post. Leap my spirit back to Cote D' Ivoire and upon that earthly rupture, Mount Nimba. Here I am on my sixth necklace of wild beads and watching *mé enat* gathering nuts and berries for me.

She seems at ease, as I am, with the cool, swollen, salty zephyr from that western blue rushing through our limbs. I watch as a young phoenix, merely a *jutte* long, pecks away in front of my feet. I could but see only his tail feathers framing my feet and this obscurity intrigues me; as does the strange *douceur* sound sweeping the air now and always at this time when Phoebus is watching. Tales from the white-man say that this sound is like their own *concertina*, but with such paragon as to repose any such comparison. These words meant nothing to anyone in my village, nor to me. We know that it is the sound of the mountain *juju* man, whom no one ever once saw, but we know he is there.

Today is special, for below where I sit, I see a *wend-lidg* about my age, three palm tree knots. He looks frightened by the black meanness of the mountain, and batters his eyes like a butterfly its wings. He must be of another village because his bodily daubs are those of another Sparrow Clan, not of mine. I walk over to *mé enat* and toll her dress until she gives me attention. I direct her attention to the *wend-lidg*, who has gained our presence and now stands staring at us. *Mé enat* and I rush over to him and start to speak *Ba-d'-lusre*, but he doesn't speak to us. Instead, the *wend-lidg* starts to cry as loud and as shrill as a hyena. *Mé enat* offers him nuts and berries, but the *wend-lidg* only drools in decline.

A man bursts through a clump of bushes and, without any civility, rudely pushes *mé enat* and me aside and scoops up the *wend-lidg*, who is silent as a lamb. This man doesn't say anything to *mé enat* or me. Instead his eyes are poised to condemn us for attempting to harm his *wend-lidg*? *Mé enat* picks me up and *jackies* me back to our village; not turning around once to be scolded by the unfriendly show of the man's eyes.

Nana-Ama sits up in bed; bewildered as to how long she has slept, and perplexed by the bizarre déjà vu dream of an incident that occurred in her childhood. She feels strong and the little tinglings of residual pain only reminds her about her affairs and her hope of bringing the joy of her life back into her arms and punishing those who took him away.

Nana-Ama ventures out of the bed in quest to find Dame Carabosse. As she enters the hallway, half a dozen guards of kerosene lamps spread their golden light in a shape like that formed between the White Nile and the Blue Nile. This illumination aids Nana-Ama in discovering a collection of old Spanish muskets hanging on the wall juxtaposed to the room she just left. A few steps down the hallway, a similar collection of Indian cutlass hangs on the wall that encloses the room she has just left. On the tail end of this virile masculine theme, and in the said hallway, Nana-Ama also sees several paintings hanging on the walls. These are French in texture and style, and are large, rather ruggedly framed paintings of slave ships and slaves working on a plantation. Nana-Ama sees herself in these paintings and hears echoes of evils of past torture on the slave ship she sailed on as cargo to Guiana. She vows never to set eyes back on Rudoyer Charnel's or any other colonist's plantation again, *deo volenté*!

She turns and descends the huge mahogany stairway. True, this house is just in its grandeur and luxury, but no right-minded European would dare step foot back in this Great House after the massacre that left its six occupants headless; they are said to still roam this plantation. Now if only the sixty-six slaves who perished here would release their free spirits to roam here also, this might be of some interest…

An awful smell of comestibles leads Nana-Ama to the kitchen. Dame Carabosse is laboring over a pot of boiling broth. A half-emptied madicra bottle stands besides a pouch with a slacken mouth displaying parts of a few gold coins on the table.

"Han' mé da cage unda de table, gyal" Dame Carabosse tells Nana-Ama, who gingerly presents the cage to her. Reaching into the cage and pulling out a rather short *fer de lance*, Dame Carabosse masterfully stabs it, slitting it from head to tail. Then, she scrapes the inside of the snake into the pot, discarding the remainder into a rusty basin nearby.

Dame Carabosse: "So, mé dear chil', how ya a feel now, eh? When yo' beena sleep, mé beena ten' to ya buss up skin. Mé see wa da man did a yo'; mé see 'im clear as riv'a wat'a."

Nana-Ama stutters a little. Until now, besides the little tinglings she experienced earlier, her wounds weren't an immediate concern. Vieille Dame Carabosse's acknowledgments is a clear sign that she is true kin to Aesailapius. "I'm sweet as jamoon and bitter like cassava," Nana-Ama replies in good report. Dame Carabosse laughs at this reply. Meanwhile, Nana-Ama walks over to the panoramic view of the tropical landscape in its evening elegance:

Chorus Canticle [G]
Breezeway in the tropics winnows the air,
Are ajar to its least breath
But hold back in a feint of architecture …
Cooling and salving us. Louvers,
Trellises, vines music also—
Shape the arboreal wind, make skeins
Of it …

How sweet and soft the air rushing in passes by Nana-Ama. A potent beam of pearly light from Heaven bounces off the green sleepers in the dark, but dissolves in the tender skin that Mother Nature suits around Nana-Ama. She retreats from this loving rapture which Heaven and Earth entwines about her. As Nana-Ama leaves the kitchen, Dame Carabosse requests: "Help mé fa tek dis pot outside. Push dis stick through de 'andle fa 'old de one side." Nana-Ama does Dame Carabosse's bidding, and then the two struggle to fetch the pot into Sylvanus' domain nearby.

As the two women reach the *purlieu* of the forest, Nana-Ama hears the familiar sound of the flute echoing its six sharp *flûtés* once more, from some pocket of the forest. This time it is more piercing and somewhat cryptic in its melody. Nana-Ama inquires: "Dame Carabosse, a who a play da thing a dis hou'a a de nite, eh? Da soun' wha' dem a mek a meking me feel fright'n."

Dame Carabosse thus absorbs Nana-Ama's complaint with a crafty *demure* and doesn't offer a reply. Instead, an artful suggestion of a smile develops on her face.

Chorus Canticle [H]
Thy soul shall find itself alone
Mid dark thoughts of the gray tomb-stone;
Not one, of all the crowd, to pry
Into thine hour of secrecy...
Be silent in that solitude,
Which is not loneliness for then
The spirit of the dead, who stood
In life before thee, are again
In death around thee, and their will
Shall overshadow thee; be still.

When the two women reach the ceremonial spot, a fire already dances fervently with the cool tropical night air. They sit the pot on the fire, throwing more wood into it—the fire, breathing with Tartarean sulfur, strengthens. Dame Carabosse, without a word, draws a circle around the fire and tosses some sort of powder into it, causing it to turn blue. She, Dame Carabosse, with her alarming stygian eyes and gourd-like figure wrapped in a stained madras frock banded with a cured snakeskin belt, is almost a single exhibition masquerade with her complementary mango-shaped-hoop earrings and red-hot cotton head-tie shaped like *astas del toro*. Dame Carabosse then begins to make frantic body movements as though in some sort of a trance. She cries out: "Yallojeeeee Yalllowjeee leee leeeee leee aaaaattooo ttoo llooomm di di...Setebos, hear mé na? Te deum laudamus, hear mé na?" Then, she grabs Nana-Ama by her arm and pulls her into the circle of obis—the fire strengthens more. Dame Carabosse tells Nana-Ama to "tell Setebos wha ya want. Tell 'im gyal!" To which Nana-Ama replies with uncertainty, "Setebos, te deum laudamus ... mé com fa beg yo' help mé fa fin' mé pickney and fa kill dem a who beena tek 'im wey." Meanwhile, Dame Carabosse continues to dance and chant: "Yallowjeee dewle vu jala scbotem. I dre lu ne me rouy nos, negdala ne yallnos."

Then Dame Carabosse jumps out of the circle and makes steadfast haste deeper into the forest, and a minute later, walks out with *chanticleer* tucked under her arm. She walks back into the circle and to the pot where she wrings the rooster's neck over it. Then, she raises the lifeless body to the heavens and spins it three times around in the air while chanting.

The nearby trees that guard the forest whisper in the wind: *qui vive*; the icy moon watches on; the six sharp *flûtés* sound stronger. Dame Carabosse and Nana-Ama begin to laugh as though reaching a pivotal ecstasy in their transcendental *sortilege*. Dame Carabosse continues to praise Setebos while Nana-Ama begins to gain confidence and joins her in praising Setebos, saying, "Yes! Yes! Setebos ze vous de ttuke shu vum huff speé dalem bacademla..." Dame Carabosse scoops up the rooster into the air again and then brings him down to her mouth where she sucks his scarce remaining blood a few times before beckoning Nana-Ama to do likewise. Nana-Ama does this and feels more entranced than Dame Carabosse, who meanwhile pulls a piece of snake organ from the pot and hands it to Nana-Ama, gesturing for her to eat it. Nana-Ama, half-crazed, wildly unfastens her head-wrap and pulls on her hair, laughs, and then pushes the organ into her mouth. As soon as she does this, she begins to suffocate. "Help...mé Cara...bosse!...Help...mé!" she cries out, as she falls to her knees. Dame Carabosse runs over to her, but instead of helping her, she kicks Nana-Ama into the fire and then over throws the pot onto Nana-Ama's face. Every time Nana-Ama tries to roll out of the fire, Dame Carabosse kicks her back in. And finally reaching for the cutlass that she planted nearby earlier, she severs Nana-Ama's head off of her body.

Dame Carabosse then turns to the forest and says, "com' out now, sha dead." Then, from behind the trees, Monsieur Rudoyer

Charnel advances to Dame Carabosse. He claps his hands, kicks Nana-Ama's head aside, and with a contented smile slashed across his face, says, *"Merci, Madame Carabosse. Votre travail est toujours fascinant. Si seulement elle m'avait donné de l'amour comme à Barrow et n'avait pas essayé de me fuir, les chose auraient été differentes."*

To this compliment, Dame Carabosse, squatting before her victim's headless corpse, begins to shed penitent tears like the water wrung out of a laundered cotton dress. She knows that the charge of death for two of her kind is the only way Monsieur Charnel will grant her complete freedom from his proprietorship. It is pitiful that such a transaction had to come at the sealed fates of a friend and her son, whose fates were inevitable at the jealous hands of Monsieur Charnel.

Dame Carabosse: "T'ank ya sir. Mé try mé bes' ta please Setebos and yu sir." This she manages to say while in a woeful slouch over Nana-Ama's body. Above Dame Carabosse's stooping, Monsieur Charnel then proceeds to pat her head and rock it back and forth—his eyes a wicked and miserable look of dementia.

Nearby, the sounds of two flutes begin to play in company.

Chorus Canticle bibliography, in order of presentation:

Richard Wilbur's *Ceremony* (1948)
William Shakespeare's *Sonnet 18* (1609)
Ben Johnson's *On My First Son* (1616)
Derek Walcott's *A Far Cry From Africa* (1962)
William Wordsworth's *Lines composed a few miles above Tin Tern Abbey* (1748)
A. R. Ammon's *Gravelly Run* (1960)
Samuel Taylor *Coleridge's The Pains of Sleep* (1816)
Barbara Howes's *A Letter from the Caribbean* (1966)
Edgar Allan Poe's Spirits of the Dead (1827)

Risa Nicole Cohen
University of Iowa

Public Transportation

The New York City Port Authority on Sunday at 4:30 was not the place to find a late lunch. The air smelled like urine and bad breath. I made sure not to touch anything with my skin. I learned my lesson the week before not to notice or be noticed. Walk fast and don't look anyone in the face. Chest or below, that's it.

Last Sunday a homeless man with soiled pants and a shirt that was struggling to stay on his shoulders followed me until I gave him seventy-five cents. That same day, as I stood in line waiting to buy a ticket, I happened to look at a black woman with a shower cap on her head. She caught me. "Bitch, what you lookin' at!" she yelled. I was actually thinking at that moment how a shower cap was a good idea for keeping all of the germs out of my hair. I didn't tell her that. I don't think she had the same idea that I did.

Really, I just wanted to get home, get out of this skirt and think about the job offer over a bowl of mint chocolate chip ice cream.

I stood in line unsure of what to do with my hands. They rested on my hips and hung by my sides several times before I decided to pick up my bag and hang it on my shoulder. The line started moving and inch by inch I made it to the bus doors. I walked up the two big steps and headed to the back. I went to the only empty seat. The woman sitting next to the window quickly filled the seat with her shopping bags. "Is this seat taken?" I asked innocently. The woman looked at me, then at the seat, then back at her magazine. *Was that supposed to answer my question?* "Ma'am," I repeated, "can I sit here please?"

The bus driver came on the intercom, his voice deep like Barry White's, "the 4:35 to Mt. Laurel/Camden will be departing in two minutes. Please be seated. We have a full house today."

Without looking at me, the woman grabbed her bags and set them on the floor in front of my seat. Her legs were thick and her knees pressed the back of the seat in front of her. My bag, of course, was on my lap.

I closed my eyes and rubbed my temples as the bus pulled out from underground and onto 42nd street. The lights from midtown flashed in the daylight as the sun descended in the sky. The woman next to me was already dozing off and we hadn't even reached the Lincoln Tunnel. *Her weight*, I thought, *must really tire her out.* Or maybe she was up all night with her kid who is dying of Cirrhosis of the liver. Maybe she was sick. Maybe not. As long as she kept her distance she was fine doing what ever she liked.

My duffel bag took up my entire lap and the man in front of me had cocked his seat all the way back. At least he was comfortable. The guy on the aisle seat next to me rested his head on the back of the seat, his hands folded in his empty lap, and his feet crossed at his ankles. I looked out the window and saw the city skyline as the bus looped around and entered the Jersey Turnpike. The buildings looked powerful as the orange clouds floated above them. I wanted to smile. I took a deep breath. I wished I could just lean my head back on the seat and nap through the trip. I looked at the man next to me again. Maybe if I can't sleep, I can watch him sleep. He opened his eyes and turned his head in my direction. He caught me.

"Sorry," I mumbled, "you just look really comfortable." He smiled and switched his left leg over his right.

"Don't believe what you see," he said, sticking his hand out, "Cal Meredith."

I shook with my left hand when I realized my right one was the only part of my body that had fallen asleep. Embarrassed, I shook extra hard.

"Jodie. Nice to meet you." I repositioned my bag on my lap to discretely wipe my hands on my skirt, and noticed the woman next to me had fallen asleep with her hand jammed into a small bag of Doritos.

"Do you live in the city, Jodie?" He asked, supporting his chin with his right hand.

"Oh, no," I said, "no, not yet at least."

"Ahhh," he said, "thinking about it?"

"Well, sort of," I replied, "I got a job offer, I just haven't decided whether or not I want to live in the city. You know."

"No, I don't know," he said. "What's stopping ya, you're a young woman, the city would be great for you."

"Well, I'm not that young," I replied.

He looked at my face carefully. "I'd saaaaay," squeezing the tip of his chin, "eighteen, maybe nineteen."

I smiled. "Close, twenty-two."

He laughed and his teeth were bright white. In one glance I could see that he probably flossed everyday. His gum lines looked smooth and shiny, not puffy like the woman sitting next to me. Maybe he brushed with that seven-day-teeth-cleaner or something. I ran my tongue across my front teeth. I had never seen teeth that white.

"Well, whatever," he said smiling, "good luck on your decision, I'd tell anyone to move here."

"Yeah," I paused for a second, "thanks." I turned away. I wanted to close my eyes and think about this job, but all I could hear was the loud humming of the bus wheels and muffled conversations of passengers near by.

"So, what company would you be working for?" he asked abruptly. I jumped.

"Disney," I said, "Buena Vista." I turned forward again. I shut my eyes before he could respond, hoping he would take notice. He continued to tell me that his ex-wife's brother worked for Disney for eight years; how the company promotes from within and how the perks were unbelievable. He and his ex-wife would get tickets to Knicks games from her brother. He went on and on. As he continued to talk I continued to nod and smile. My blinks became slower and slower until finally he ran out of things to say. When his voice stopped I shut my eyes.

He was right, Disney was a great company. Who wouldn't want to live in the city? Bars, restaurants, antique shopping, Italian markets, brownstones. I pictured myself strolling through Union Square with a long suede coat that I had picked up at a little vintage clothing store in the West Village. Holding my hand was the dark-haired Venezuelan guy who had been sending me email messages over the company computer. Maybe he worked in the next office or on the floor below me, but we walked and shopped and ate a late dinner at a small Lebanese restaurant on Fifth Avenue. That could happen, it wasn't too far fetched, and he didn't have to be Venezuelan, maybe he was just really tan. Christmas parties, company picnics, tickets to Broadway shows, it could be mine. I'd just go home on the weekends to see my family, how hard was that? Jodie Hughes, Walt Disney Regional Sales. It sounded good. With a firm handshake and a wide smile, I could picture the end of the month bonus checks in my mailbox. Shining.

I scratched the back of my head. I quickly sat forward when I realized I had been leaning my head on the seat. The woman to my right had her face smeared against the window. Her lips were slightly open, bronze lipstick and a thick etching of lip liner colored her mouth. I can only imagine what it looked like to a passing car.

I heard what sounded like a closing door. I looked behind

me without peering too far over the seat. Locating the bathroom, I suddenly had to pee. I thought about the cleanliness of bus lavatories and turned down the idea immediately. The hidden bacteria and the droplets of a stranger's urine were probably resting on the rim of the toilet, waiting for me to sit down. I could definitely hold it in. I sat forward in my foam cushion seat that was covered with fabric from the early seventies. Oranges, reds, yellows, with several tricolored zig-zags and thousands of tiny fuzz balls. I thought fuzz balls came from frequent washes, but apparently there are other ways.

The bus driver had been braking regularly for the past few minutes. Maybe there was an accident. The New Jersey Turnpike was known for two things: accidents and traffic. In this case it was both. I could see flashing red lights reflecting off the window. The jerking from the brakes became constant. I held on to my duffel bag a little tighter to give myself some leverage. My mouth tasted sour and the bus was quickly getting warmer and warmer. I took a deep breath. It felt like turbulence. Leaning my elbow on something stable, with one hand supporting my head, is the only thing that works for me. It would be working now had I not gotten the seat with the broken armrest.

I could hear a toddler fussing a few rows in front of me. He probably felt like I did, so I couldn't blame him. Poor kid. His cries were screeching. I couldn't imagine being the mother of an hysterical child on a public bus. I'd probably start crying right along with the kid. I heard a firm smack, like the sound of two palms clapping together, no fingers. The kid's cry became erratic. Inhale, inhale, inhale, scream, it was a pattern that lasted for nearly ten minutes. *SHUT THE HELL UP*, I thought. I screamed it so loudly in my head that my throat hurt. There was no one sleeping now except the women next to me. The lady kept slapping and the kid kept crying louder. It was a face slap, firm and hard. The kid was going to die or pass out from crying.

He puked. I heard it, I smelled it, and for a second I felt like I could taste it. It sounded like the wringing out of a wet sock, splashing as it hit the runner down the center of the bus. It didn't stop. I kept hearing the splash and it sounded as if it were getting closer and closer. Then I realized the mother was rushing the kid to the bathroom and coming my way. I squeezed my eyes shut and plugged my ears with my index fingers and my nose with my pinkies. *This can't be happening.* The little boy cried and puked as he headed up the aisle. As I watched him pass by, my chin wrinkled and my stomach contracted several times. His mother was holding the bottom of his shirt up to his mouth. I looked at the man next to me, not to talk, but to see if his eyes were tearing too. They weren't.

"So," he said turning in my direction, "are they offering you a decent salary?"

I thought about not answering at all. Didn't he see what just happened?

"Ahhh," I couldn't think of what to say, "yeah, pretty good, commission, and what not." I was squinting as the smell of greasy food and sour milk rose from the floor of the bus. I turned forward and put my face in the palms of my hands.

Please stop talking to me, you're nice and you've got great teeth, but I'm concentrating on keeping the bowl of oatmeal I had this morning in my stomach.

"So, you live with your parents?" he continued.

"No, near 'em," I said with my face still in my hands, wondering when the bus was going to move faster than fifteen miles per hour.

"They think you should stay close to home?"

I sighed and dropped my hands on my duffel bag making a slapping sound against the leather and turned my head quickly in his direction.

"No," I said creasing my eyebrows, "no, they think I should go, they think it's a great opportunity, I can't talk—" his wide eyes became smaller—"I'm sorry," I continued, "I can't talk to you, no offense but this bus is freaking me out, I can't deal right now, I just, I'm sorry." There was a long pause.

"No, I'm sorry, " he said, "I shouldn't be so intrusive."

"It's not that at all," I said looking down. As my eyes faced the floor I noticed vomit streaming down the ridges of the runner, "It's that." He looked down and back up at me and grinned. He didn't show his teeth this time.

The kid and his mother made it back to their seats and the bus actually began to move again. The woman next to me woke up after the commotion and gave me a look that suggested I had created the smell. She leaned her head back on the window which had a grease spot where her face rested. She was asleep again and snoring within minutes.

The man in front of Cal had put a light blue bus-blanket, which clashed with the rust color of the seats, over his body, exposing only his head and his left arm. He was reading a magazine. I wished I had a magazine too, something to get my mind off of this germ-infested, kid-beating, vomit-dripping bus. I leaned over into the aisle a little, trying to keep from being directly above the pinkish liquid on the floor. He was reading a cartoon. *Oooh good, I love cartoons.* Just as I focused on the words, he turned the page. I turned my head firmly down to my lap. I was staring at the top of my duffel bag. *Did I just see breasts, naked breasts? Tell me I didn't just see a still shot from a dirty porno.* I looked up again. I was right. This time I was looking at his arm, and not the one holding the magazine. There were quick little movements. *Quick* ones. I glanced down at his legs and saw his silver belt buckle dangling down the side of the seat. *Oh my God. Get me off of this shit hole and into my house! If he leaves the blanket on the bus I'm telling the Greyhound ticket guy.*

I looked at his belt buckle again and rested my forehead in the palms of my hands and cried. I held my face firmly and tried not to make noise. I didn't want anyone to think I was just another weirdo on a city bus crying in her seat. *I* wasn't mixed-up like the other passengers. I was crying for a reason. I had every right to be upset. *Did this happen all the time? Was every bus out of New York City filled with passengers who openly indulged their sexual appetites? Who are these people? And what am I doing here? It smelled. It was hot. I couldn't do this. How would I ever see my family? Puffin? Who would run Puffin at the lake on Saturdays? If she doesn't get enough exercise she could get sick again. Mom wouldn't drive to the city. What if somebody nicked her car door?* I felt a warm hand on my right arm. As I looked up, a tear rolled down the side of my nose. I wiped it with the back of my hand.

"It's not always like this," said the woman next to me as she held out a tissue. I was startled by her sudden kindness and by the fact that she was awake. I tried to smile.

"Thank you, ma'am," I said, "you're very kind."

"Well," she said, "I take this bus every weekend, I see all kinds of people."

"Really," I shifted in my seat, "really, every weekend?" I wiped under my nose with the tissue.

"Every weekend to Camden," she gave me another tissue, "my daughter and my grandson moved there three years ago."

"Wow," I responded, "I mean, I couldn't do it."

"Aww, it's nothing, child," she turned away.

"No, no I couldn't. I mean I couldn't even take the bus to school as a kid," I said. "My mom had to drive me until I was sixteen."

The woman smiled and rested her head on the window. She closed her eyes. "Get used to it girl," she said, "get used to it." I turned forward and pulled at a loose thread on my bag. "I wish it were that easy," I said under my breath and more to myself than to her. I could tell she didn't want to hear my life story. I unzipped my bag and jammed my hand in the bottom and felt for my package of wet-naps. I took my last one and wiped my hands and arms. I blew my fingertips dry.

The people on the bus were restless once they realized our stop was only two miles away. I had never wanted to be in South Jersey so much in my life.

I didn't really feel like discussing the Disney job, but I knew it would be the first thing out of my mother's mouth. I could picture it now. I sighed and looped my hand through the handle of my bag. The woman next to me reached for her shopping bags. As I watched her, I hoped that her kid wasn't dying of Cirrhosis of the liver.

There she was, sitting in her new Lexus. I could see her smiling and waving. As the passengers started getting off, I stood up in the aisle making sure no part of my shoe touched the mess. The jerk-off left his blue blanket lying on his seat. He took the *Hustler* with him. The aisle was scattered with towels, making a sorry attempt to cover the vomit.

The bus depot was empty. When I clunked down the two big steps I took the biggest hit of fresh air and held it for a few seconds before letting it out slowly. I walked to the car and motioned for my mother to open the trunk. She rolled down the window.

"Well, how'd it go, kiddo?" she asked. I pretended not to hear her and took my time putting my stuff in the trunk. I walked around to the side of the car and got in the front seat.

"Huh?" I asked, wiping the oil off my nose and cheeks with the tissue from the woman on the bus. She put her hand on my leg and patted it.

"How'd the second interview go, did you get it?" Her smile took up the whole of her face. "Well?" she waited with her eyebrows raised high above her eyes. I couldn't bear to see her face if I said, "Yes Mother, but I decided not to take it." I didn't want to answer all the questions that would follow. She wouldn't understand. If she saw a man beating off or sat in traffic for an hour inhaling the fumes from a stranger's stomach, she might. She knew I hated public busses, or public anything for that matter, but it was a job in the city. Possibly a career, a chance to find my independence, a chance to leave home. All of the opportunities that my mother never took. She wanted this for me. I could feel it in the way she hugged me and the way she looked at me. I didn't know what to say and in the four seconds that went by, thousands of things went through my mind. She was waiting.

"Ahhh, no I didn't," I said looking out the window, "the other woman got it. They said they'd let me know if there were openings in the future." I didn't look at my mother. I couldn't. Her hand was still on my leg only the patting had stopped. I closed my eyes and she was quiet. I wondered what she was thinking as I heard the clink-clunk, clink-clunk of the blinker.

"That's okay, Jode," she said as she squeezed my knee. "There's other jobs." I didn't say anything.

We drove to the end of the bus station. There were several cars in front of us waiting to pull out onto the highway. The red lights from their brakes hurt my eyes.

I glanced out my window and noticed the woman from the bus walking along the sidewalk with her bags in each hand. I could see her breath in the cold air. I wanted to offer her a ride. Instead, I just watched her walk. She caught my eye and I grinned, as each of my fingers gently pressed against the window. She stopped and watched our car pull out onto the highway. She had a beautiful smile. I closed my eyes and leaned my head against the headrest. I thought about Cal and the sick little boy. I wondered if the boy was okay.

"Well," my mother said, "how was the bus ride?"

"Just traffic in New Brunswick."

I turned and looked at my mother, "But it wasn't a bad ride, Mom."

Ryan Bachtel
INDIANA UNIVERSITY

The Rescue

The stillness of the night was permeated only by the wheezing of the wind outside my bedroom window. A stream of light squeezed through the crack of the door leading to the hallway. Most nights, that slim beam of light was the only defense I had against the monsters that leapt from my budding imagination and brought life to every fear. However, on this night, which was to be branded into lifelong memory, the imps and ogres did not appear. I did not cower beneath the covers preparing for flight to my mother's room to seek asylum from the darkness. Though my body was exhausted, something besides my body raged within. It was the most elusive, subtle suffering I had ever known. A moral crisis had arisen for me which I believed was a test of my soul by God.

Every child knows that the world is a polarity between good and evil. These forces battle each other in every perception of the young observer. I always knew as a child that I was a chosen one, destined to fight on the side of goodness. My favorite picture was one I'd seen at the library, of angels wielding swords, fighting Satan and his minions. Though I was no angel, I considered myself a knight in training. One day I would vanquish evil in the service of righteousness.

For the youthful knight, membership in an Order was essential. The primal, archetypical elements of each warrior were melted down, distilled and amalgamized into the liquid fire coursing through our veins. In the forge of youth, the mold of the heart was poured and took shape, pounded and tempered by our shared experiences. Each of us was armed with weapons of subtle energies we were only vaguely aware of. The nuclear forces binding the atoms in steel are minuscule next to the alloyed being the five of us formed. Taken as a whole, it was as if we made up a perfect, superior excellence which the individual could not attain. The four fellows who I considered my companions in the quest were: Marcus, the powerful and foul in temper; Andre, the agile and sly schemer; Raymond, the gentle and intelligent; and Phillip, the forgiving and dispenser of compassion. The five of us borrowed from one another what was best in each of us.

So it was the five of us one afternoon tromping through the woods a bicycle ride away from the neighborhood. It was our woods, or so we considered it. Many days had been spent exploring and adventuring among the maple and oak trees, there were contests, games and attempts to discover hidden passageways to other worlds.

We were on our way to winding up another of our countless, benign campaigns when we came upon the most perfect, magnificent spider web that our collective memory had ever seen. No human architectural achievement could have matched the symmetry or wonder of this stretch of silky thread so delicately woven. Our first inclination was to destroy it. Silently we all came to realize that it was sacred, and to desecrate it would be an insult to all of nature. Contrasting its entrancing beauty were various insects, or the skeletons of insects, frozen in stillness, wrapped in enough of the milky white webbing to ensure their woeful imprisonment. One of these graves was filled by the mighty wasp, the likes of which had chased five screaming young knights through the woods on previous occasions. The sight of such a worthy opponent bested told us that this spider must be the spider queen herself.

"Where's the damn spider?" Marcus spoke out.

Profanity was our secret battle language, it was spoken like a code and it had special undercurrents to it that communicated more than the words themselves.

"Marcus, it's on yer neck!" Andre shouted, pointing.

"Where! Get 'em off! God dammit!" Marcus flailed his meaty arms in a dance of wild slaps and swipes. It took him a moment to notice our laughter that unmasked the ruse. Andre, always prepared, was already twenty steps away from Marcus and still laughing.

"Yer on my shit list now," Marcus said with the sureness of revenge. "Dork!"

"Knock it off you two. Let's find the spider." A truce, the work of Phillip.

"He's probably up in the trees. Either that or he was on the ground and we stepped on him already," Raymond offered. We all inspected the bottoms of our shoes with no findings and then redirected our attention back to the web.

"How do ya think spiders learn to make webs?" I asked the group.

"They're just born knowing," Raymond replied. I found that puzzling.

"That don't make no sense," Marcus answered. "No one is just born knowing how to make a web."

"It's just like no one having to teach us how to eat or cry when we're born, except with the spiders they know how to make webs," Raymond continued.

"I get it, just like no one ever had to teach Marcus how to crap his pants when he was a kid. Or do you still do that?" We all laughed.

"How about I beat the crap out of you smart aleck, that'd be a lesson you weren't born with." We all stifled our giggles, Marcus had his boundaries.

"Hey! Let's find us a bug and throw it into the web and see

what happens!" Andre, the Napoleon of strategy, said.

"What'll happen then Raymond?" I inquired of our information source.

"The spider might come out to get the bug."

His answer set Marcus into action rolling over a nearby log to unearth a city of insects beneath. Andre was directing, Raymond was still talking but everyone had ceased to listen. Phillip and I exchanged curious looks, unsure of where this was going.

"That one!" Andre declared pointing at the unlucky selectee.

Marcus carried a black beetle in his large, clumsy hand. I was thinking that the thing was probably already broken from the trauma of being handled by Marcus. We gathered around the web to get a view while Andre instructed Marcus on the proper bug throwing stance.

"Don't be throwing it with all yer arm or the damn thing will end up by the road."

Marcus always took an amazing amount of abuse from Andre, but they made a pretty effective team. I was still uneasy, but intrigue had taken over. I was caught up in the possibility of seeing the awesome monster who had constructed this web come to claim its prize.

"Fire!" Andre ordered.

The beetle sailed up to and on through the web, leaving in its wake a few dangling strands that broke under the stress. It landed somewhere beyond sounding like a small stone.

"Ya big lummox! I told you not to go launching it."

Marcus was already stomping back to the log for more ordinance.

"Hang on a minute. I'll tell ya which bug to use," Andre chased.

While they searched, the rest of us warily inspected the damage to the web. It would not take many beetle blasts before the entire web hung useless. Our concern reflected off of one another until we silently agreed to intervene. This could be touchy.

Coalitions sprung up among us in times of conflicting interest, so this had to be handled carefully. I was pushed to the head of our spear tip.

"Hey, Andre, maybe we outta leave the thing alone. It is a really neat web and well, um…if another couple more bugs go flying through there, it might wreck it." It was the best I could do in the immediate circumstances.

"It ain't goin' to go flying through this time is it, Marcus?"

"Nope."

"There, ya see, the spider will be thanking us for a free supper."

"It probably won't be too happy about that hole it's got to fix now." Raymond was on our side. That was good.

"That's why we have to get a bug for it now, to make up for the hole in its web." Andre shot right back. This was not going in the right direction. I gave Phillip and Raymond the look that told them to leave it to me. I had to switch tactics, go to the base of the problem.

"Marcus, ya remember that tree house we built out here last summer?"

"Yeah, I remember. Who do ya think carried all that stuff up the tree?"

"Right! And you remember what happened with it when Kip and Randy came and tore it down? You remember how mad all of us were?" I knew he remembered that he had cried in front of us over the destruction of our fortress; I was playing a dangerous hand by bringing it up.

"Yeah, so! What about it?" He replied bitterly. I was close now, if I could just hold the rope.

"Well, what if this spider kinda feels the same way about its web as we felt about our tree house. I know ya don't mean no harm, but that spider might be awful upset if something was to happen to its web… I mean, after all that building and crawling around and stuff…"

It was working, I saw the change come over his face, I just

kept slashing, forcing him back on his heels. "...and our tree house was just for fun, the spider needs the web to get its food."

That was game and I knew it. At that point I could have had him apologizing to the beetle he threw. Phillip and Raymond were grinning, happy to be in the winning corner. Andre of course was livid, he had stood helplessly by and watched his plans evaporate. He tried to react, to regain the upper hand, but it was too late. My influence was a weapon too powerful to now be subverted by Marcus. He rolled the log back into place apologetically; I'm certain he wanted to say sorry out loud to the bugs underneath. Andre watched, dejected but already recovering; he would have his day.

With the impending catastrophe averted we all returned to give a farewell glance to the web, enough damage had been done and darkness was inimically driving back the blueness of the sky.

"Look at this," Phillip said with overtones of interest.

"What is it?" I asked.

"I think it's..."

"It's a cocoon," Raymond said ominously.

He was right, and his dark tone immediately registered its purpose in my mind. Inside the cocoon was a butterfly, we saw cocoons every year before the woods filled with fluttering colors. It was obvious that the butterfly would have no chance to dance on top of the wind like all the others. As soon as the cocoon would open the butterfly would find itself entangled in the sticky fibers of death that the spider had prepared. I was furious, the spider was not following the rules. It couldn't just build a spider web right where a brand new butterfly was going to try to leave its cocoon. It was a preposterous crime against the woods, all the woods.

"We gotta move it," I said and was met with silence. I did not notice any gestures of agreement or disagreement, nor was I concerned about it. Something in me had taken it personally that this spider was guilty of such an evil scheme. I reached out my hand to lightly take hold of the cocoon and was surprised when the iron clamp of Marcus' hand fastened on to my wrist.

"What are you doing? Let go!" I said, frustrated that my plan hand been interrupted.

"Wait a minute. I say that spider has got a right to its butterfly, it's his web."

Oh no, I thought. It was the Frankenstein effect.

"That's totally different, Marcus. I'm not gonna even touch the spider's web, I'm just gonna move the cocoon so it'll have a chance, the spider has a lot of other bugs that'll fly into the web on their own."

I had him considering while he loosened his grip on my wrist and allowed the color to return to the hand. It might have worked had Andre not chosen his moment with a smirk.

"I understand what you mean, Marcus. That spider probably chose this very spot so it would have something to eat when that cocoon opened up. Remember why we chose our place for the tree house?"

"It was 'cause the tree had perfect climbing steps built right into it," Marcus said nostalgically. I was disgusted.

"Yep, that's right. Remember how you were going to show it to Stacy when it was all done?"

"Yeah." Marcus was really reminiscing now and Andre, the scoundrel, was milking it for every drop of mockery he could assault me with. I was completely fed up.

"You don't get it, Andre, you're such a shithead! I'm moving it."

He didn't grab my wrist, but I would have rather had that than the push that sent me sprawling onto the leafy floor. Every muscle in my body was charged with a surge of adrenaline and I was swollen with rage. I heard nothing. Although I do recall being spoken to. I said nothing. But yelled a string of blasphemes and profanities. When I regained my feet, I lunged at Marcus: he was not Marcus anymore, he was the spider. All of my repulsion at the notion of the innocent butterfly being eaten by that glutenous, damnable, hell spawn of a spider, manifested itself in my anger. My fists whipped through the air uncontrollably. It was only a few seconds before I was on the ground with Marcus on top of me, holding me in a suffocating headlock. I tried to scream in rage, but was muffled by the forearm that was covering my mouth. I fought for a moment more before giving up so that I might be allowed to breathe again. I was released and the world looked splotchy from the rush of blood to my head. My nose was bleeding and Phillip was trying to speak to me while looking me over at the same time. I remember how shocked all of them looked. They never had the slightest idea that I was capable of such a thing. I hadn't either until that day.

"Are you crazy?" Andre was asking.

He wasn't taunting now; after all, we were all friends and he was as shocked as any of us.

"Marcus! Where you going? Wait up," Andre called before he went chasing after a pouting Marcus. He was much angrier at himself than at me. He wasn't a complete dolt, he knew how silly it had been for him to throttle his physically inferior friend who considered him a blood brother. For both of us, anger had exited and left only shame.

"You alright?" Phillip asked.

I nodded. I didn't feel like speaking. I was afraid that I would start crying, which would only humiliate me further. Best to put on an air of indifference, which of course was totally transparent to Raymond and Phillip.

"You guys go ahead and go, I wanna be by myself." They knew full well what was coming.

"Ya wanna go move the cocoon? We'll help ya find a good place for it."

"No, just go. Tell Marcus that I'm not hurt or sore at him or anything."

"You gonna ride home by yourself?" Phillip asked.

"In a little while."

"Well, we'll see ya back home. Ya wanna catch lightning

bugs tonight?"

"I dunno, I just wanna be alone."

"Ok, we'll see ya later." Reluctantly, they left. Part of me wished that they would have stayed and insisted that I go with them, but I was still trying to save face when it was unnecessary.

The task that begged completion now was also my chance at redeeming this disaster of a day. Now was the time to prove myself a worthy candidate for the quest. I just knew that God was watching and that this was the right thing to do. I was to play an important part in the battle of good against evil. Marcus wasn't evil; he just didn't understand. It wouldn't be right if all the spiders could just go around setting up webs to take advantage of infant butterflies. What if someone was doing that to humans, not even allowing them a chance to live? Maybe this was His way of training me for the future, when I was to be a real warrior, a champion of justice, defender of the defenseless. Surely there would be rewards. I would be a hero, rescuing all life from annihilation somehow, because God made life and everything, so there is no way it should be wasted. I would do the right thing, no matter what.

I walked to the web feeling like a divine hero already. I could feel God's smile upon me. It was growing darker and the woods were getting a little creepy; this required God's speed. I reached for the cocoon, having a flashback of the events that followed the last time I reached for it. It was in my grasp, a slight tug and the extraction would be complete, the cocoon safe and intact. I drew my hand slowly away from the web, and just then a small breeze came flowing from the tree tops and blew a piece of the web onto my hand. It stuck there for a moment, just long enough for the queen of the spiders to come out of hiding, and make a dash for my hand. I froze. Its body was the size and shape of an acorn. I swore it was laughing the maniacal laugh of a deliverer of poisons. I prepared for death.

The queen made her way onto my hand just as I jerked it away, frantically slapping the spider with my other hand. It ran in circles around my hand avoiding my strikes, no doubt looking for an opening to deliver its deadly bite. I was now convinced that this was no ordinary spider. It must be some demon in disguise—perhaps it was Lucifer himself, he was known to wear disguises.

My hand came down squarely on top of the spider, and I stared in disbelief. I just held it there. I knew it was a fatal blow, as I could feel the juices of the spider, slimy and slippery, under my hand. When I lifted my hand, a million tiny spiders scattered and spread across my skin. I screamed and dropped, beating my hand against the ground. Still bewildered and stupefied, I got to my feet and took flight on my bicycle.

That night I lay in bed after a long bath which insured no spider, no baby spider, was making camp in some crevice of my body. I tried to organize the events of the day into something that made some kind of sense. I kept scratching my hand, imagining I felt the tiny spiders scurrying, and wondering what kind of world they had come into where upon birth they were being squashed and smashed. Wondering about the kind of world I had been born into.

The web was destroyed, with it went the frail, meticulously arranged structure of reality that shielded me from the uncertainties of my universe. The ghosts of infant spiders were spinning patterns of conceptualization in my consciousness. The trembling child that had once tightly wrapped the covers around his body at night to stave off the darkness, was exiting the age of innocence.

Clint Connely
UNIVERSITY OF WASHINGTON

The Two Minute Myth

Sully is my friend. Shawn Howell Sullivan, III. Sully for short. I don't have many friends, but I do have him. He has only two talents in this world: he can feed an incredible line of bullshit to anybody at anytime; and he can do tricks with his scrotum. Sully has an enormous scrotum, almost freakish in size. His penis is of average length, but looks small in comparison to the veiny sac underneath. For some unknown reason he thinks it is necessary to take advantage of this mutation to make people laugh. He can contort it into a replica of the human brain or the human heart. It has been social suicide for us at every party since I started hanging out with him during my senior year of high school.

I am twenty years old. I was supposed to have the world by the balls at least two years ago. But it hasn't happened yet. In fact nothing has happened yet. I am still working at the same damn pizza place that I worked at in high school, I am still driving my little, 1977 Volkswagen Rabbit, and I have never had a steady girlfriend, let alone entered the dating scene. So, it is wisc to assume that I am still a virgin.

Fear must be the reason my life is like this. I am afraid of rejection, afraid of taking that chance. I am, however, growing tired of it, beginning to feel trapped. I have to do something. Something that nobody would ever expect me to do in my little, white-bread, Sunday school world.

Sully is in the same boat as me. He is a twenty-year-old virgin, although he would never admit it to anybody else but me. If you asked him, he would tell you stories of discreet, romantic interludes in the backs of cars and in hotel rooms with women who didn't have names, smoked Virginia Slims, walked around in their lace and spoke in raspy, low voices. But it's all a lie. The truth is, women don't want to date a man that is tall and lanky and can make his scrotum beat like a human heart. I think Sully knows this, and he knows that eventually he will have to grow up. He is just as afraid of growing up as I am of rejection.

So here we are, two lonely, horny, young men on a Saturday night with nothing to do but split a pack of cigarettes and cruise around in my little Rabbit.

"Hey, Hoss, I got a plan," says Sully.

"Don't call me Hoss," I say. He always calls me that, and it really bothers me. I don't even know where the name came from.

"A plan for what?"

I slow down and pull into the all-night burger joint, our usual stop on Saturday night. We hope that if we sit here long enough and often enough, the women of our dreams will walk up, get in my car, and we would all drive off into the sunset. So far, after two years, the only woman at this place that has ever talked to us is the fry-woman, a harelip who is grotesquely overweight and always calls us "Sugar."

I cut the engine. Usually his plans get us into trouble. Like the time he tried to meet Donna Ritzen by way of an auto-collision. He thought it would be a great way to break the ice. All it got him was a sore neck and a car thrashed beyond repair. Donna had busted her head on the steering wheel and Sully felt too guilty to ask her out in the hospital room where her father and mother stood crying. So naturally, I was wary of his ill-conceived plans.

"I heard of a place."

"What kind of place?" I ask, fully knowing that I have just asked the wrong question. I should have kept my mouth shut. I should have just turned up the radio. But Sully keeps my mundane life interesting. Maybe that's part of the reason we go so well together: I keep him from killing himself, and he keeps it exciting.

"There's a place downtown where we could pick up some of the most exotic women in the world." He smiles. "And it's guaranteed that we'll get laid." He lights another cigarette and blows the smoke out the window. "How much money you got, Hoss?"

"Don't call me Hoss. What kind of place?" He had me. I was interested. I was up for anything that would brake up this boredom: the boredom of working and then going home and reheating the leftovers my mother had made that night, jacking off to the outdated Hustler I kept under my bed, and drifting off to sleep, only to repeat this process the next day.

"A brothel. A whorehouse. Women who couldn't say no even if they wanted to." He blows more smoke out the window and starts picking at his teeth with his fingernail.

"How did you find out about this place?" The farthest I had ever gone with a woman was a kiss on the cheek; I was shy. But the idea of a woman being bought, guaranteed satisfaction, was exciting. How could I go wrong?

"Gooch, at the plant, gave me the address. He says fifty dollars to get in the front door and about a hundred for an hour." Finished with his teeth, he pops down the visor mirror and begins to pick at his face, carefully priming the puss-filled zits before popping them and wiping the fluid on his jeans.

"That's a lot of money, man. What about diseases and shit like that?"

"Condoms. No problem. Aren't you tired of being a goddamned virgin? I know I am. Let's do something about it, before we get old and they rot off from lack of use."

"I don't know, Sully." He is still picking at his face. "Are you serious about this?"

"Trust me." He smiles.

I laugh. Trust is a funny word with Sully. I know he will always be there for me, but when he thinks with his dick, there isn't a lot to trust. I watch him flick the cigarette out the window and pull out a little piece of paper.

"You still got that map?"

"Yeah, in the glove compartment," I say.

Sully pulls it out and pinpoints the whorehouse on the map. "Here, on 12th. Gooch said it's in the back of this apartment building, on the first floor. Just park across the street and knock on the door, and we're in."

"What if he was bullshitting you?"

"No, not this time."

I take a deep breath. A hundred and fifty dollars is a lot to drop in one night. But I only spend my money on cigarettes and car insurance anyway. I know this is wrong, not at all socially acceptable, taboo. Yet, exciting too. Maybe it will be worth the money. Maybe this is what I need to get over my fear of women, to finally become a man in my own eyes, to lose the yoke of baseball cards and comic books. After all, I have nothing to lose but a hundred and fifty bucks.

"Okay. But if there's any trouble we're out of there. I don't want to get caught. And they have to be good-looking. I am not screwing anybody that looks like that harelip behind the counter."

"Okay, Hoss, we're in business." Sully says, smiling. Yet, somehow he looks disappointed that I have agreed. "Let's get on the road."

"Don't call me Hoss."

We fall silent. My little Rabbit takes control of our destinies and leads us down the path to debauchery. Sully isn't smiling anymore. He lights a cigarette and stares out the window. I think he is having second thoughts. Too late to back out now, I've jumped at the bait and now he has to reel me in.

My stomach turns over in anticipation. A real woman, with breasts, and legs, and hot breath to whisper in my ear. No more pictures and wondering. No more will I be a little boy. Now all I have to do is muster the intestinal fortitude to follow through with it. I coast to a stop in front of the ATM.

We both withdraw the money. We are at the point of no return, neither of us can back out now. All I have to do is drive.

"This is 12th. Park over there. I think this is it," Sully says. He combs his hair with his hands and checks his teeth one more time.

I park and we sit in silence, contemplating.

"You ready?"

"Alright, Hoss," says Sully, "let's do it."

"Don't call me Hoss, asshole," I say in a low whisper. I am beginning to sweat. Unchartered waters lay ahead for us. I am scared, but for the first time in my life I'm not going to give in to fear. Maybe it's the money in my pocket acting as a guarantee against rejection, or maybe it's the fact that I can be anybody when I walk in there, and nobody will know the difference.

We walk across the parking lot. Sully, a half-step in front of me, stops in front of a green door. He looks at me and I nod. He knocks.

Something deep inside of me hopes that the door will not open. That this is all a mistake and we will go home with our pride intact.

But the door opens and the biggest black man I have ever seen stands before us. He is bald and dressed in leather. The cigar that hangs from his mouth is mostly ash, and cheap perfume engulfs him as it wafts from the innards of the room.

"What do y'all want?" His eyes bore down on us.

"We're looking for some action," Sully says. Action? Where the hell did he come up with a stupid line like that? This isn't a movie. I'm not Bruce Willis, a hitman for the mob, or some cool undercover cop. And Sully isn't my steely-eyed partner. I'm a twenty-year-old kid who still gets yelled at by his mom.

The black man scratches his head and blows smoke in our faces. "Fifty dollars. Then settle the rest inside."

We each peel off the money and give it to him. He puts it in his pocket and ushers us inside saying, "follow me."

The hallway is dark. The smell of cheap perfume and cigarette smoke overwhelms us. Sounds of beds thrashing against the wall and of men grunting and groaning resonate and pound in our ears. What lays behind these doors is the answer to all of my problems. The mystery of Woman, about to be revealed.

We're led into a lounge. Women of all shapes, sizes and colors rest on the couches that line the wall. I look at Sully, who looks at me and nods. I have to admit, this is better than cruising the strip and spending the night admiring beauties we could never have.

We stand against the wall, too shy to say anything. With our hands shoved deep in our pockets, we take in the sights and smile little nervous smiles.

"Wanna party?" A petite woman has approached Sully, rubbing her hand over his chest. Sully simply nods, and is led away, back down the corridor.

"Hey, sweetheart, wanna come with me?"

I nod to the blonde standing in front of me. She's wearing a dental floss bathing suit which reveals each and every curve. I let her take my hand as she leads me down a corridor into a room

"A hundred dollars for an hour, fifty for half an hour."

The room is small, with a twin bed and a picture of Robert de Niro from the movie *Taxi-Driver*. Other than that, the room is bare except for an overflowing ashtray near the bed and a pair of black high heels in the corner.

"My name's Cindy. What's it going to be?"

"Half-hour" I say, barely managing to get the words out.

"Okay, honey, let's see the money."

"Here." I give her the money, she puts it in her purse and turns out the lights.

My first sexual experience lasts about ten minutes. Two minutes to fumble with my clothes, one minute to find the bed in the dark, two minutes to reach orgasm, and five minutes to get dressed and find the door.

I am sick to my stomach. *That's it? I paid a hundred bucks for this?* I'm embarrassed. *Two minutes! And I had no idea what I was doing!* I don't want to stick around for the next twenty minutes. I feel absolutely empty. I just want to get out of here, go home, eat some leftovers, and look at my *Hustler.* I walk into the hall, past Baldy, and head toward my car. Sully is there, waiting for me. He doesn't say a word, just lights up a cigarette and nods.

Matt Norman
UNIVERSITY OF NEBRASKA, LINCOLN

When It Rains in California

Every time Mark came home to visit, it rained. This was no exaggeration. Every time. And this particular trip was no exception. Swaying palm trees and the familiar roar of a California downpour greeted him once again.

This used to be a kind of joke in the family, "Marky's just bringing the bad weather home with him." But lately, Mark's mom actually forbade this topic at the dinner table on holidays. She came from a long line of superstitious women and this strange phenomenon made her uneasy. Mark and his brother, James, liked to antagonize her by talking about imaginary, old friends who'd been struck by lightning or washed away in floods, never to be seen again. Their wives would kick their shins under the table and whisper for them to stop it.

Mark flipped the wipers on his Range Rover to high and they quickly became a blur on the windshield. Its huge tires pushed through the steady down pour, throwing water all over the street. It was almost ten o'clock at night and the roads were nearly deserted. Californians don't like to come out in thunderstorms. They'll go jogging during earthquakes and riots, but a little rain sends them cowering in their homes.

He picked up his cell phone and dialed his parents' number.

The phone rang weakly, due to low batteries. He figured it had enough juice left for the call, as long as his mother didn't answer the phone.

"Hello," a gruff voice said.

"Hey, Pop, how's it going?"

"Mark. Hi." His father sounded happy. Mark could hear his mother chattering in the background.

"How's it going, Dad?" he asked again.

"Oh, I'm fine. Hey, are you in town? We figured you were. Been raining all goddamn day."

"Yeah, I'm about a half hour away."

"Good. Is Mary with you?" Mark was dreading this question.

"Uh, no. She had to work this weekend. She sends her best though."

This was bullshit, of course, and there was a moment of silence, during which his father made it obvious that he knew it.

Come on Dad, let's not get into this now, please, Mark thought.

"Oh. Too bad," his father said.

"Yeah, but that's OK. Now I can get nuts at your retirement party. If I know one thing, it's that women hate it when their husbands get piss drunk in public."

His dad laughed. "Yeah, tell me about it."

He'd been mentally preparing for his retirement party for about twenty-five years. The time had finally arrived. Mark had offered to help his parents out with money, maybe try to push that retirement date up a little. But his Dad would hear nothing of it. "I'm not taking my son's money. I don't care how much dough you've got," he'd said loudly.

A wave of static started to break them up. He figured he only had a few seconds left. "Hey, Dad, listen, my batteries are low. I'll be home soon, OK?"

"OK, but hurry because it's getting late and…" static claimed the rest of his sentence.

"Yeah, Dad. I'll be there soon."

Mark barely heard his father say good-bye. He hung up and put the phone in its cradle.

A huge semi tore past him on the left. The Rover was suddenly rocked by wind, rain and street-grit. He felt the car try to veer off the road but Mark gripped the wheel hard. The semi passed on, dousing the windshield. The wipers fought hard but did little good. He slowed down some to let the truck get ahead.

"Fucking rain," he said to the empty seat next to him.

A picture of his wife, Mary, hung from a piece of sticky-tack next to the volume knob on the radio. It was the best picture he'd ever seen of her. It was taken about seven years ago, just after they had been married. Her hair was pulled back in a tight pony tail, and she wore a San Diego Padres sweatshirt and a pair of tight, khaki shorts. Their dog, Trevor, sat in a ball at her bare feet. He was just a puppy then. Now he outweighed her by almost ten pounds. She always said she'd be happy as long as she didn't weigh as much as the dog. Mark wondered if she ever over-fed Trevor, just to pad the margin a bit.

Mark's stomach warmed slowly as a steady wave of guilt hit him. When he left, Mary had been crying. He had taken her overnight bag out of the back of the car. It was packed full of jeans and t-shirts, along with her favorite dress for the party. Another visit home, full of fake smiles and false hugs, would be just about unbearable.

"I don't think you should come with me this weekend."

He couldn't believe he'd said it. That was a lot to put out on the table while standing in the driveway, ready to leave.

She looked at him, wounded. Her lower lip curled a bit and her eyes flooded. The distance between them had been growing for months. He kept finding reasons to work longer, go on research trips, whatever.

It wasn't Mary. It was Mark. He had gone and gotten himself almost-famous. Not like "can't go out of the house" famous, but famous within some fairly prominent circles. Just the other night at a premiere party, a model smiled at him. Like, really smiled at him. Right in front of Mary.

It was starting to happen all the time. *They* cared what he had to say. *They* wanted to talk to *him*, Mark Winter. Some of the most glamorous and beautiful people in the world waved at him and called him by his first name. It was amazing.

How could he go on like this, married to a woman that didn't excite him? There was so much out there. So many flirtatious smiles through crowds at parties. So many nights ahead and so many people to meet. He had just turned thirty-one last month. He had his whole life ahead of him.

His dad and his brother thought he was about the biggest asshole in the free world for even thinking about leaving his wife. Neither of them admitted it sober, but they both harbored boyish crushes on Mary. They'd always thought she was the best—a beautiful girl who knew how to read a box score—the perfect woman.

"You'll be just like all those other pricks in Hollywood who leave the woman who loved them when they weren't shit," his dad said. His brother chimed in, "Yeah, like Sly Stallone. The son of a bitch is living in a piece of shit apartment with his wife. The guy can't hardly speak English and he looks like the Cro-Magnon man. He does Rocky, gets an Oscar, then cans his wife for Brigette Neilson. I mean, Jesus Christ!"

They didn't know what the hell they were talking about. His brother was a high school baseball coach and his dad was an almost-retired fireman for Christ's sake. Like these two guys have ever been smiled at by a model.

"What are you going to tell your parents?" Mary asked him as he climbed into the Rover.

"I don't know. I'll just tell them that you had to work this weekend. The hospital wouldn't let you off or something. Whatever."

Her face seemed to grow heavy and she bit her lower lip. This used to drive him crazy when they were dating. She would chew on her lower lip when she concentrated, like during the suspenseful part of movies or while having a conversation with his mother.

"I guess you make things up for a living, right?" she said quietly.

He tried to brush this off, like it didn't bother him. But nothing offended Mark more than reducing his life and passion to a collection of well-constructed, commercially lucrative lies. "Yeah, I guess so," he said. "I'll call you when I get to my mom and dad's."

She said nothing and stepped away from the car. Her eyes never left his. He could see in the rearview mirror that she was crying. Mark felt a wave of guilt laced with relief. Her reaction affected him the most: she didn't yell or run away from him, she just watched him leave, as if she'd been expecting it.

It's OK, everyone in the industry has been divorced three times, he thought as he left his gated neighborhood.

Mark coasted off the interstate into Escondito. Through the downpour, the street lights offered little more than a cinematic eeriness straight out of an apocalyptic movie, and the signature palm trees drooped sadly on the side of the road— they had been beaten down with more rain in the last few hours than they had seen all month. The occasional gust shook the Rover and Mark's fingers began to cramp as they gripped the wheel tighter and tighter. *Jesus, I can't get myself killed in a rain storm,* he thought, *I'd feel so stupid for making fun of my mom all these years.*

It was strange coming home. He felt like he was climbing into an old tree house—it used to be so big, but now he could hardly fit. He passed the grocery store were he'd bought beer legally for the first time. Just up the road a mile or so was his high school—a place he wouldn't mind forgetting.

An old U2 song came on the radio. He took his eyes off the road to find the volume knob, catching a glance of the picture of Mary and the dog, as Bono's voice got louder. He should probably call her when he got to his parents'.

Mark looked up and saw a man in the middle of the street. He was waving his arms and jumping up and down. "Jesus Christ!" Mark yelled, slamming on the breaks. Sliding, fishtailing, swerving on the wet pavement, Mark barely missed the idiot in the street who moved out of the way just as Mark came to a screeching stop where the guy had been standing.

"What the fu...!" The electric window came down slowly, not keeping pace with his anger. "Jesus Christ! What the hell is your problem, you moron!" Mark yelled.

The guy ran around to the driver side window. He stumbled and slid in the rain as it beat down on his head.

"Shit, man, I was waving at you for like, ten seconds. I thought you saw me!"

"Well, I didn't. And I just about ran your ass over!" Mark yelled at the stranger, their faces only inches apart. Even soaking wet, in the midst of a raging California storm, the guy smelled like the floor behind a bar.

"What are you running out in the goddamn street for anyway?"

"Check it out, man, " the guy said, shouting over the roar of the rain. "My car, it's all fucked up." Mark followed his gaze to a rusty Ford Tempo on the side of the road. It looked like it was going to dissolve in the rain, right before their very eyes. "You got a cell phone or something I can use?"

Mark looked at the guy and then back at his car. *This is California. You can't just stop and talk to people on thc side of the road, you're liable to become a lead story on the local news.*

As if reading his mind, the guy pleaded, "Hey come on. I don't got a gun or anything. I just need a phone." His hair hung in his red eyes. "So you got one or what?"

Mark heard a car door slam. A woman got out of the Tempo and ran to Mark's passenger window. She was instantly drenched. She tapped on the glass and tilted her head.

Oh great. They're working as a team, he thought. Mark lowered the window and she stuck her entire upper body into the car. She was dripping all over the leather seats. Mark had driven without incident almost four hours in the pouring rain, and now, ten minutes from his parents' house, he'd found himself in this situation.

"Mister, please. Just let us borrow your phone. That's it." She smiled at him and peeled the wet hair from her face.

Mark lost his breath for a second. All at once he realized that he knew her. This was not a stranger begging to use his cell phone. He looked her in the eyes. She stared back, pleading, but with no hint of recognition.

Mark flipped the lock button on the door. "Yeah, I got a phone. Get in." He snatched the picture off the dash and threw it into the center console.

The guy opened the back door. There was a splat as his wet jeans met leather. She climbed in next to Mark. It had been years, but she was still amazing, even soaked and haggard. She looked at him, shivering. Mark rolled up the windows, pushing the rain outside again where it belonged.

Before escaping to Hollywood, the farthest Mark ever made it away from home was Emitt College, twenty-five miles outside of Escondito. It was a dumpy little school that hardly anyone had heard of, other than the two thousand or so students that went there. The joke around campus claimed that it was actually a mental institution years and years before some guy with the last name Emitt decided to found a crappy college. And supposedly, all of the patients were hired cheap to be janitors in the few buildings where classes were taught. This was funny for the students, but unfortunate for the janitors who the students avoid to this day like mangy stray dogs.

And it was at this said-to-be former nut house, in a tiny freshmen dormitory, where Mark first came into contact with Stevie Klien.

She was the kind of college student who didn't seem to actually be a college student. Mark never saw her studying or doing anything particularly intellectual. But every morning before classes, classes which she was only rumored to attend, she would put on a show for every guy in the dorm. At promptly 9:00 a.m. she would walk down the hall en route to the bathrooms wearing nothing but a tiny, white robe. About ten minutes later, she would stroll right back down that hall, her robe clinging to her wet skin as she left a trail of watery footprints in the matted carpet leading back to her room.

Interestingly enough, between about 9:00 and 9:15 in the morning every guy in the dorm decided to hang out in the hall, fill up his water jug at the drinking fountain, or meander down to the men's room. Mark actually dropped one of his morning classes so he could join the crowd of loiterers.

After about seven months of daily peep shows and the occasional on-campus sighting, Mark decided to make a move. He was a skinny, short guy with oversized glasses, but he had spirit. And he was sure that spirit was worth something.

One night in early April, Mark and his roommate, a guy who smelled strangely like soup, and was never seen or heard from again after finals that year, snuck a case of beer into their room. They had waded though about half of the lukewarm Buds when Mark realized that you never really buy beer, you just sort of rent it: he had to go to the bathroom. So he stumbled through the deserted hallway and did his thing. On his way back, there she was. Stevie was at the drinking fountain filling up her iron. He couldn't believe it. It was odd to see her alone. She usually generated a lot of attention, but apparently she'd snuck out into the open, undetected.

Stevie looked at him and looked back down at her iron. It made a comic dribbling noise as it filled. Mark stopped, his body warmed by alcohol, his head floating a bit.

He suddenly heard himself speak, "What's a girl like you doing all alone on a Friday night?" Did he say that? Where in the hell did he get a line like that? It sounded like something out of a porn movie. Did he expect her to say "Well, I'm not alone now," and lead him back to her room, a snare-drum-lead blues tune in the background?

She looked up, unimpressed, "I won't be alone for long."

"Oh yeah? Big plans tonight?" He asked. Why was his voice suddenly a few octaves higher?

"Some friends from USD are coming up tonight. Nothing cool happens in this city until after eleven."

"Yeah, I hear ya," he said. Was this true? What happened after eleven? He thought about asking her if she wanted to join him and his roommate, who smelled like soup, for a few beers, but he wasn't sure she would place that in the category of "cools things that happen after eleven." Plus he didn't think it would be fair to put his roommate through that kind of a shock. He leaves to take a wiz and comes back with the hottest girl either of them had ever seen. It could be disastrous.

"Well, I tell you what," Mark said. Why was he continuing to talk? "When you come back tonight, why don't you stop by room twelve. A bunch of people usually end up hangin' out there pretty late."

Stevie laughed a little. "Uh, I doubt I'll be coming home tonight, but if I do, I'll be with my boyfriend. He plays football for USD. We don't really like to hang out with people from around here." She should have just bashed him in the face with her iron.

Mark, wounded, frowned and looked at the floor, "Uh, cool. Well see ya." He scurried back to his room, imaginary tail jammed between his legs. He heard from behind a mocking, "see ya." Mark's buzz was gone.

After that school year he never saw Stevie again. Much like his roommate who smelled like soup, she sort of vanished.

"Shit, man, I haven't seen rain like this forever," the guy said from the back.

Mark wondered if this guy was the football player from USD. He didn't look like an ex-football player. He was pretty short and he had one of those skinny bodies with a bulging gut. In a few years he'd look like a man shoplifting a basketball.

"Yeah, sure is coming down," Mark said.

Stevie grabbed the cell phone and put it to her ear.

"Give me that," the guy snapped. She cringed at his raised voice.

He pushed some buttons and shook the phone, as if this hand-held piece of technology would suddenly come to life when properly shaken. "Thing's dead," he declared.

"Oh God, yeah, I'm sorry. I forgot to charge it," Mark said, overly apologetic.

Stevie sighed, "What do you want to do, John?"

Mark saw him glare at her in the rearview mirror.

"Shit, I don't know." He said. His face darkened. "Tow truck costs like eighty bucks."

Mark realized how badly this guy was slurring his words. *Jesus, was this guy driving? No wonder the car is screwed.*

"Uh, sorry about the phone. Listen, I'm just heading to my parents' house a couple of miles from here. Can I drop you guys off somewhere?"

"What about your brother's?" Stevie asked timidly. "That's not too far." She talked to the guy like she was asking permission.

"Yeah. Maybe tomorrow after it stops raining you could come back for the car," Mark said, trying to keep this guy from getting mad. "Who knows, it might start right up." Mark knew about as much about cars as he did microbiology, but this sounded like a logical suggestion.

The guy sunk down in the seat and closed his eyes. "Yeah, that's fine," he said. Mark looked at Stevie. She smiled. "You know where El Torro Boulevard is?" she asked.

Her hair was soaked but she'd pulled it off her face and tucked it behind her small ears. A hint of mascara ran from her left eye. She wore a short, brown skirt, blackened by the rain. She wasn't wearing a jacket, just a white, long sleeve blouse, which had a low cut v-neckline. Beads of water slowly rolled from her neck down her tanned chest, disappearing between her breasts. Her nipples stood firm against the thin fabric. Mark felt his face flush, *she's not wearing a bra.* Mark gave it his all not to look at her chest, but he couldn't help himself. His eyes dropped for a second. She didn't react, but women always know.

"Yeah, I know where El Torro is," he said. It was about ten minutes past his parents' house. He thought there was a trailer park out in that direction, but he hadn't been out there in years.

They drove for a while in silence. He glanced at her legs. She'd slipped her wet sandals off and was rubbing her bare feet against the plush floor mat. Her skin was covered with goosebumbs. Mark flipped the heater on. He was struck with sudden anxiety. *Could she tell I was looking at her legs? How did I know to turn the heater on?*

"Oh, thanks," she said, "I'm freezing." Her tone wasn't friendly or hostile, it floated in between, close to indifference.

"I can imagine," he started. "You're soaking w…"

"So, this is a nice ride," the guy interrupted from the back. His eyes looked heavy in the rearview mirror as he slumped further down in the seat. "You a doctor or a lawyer or something?"

"No. No. Not smart enough. Actually, I work in film." In California, everyone with a nice car and a decent haircut claims to be, in some way, connected to the film industry. This, in itself was not impressive.

"What, you an actor? You don't look like an actor," the guy probed on.

"No. I'm a screenwriter."

"A what?"

"A screenwriter. I write the movies. You know, like what the actors say to each other," Mark said. He wondered if this red-eyed idiot in his back seat realized how stupid he sounded. Did he want it written out on a chalkboard or something? He probably couldn't even read. Jesus, the guy didn't even know what a screenwriter was.

Mark glanced at Stevie. She looked straight ahead.

"Well, no one really knows who screenwriters are anyway," Mark said, trying to ease the sudden tension he'd created.

"What movies have you done?" the guy asked, seemingly prepared to give the famous "I never saw that one" blank stare.

Mark cleared his throat. Even Stevie seemed to be paying attention now. "You guys seen *Jerry's Bride*?"

He jumped and the car swerved as a hand grabbed his thigh. "Oh my God!" Stevie said, "You're Marcus Winter."

Mark smiled. He wasn't used to a genuine reaction from someone outside the industry. But then, he *was* a local celebrity. The Blockbuster Video by his parents' house had a "Marcus Winter" section with all four of his movies and a little picture of him standing by a big tree in his old neighborhood. He'd cut his hair and started wearing contacts since than, so it didn't even really look like him anymore.

"I can't believe I didn't recognize you!" she yelled.

"Oh yeah, I remember you," came slurred words from the back seat. "Yeah, 'bout a year ago they were talking about how *Jerry's Bride* didn't get nominated for an Emmy or a Tony or whatever."

Listen to this asshole. "An Oscar," Mark said, unscathed. "It's OK. Just an award, you know?" Mark's eyes met his in the rear-view mirror. Mark smiled.

"I never saw it, so I don't know what to tell you," the guy said, looking out the window at the darkness, defeated. His voice was slow and slurred.

"Well, I did, and I loved it," Stevie said, "made me go out and rent your other three, those were great too. They're just so different, so not-Hollywood."

Mark wondered if she really thought this or if she'd just run across an *Entertainment Weekly* in the last few months.

"Thanks. I just try to write about real people." He'd used this line on nearly every female in the state of California. She removed her hand from his thigh, but not without a light squeeze.

She said her name was Stevie, as if he didn't know, and they chatted for a while about his work and the industry. Mark drove slowly, deliberately in the rain. He was in no hurry to drop these two off. Well, that wasn't entirely true. He was in no hurry to drop her off. The lump in the back seat could exit stage left as soon as possible. She looked at him, hanging on his words.

Mark laughed when he discovered that, although the guy hadn't left, he might as well have. "I think your friend's had enough," he said

"What," she asked, as if she'd forgotten someone was even in the back seat. Mark nodded at the rearview mirror. The guy had passed out, his labored breathing echoed through the car over the sound of the rain.

Embarrassed, she looked at him, face flushed. "Oh. He had a rough night."

Mark glanced at her hand. No ring. "You guys married?" He wanted to hear her say it.

"Oh, no, no. We're not married."

"Been together awhile?"

She said they'd been together about a year. They'd met at the bar where she waitressed. She'd lived in Escondito for about twelve years after dropping out of Emitt College. He saw in her the same beauty from those days, the same beauty that had nearly stopped his heart when she climbed out of the beat-up Tempo a few miles back. *Stevie* was talking to him, a man who'd never caught a passing glance from any beautiful woman before Hollywood had found him.

Mark caught sight of his own reflection in the windshield. He saw a skinny, little man smiling and nodding at the beautiful woman next to him. His hair was jet black and where it wasn't curly and out of control it was falling out all too quickly. His eyes were too small for his strange nose, left crooked by a little league line-drive years before. The red sweater he wore was too big and bulging in all the wrong places. He was looking at a man who'd been left at many drinking fountains, awkward and embarrassed, doubting and hating himself.

She had been talking about how exciting it was to meet him, asking who all he'd met in Hollywood, then suddenly, "You're coming up on El Torro," she said, startling him. "Go ahead and go left at the light."

Mark came to a long, slow stop at a red light on El Torro Boulevard. The rain was still constant, fighting the wipers every inch of the way. The speed change seemed to rouse the sleeping drunk in the back seat. He moaned, opened his eyes, and sat up. "Jesus Christ," he said, grabbing his forehead.

Stevie turned around. "You OK?" she asked tentatively.

"How far we got?" he groaned, not looking at her.

Stevie glanced at the rain splashed El Torro Boulevard sign that dangled from the stoplight. It swayed in the wind like a green shutter. "'Bout a mile or so."

"Hurry up, man, I think I'm gonna puke," he said, eyes closed. He gripped the armrest, undoubtedly trying to stop the interior from its out-of-control spin.

"Shit, is he serious?" Mark asked her.

"Can you hold it, John? Are you gonna throw up?" She was less tentative now. "Come on, we'll be at your brother's in two minutes."

Mark turned left onto El Torro and gunned the engine. He sure as hell didn't want to have this guy spill used Jim Beam all over his back seat.

"OK, you're coming up on it," she said, her hand finding the same spot on his thigh again. "Turn left up here at that sign."

"El Parque de Paradise," Mark read the sign aloud. "Jesus, how come every place in this city sounds like it should be on a Taco Bell Menu card?"

Stevie forced a laugh.

Mark pulled onto a gravel road. Rain danced in puddles like boiling water. A long line of trailers stood before them. It seemed that at any second a gust would come along and scatter them all over the park like playing cards.

"It's the third one, over there," she said, pointing to a small, silver trailer with a set of lawn furniture overturned in the yard like fallen soldiers.

The guy in the back groaned as Mark pulled to a stop. Mark watched in guilty amusement as he jumped out of the car, scurried through the rain and mud, then crashed through the trailer's front door.

"I hope his brother doesn't scare easily," Mark said, laughing. "Guy's gonna get his head blown off crashing through front doors like that."

She was looking at him. He smiled at her. She was suddenly close to him, her seat belt off. Her hand rested on the center console. "I'm sorry about that," she said, eyes locked on his. He could smell her perfume.

"Oh, no problem. No harm no f…"

"How long are you going to be in town?" she interrupted. "Maybe we could get together." She was a different woman now. She arched her back and tilted her head at him. The damp clothes clung to her body like the short little robe from long ago. The robe that she wore back when she was too good for him; back in the world where she didn't like to hang out with people from around here and the cool things didn't happen until after eleven.

"I could make it worth your while," she said, running her hands through her hair, letting it fall over her right eye playfully.

Mark knew Mary was at home listening to the rain drum against their bay window. She was lying in bed thinking of him and whether or not he'd call. And she'd also be there if he'd never even been to Hollywood and they still lived in the shitty apartment with the broken elevator.

"You know, Stevie," he said, looking at the steering wheel. "Thanks, but I'm married. Have been for a while."

Her smile vanished and her body slumped in the seat. Silence found them, pushing the rain away for a moment. Mark listened to her awkward "thank you," and "good-bye," and he watched her step out into the rain and walk slowly to the trailer door. She didn't even seem to notice the rain crashing down around her.

Mark put the Rover in gear and pushed back out onto El Torro Boulevard. He dug into the center console and found the picture of his wife. Hopefully his parents would be awake when he got home. He didn't want them to worry about him. His mother hated when he drove in the rain.

Alexis Taylor
California State University, Long Beach

Sundogs

A skull, executioner-black, woven into spattered crimson, is tattooed onto Frankie's right forearm. It sits perfectly proportioned, elbow to wrist. His arm is thick where the stain penetrates, with veins straining outward because the muscle has left them nowhere else to go. This tattoo covers another tattoo, one that reads "Tiffs." No apostrophe, but possessive all the same.

Tiffany is Frankie's wife. They have been separated almost seven months. I am not particularly jealous of their past together, because with Frankie all endings seem sad and inevitable.

The skull was applied eight weeks ago, a gesture of commitment I neither requested nor desired. The scabs have barely healed. They flake off onto the sheets, and I brush them away when I make the bed each day. Frankie has reluctantly kept his own apartment, but as the weeks have stretched into months, more of his t-shirts and Levis have been mixing with mine in the laundry hamper. This is good or bad, depending upon the day.

At breakfast this morning he laughed and said if he really ends up hating the new look, he can keep covering it until his entire arm is an obliteration of tattoo.

I repeat the odd phrase "obliteration of tattoo," then say, "maybe," but both of us are on edge and it comes out flat instead of hopeful. There is less and less to be hopeful about. We have spent our allotment quickly.

Frankie is mostly quiet about his life with Tiffany. Hints of how they loved are buried in his conversation as softly as seeds tucked into pockets of thick soil.

One story: Frankie and Tiffany dropped acid together. Under the influence, he cut up an old extension cord, fastened it to the ceiling using a thumbtack and then set it on fire with a disposable lighter. After everything had been prepared, the two of them laid together on the bed, under a patchwork quilt made of old Catholic school uniforms. From this safe place they watched the melting cord drip and crackle into a bucket of water. Acid, he explained, as I feigned interest, is an intense experience.

And now, there is the persistent knowledge that we have lost something, although I don't yet know all of what there is to lose with Frankie. I am thirty-three years old, seven on the plus side of him. I have never seen a tab of acid or even thought much about it. Frankie, as an odd kind of balance, has never heard of Joseph Conrad or William Blake.

He abandons the bed late at night to draw, and sleeps during the day while I am out teaching English to accelerated high school seniors. Frankie claims to be jealous of my knowledge. He once sat in the back of my class and sketched me behind the podium unmasking a hidden *leitmotif* in Beowulf. One of my students asked if he was my lover. "No," I explained. "He's just another student." He overhears and later ruins my detachment with his lovemaking.

Frankie and I are sometimes so taken with the idea of who each other is that the in-love aspect of our relationship becomes a lost edge. Family and friends on both sides are confused, cautious in a way we haven't been. Opposing camps have been established on our behalves. I give my side the easy answer—his carelessness awakens my imagination, his touch cauterizes old wounds. Frankie's motives are his own.

Our common ground—Scrabble. It was through the placing of the tiles that we moved from friends to lovers. When we sit at the round, oak dining table we are almost equals. Each time Frankie's thick arm stretches across the board to make a word, I look for the faint outline of "Tiffs" hidden beneath the skull. He has never disclosed its location, but I imagine it to be in the blackest part of the tattoo, the empty socket of one absent eye.

"Play, Olivia," he says, tapping a Marlboro to the front of the pack, "or I'm going to put a time limit on you."

I shuffle the tiles around on my rack, pretending to have a word. He won't push the time limit rule, because I let him look up words in the Scrabble Dictionary.

Frankie is not fooled by my letter shuffling and leaves the table with his cigarette fixed in a Teddy Roosevelt clench between his teeth, a joke once funny, that has quickly faded into tradition.

After a minute, while I'm still mulling over possibilities, he sits back down with six unsmoked roaches. He pulls the papers apart gently, reminding me of his watercolor of a young Mexican girl husking tamales. He rolls the six roaches into a new joint, puts out the cigarette in a ceramic ashtray given to me by one of my students and lights up the tightly twisted paper.

I open the window behind me and hope the neighbors have closed theirs. It's a very tight board. "Pass," I say and throw back two 'I's, a 'U,' and a 'V,' keeping the "ing."

Frankie holds the smoke in his lungs and lays down "balance" for twenty-three points before exhaling.

"Play," he says when the new joint is smoked down to a new roach.

I have drawn an 'X' and can play it alone for twenty points, but decide to hold on to it. This may be my inevitable downfall with boys like Frankie who paint with genius and make oblique gestures aimed at what they imagine is commitment: resisting the pull to let go in a timely manner. The word "luck" is on the board. I add a 'P' to the front and my "ing" to the back. "Plucking," I say out loud because Frankie has left the table again. "Triple letter on the 'P' and double word for forty-six points." Smug.

Frankie walks back in the room carrying his frayed, orange backpack. He places it by the door without a word, then sits. He looks at my score and I watch the backpack slump into the carpeting. He is unnerved by the number of points I have accumulated. Frankie plays frantically, always looking for the big plays, the clever links, while I play the tortoise's game, slow and steady. Neither of us has ever thrown a game, but I have scored the most points for one word—vanquish—two triple word scores, a double letter on the 'Q' and fifty bonus points for using all my tiles, a total of two-hundred-and-forty-eight points. Since I'm sure this feat will never be repeated, I slip it into conversation whenever I think it will sound like a natural addition.

Three nights ago I saw a photograph of Tiffany, shuffled between two pages in a book of short stories by Woody Allen. Her youth startled me, as did Frankie's at first—twenty, maybe twenty-one, pretty except for a slight plumpness, and lips that stretch her smile thin. I pinched the photo between two fingers like one of Frankie's joints, and held her to the light, looking, as with the tattoo, for the reason she was no longer there, and for assurance that she wouldn't seep back to the surface.

It is Frankie's turn again. I call to him in the bedroom.

"Have you seen my Social Distortion t-shirt?" he yells back.

"Second drawer. Wicker dresser."

"How about my cross-hatch of the bunnies sucking fish heads?"

"Under the bed. Come play." Now I am the impatient one.

He comes carrying the cross-hatch, a recent diversion from the watercolors. Frankie has two distinct styles. His earlier works have dark, alluring shadows, like the skull. They are private and demonstrate the inexhaustible extent of his talent. The newer works are conundrums meant to amuse and impress, like a seven-letter word laid so quickly across the board that the tiles make a clicking noise against the plastic. He rests his portfolio against his pack and sits restlessly at the table. "The shirt wasn't in the drawer."

"I'll look," I say, anxious now to have it finished. Before I go, he takes my hand and squeezes. A familiar rush of heat travels through me at this simple physical joining.

"You know why it has to be now," I say, sensing he won't press me for words that will merely refract the truth.

"The long nights?" he murmurs.

"You leave the bed before the sheets have cooled."

"Yes," he says, thinking we have hit upon both problem and solution. "I grind my teeth during sleep."

I pull my hand from his and start toward the bedroom, the warmth has already begun to dissipate. Frankie is still speaking.

"My jaw is so tight by morning I can hardly move it." He sets his teeth, ready to demonstrate.

"Stop," I say.

"I don't know the things you know," he says, and I can't recall if this is its first airing or a repeat of previous conversations. It has a familiar truth to it anyway.

Here is something I know: Frankie is good at anger. He is a self-motivator.

I find the Social Distortion t-shirt in a drawer with others of his I've worn as nightshirts because I like their musty marijuana fragrance. His fingers smell the same way from holding the roach until it is nothing. I take all the shirts but one and stack them neatly, one on top of the other, then place them by the front door next to the growing pile.

Frankie has not yet played a word, although he is looking something up in the dictionary when I sit down. I notice for the first time that when his arm tenses, the cheekbone of the skull also tightens.

I stand. "Something to drink?"

"Beer's good."

I open a bottle for Frankie and at the last minute, one for myself.

As I set his beer on a coaster, he plays "sundogs" for thirty-four points.

Challenge, I start to say, but it must be verifiable because he's been scrambling through the dictionary.

He looks at the beer in front of him, says nothing.

"Good word," I say, pretending the mood is light. "What does it mean?"

"If you find any more of my things, just throw them out."

"I have an unused 'X.'"

"Play it then." His voice belies his anger and I think, *good, this is where we should be.* I am finally standing on familiar ground. I know where this path leads. We stare at each other's beer. Frankie reaches for my hand again but this time I pull back, my knuckles scraping the board. A few of the letters are jostled. Frankie thinks I've done this maliciously. It's there in his eyes. It's there in his tensed muscles. I grip the edge of the board as if it were a Frisbee and send it spinning, around and around and around, until the tiles are flipping and flying in troubled arcs to the floor.

"Bitch."

I begin peeling the gold foil off the neck of my beer. I know he's desperate for a sign that he should stay, but I continue unraveling the foil. I want him to leave. He knows I've orchestrated it. He can't prove it and he'll never understand it. The ones before him have lied if they say otherwise.

When a small pyramid of gold builds up next to the bottle, I shape it into a makeshift band and slide it over the neck. Frankie is at the door, arms loaded—waiting, hopeful, powerless.

There is something I want to say, but the words won't come while he is standing half-in, half-out of the doorway. I think about taking him to bed and dismiss it. Twice.

He leaves.

When the words do come, it is inside a deep and unsettling sleep—clay fish heads are sucking bunnies and Woody Allen is holding a picture of a plump Mexican girl peeling, gently peeling, the scab off a fresh tattoo. Golden beer bottles fly around and around the table, and the smell of marijuana hangs sweet on a severed hand. Sundog—a small rainbow. Why did I think it was another word for good-bye?

Aaron Reid
University of Alabama at Tuscaloosa

Cleveland Flight

Sweat dampened his forehead. He reached up with a shaking hand and wiped the moisture onto a linen handkerchief. Licking his dry lips, he peered around the chair and glanced down the aisle. Empty.

The plane jumped and turned. Gary closed his eyes and gripped the arms of the chair, curling his thick fingers around the upholstery.

One flight, he thought, *and then I will start my new life. Cleveland. A fresh start. Just me, a dog, and a city of strangers. I'll put everything behind…*

"Here you are, Mr. Hinman."

He opened his eyes and tilted his head. The reading light above him caused his balding scalp to glimmer. His thin lips parted into a half-smile.

"Your drink," the stewardess said, placing the plastic glass on the fold out tray. Her crystal-blue eyes searched his pale complexion. Her blond hair fell about her shoulders in curls, and her triangular face was painted with make-up, accenting her high cheek bones and deep-set eyes. "Would you like a pillow?" Her red lips smiled.

The plane tossed again, dropping.

"Oh God." Gary shook his head, spinning his thinning hair.

"Only turbulence," she patted his arm. "It'll be over soon, Mr. Hinman. I brought your rum and Coke. Three ice cubes, just like you asked." She smacked her lips, and anchored her hands on her hips.

"Uh, how do you know my name?" He asked, rubbing his chin. He scanned her face, her hair, her figure. "I don't recognize…"

"You're such a kidder." She patted his arm again, laughing softly. "Let me know if you need anything else," she winked.

"I've never seen you before," he said, his forehead folded into rivets.

"You're so cute," she pinched his cheek, held for a moment, and snapped her fingers away.

A voice came over the intercom, then static.

"That's for me," the stewardess said. "Let me know if you want another." She patted his arm again, and disappeared down the aisle.

He massaged his cheek, kneading the numbed flesh. His eyes lowered. *I didn't order this*, he thought, eying the glass. He rolled up his shirt sleeves and loosened his seatbelt from around his generous belly.

The reading light flickered. The plane rocked. He grabbed the cup, squeezing the iced plastic, and drew it to his bulging lips. Two swallows and the cup was empty. It fell from his hand to the floor. He reached for it, resting his round head on the foldout tray. His fingers squirmed in the air. It was out of reach. He sat up, heaving, and leaned back.

"Calm down," he told himself, clasping his hands together and resting them on his stomach, "if I can sleep, it will be over soon."

"Go, then, you coward." Emilie's words echoed through his mind. He could see her sitting up in bed, hugging the white blanket close to her chest. Her graying hair was done up in curlers, and her long, wrinkled face swirled into a hideous expression.

"Leave everything you've worked for," her raspy voice lashed about the small bedroom.

Gary sat at his desk, facing his wife. His face was blank. All he could think about was Cleveland. It would be *his* city. His dreams would come true there. Everything would work. He had been wrong before: Dallas, San Diego, D.C. and the others, were not his. Cleveland would be.

"Are you listening?" She shouted. "You can't keep doing this to yourself. You're going to find yourself all alone. You promised it was in the past. You promised."

"I've got to go. There's nothing here for me. I'm leaving." He stood, a suitcase in each hand. "Good-bye, Emilie."

"Bastard." Her eyes were fierce. "Bastard."

He opened the bedroom door; the hinges groaned.

"I'm begging you," Emilie turned him around, struggling to keep the comforter around her body. "Don't go. I'll make breakfast. I've got eggs," her bony fingers squeezed his arm, wrinkling his shirt.

He cleared his throat.

"We'll sit on the porch and talk like we used to. You remember?" Her eyelids fluttered. She tugged his shirt. "You're settled now. With me. You have a wife now."

"I've never changed."

"Yes, you have!" The veins in her neck bulged. She held on to his shirt, stretching the fabric, preventing him from walking down the hall. A curler slipped from her hair, bounced on her shoulder, and disappeared into a crease in the blanket. "You're not the man you told me about. You've settled."

He shook his head, pulling away, trying to break free from her grasp. He twisted, facing the narrow, tomb-like hall, and pressed his sight on the stairwell.

"You're fifty-nine." Her voice heightened. "You're not the twenty-five-year-old boy you told me about. You're happy now. And your job?" Her fingers slipped from his shirt. "You said you loved your job. You told me!" She began to scream. "You told me!"

He was halfway down the hall, passing paintings of mountains, his paintings for Emilie. They were blurs in his vision.

"Gary, you're not leaving." Her feet pounded the hardwood floor, thumping, rattling the paintings on the wall. "Look at me!"

"Another drink?" The stewardess leaned over him. Her hands were tucked between her knees.

"Um," Gary looked up. "I guess..." He wiped his eyes with the back of his hand "Yeah. One more," he sniffed softly, "please."

"Feeling better?"

"Yes, I'm okay. A little shook up." He nodded, firming his lips.

"I'm glad."

"I still can't piece together where I know you from," his eyes fell on her face, searching for familiarities.

"Gary," she laughed.

He tried to smile, only managing to open his mouth.

"Be right back."

She didn't return. He leaned back, eyes closing, mind drifting back.

"And how may I help you?" the young man had asked indifferently. The bank lobby stirred with silent, tranced people. Gary was in the front of the line, weaving in his steps. "Sir?" The clerk rapped his hand on the counter, "You're next in line."

"Oh. Yes." Gary said, darting to the counter. He spoke sluggishly, "I need to close an account." His head throbbed painfully. He fingered his moist scalp. "An account," he repeated sharply.

"What's the number?" The bank attendant's face was narrow, harboring a needled nose, tiny lips and a forehead that sloped to his bushy, chestnut hair. "Sir, the number?" The scrawny man blinked impatiently, thumbing his mustache.

"It's under Emilie Hinman. I can't recall the number." Gary scratched at his cheek. The clerk's face appeared to dissolve. It swam in a murky pool of flesh and bone. Gary shook his head, batting his eyelids. "Savings account."

"I need to ask who you are, and I need to see identification," the attendant clasped his hands on the counter and squinted his eyes. "You do have identification?"

"Gary Hinman. Her husband." The attendant's lips vanished, melting into his skin. "Here," Gary placed his license into an eight fingered hand, "I'm on the account also. Please hurry. I feel dizzy." Gary shielded his eyes with his hand, "I want to close it."

A baby was crying. Someone whistled shrilly. Gary's head thumped, thumped, thumped.

"Of course," the man rattled the keyboard buttons.

Someone caught his shoulder, turning him from the counter.

The plane rocked back and forth, the front end sinking, startling Gary, waking him.

I must be coming down with something, he thought, squirming in his seat, *I must have been...* He exhaled, twiddling his thumbs in rapid circles.

She'll manage without the money, he thought suddenly, cracking the blind on the airplane window. It was dark outside. Cloudy. *She'll work overtime at the school. She'll manage, and one day she'll understand why I had to leave. I'll write to her first thing. I'll apologize, and tell her I'll miss her.*

The stewardess returned, "A rum and Coke." She placed it on the tray.

"Oh." Gary reached for it.

"Three ice cubes," she said as she nudged her elbow into the head of his chair, crossed her legs, and hovered over him. Her blond hair tickled his head and ears. "Just how you like it."

"I must tell you," he shifted, making it possible to look in her eyes, and to get free from her teasing hair, "that you've mistaken me for someone else." He sipped the drink. The center arm of the seats burrowed into his side. "I've never seen you before."

She was silent.

He averted his eyes to his drink. She was smiling, arms at her sides.

"Do you mind if I sit with you? My legs feel like putty." She ran her fingers through her hair, wound it together and deposited it over her left shoulder.

"Um," Gary scratched his head, "sure. Let me slide over." He moved from the aisle seat to the window seat, straddling the intruding center arm.

"Thanks," she collapsed into the chair, "I'm on my feet all day." Her smile faded.

Gary nodded, drinking. He kept his eyes straight, glaring at the safety manual for accidents.

"Let me ask you something," she clutched his arm and leaned close to his face. He could smell her breath. Minty. "It's kind of personal." Tiny lines spread beneath her eyes.

"Um, OK," he said, moving the glass from his mouth, eyes still on the manual.

"Have you ever felt really guilty?" a hoarse whisper.

"What? What kind of a question is that?" Their eyes met.

"I was just wondering," she moved away, resting her head on the seat. "I feel guilty all the time."

"I don't understand what…"

"Nevermind. I shouldn't have brought it up. I've got to get back." She stood, adjusted her skirt, and was gone.

Gary finished the drink in a swift gulp.

Again, the cup fell. He watched it roll under the chair in front of him. He tried to reach for it, stretching his arm in order to…

"Gary, you'll be fine," it was Emilie; it was her voice.

Gary opened his eyes wide, sitting upright. "Emilie?" His legs had fallen asleep. A piercing screech penetrated his hearing. The plane's engines rumbled violently, shaking the plane. "Where are you?" He peeked over the seat. Faces. He turned, blushing.

"I understand, Gary."

"Where are you?" He lurched over the aisle seat. "Emilie?" There wasn't anyone in the aisle. "Emilie?"

Silence.

Could she have followed me aboard? he wondered silently, *to the bank? If she knew about the money...*

He checked his watch. The silvery hands were dormant. The second hand rested in an unmoving slumber.

She'll find me. And this time...

He was instantly warm, hot, burning. He climbed over the aisle seat, crawling. The plane lurched forward. He slipped, rolled off the seat, and wedged himself partly in the aisle. The cushions compressed his stomach, causing his heart to hammer against his ribs.

I'm going to suffocate, he thought, These seats. I can't breath.

He wriggled from between the seats, using the legs of the seats as leverage, and fought his way into the casket-slim aisle. He pulled himself to his feet, hitting his head on the overhead compartment.

"What's the problem?" an elderly woman asked from behind.

He whirled. She was two seats back. She wore a black fur hat that sat on her head like a bundled towel and a silk scarf around her neck. Her eyes and face drooped, melting from her skull. Her body slouched awkwardly, crookedly, as if her spine were kinked in various directions. Her leathery lips parted, revealing a crusted tongue. "You're not supposed to leave your seat," her voice was like tearing, crumpling paper.

"My seat?" His hand went to his chest.

"Sit down," the old woman ordered, clapping her hands together. "You've got some nerve." She arched her back, crackling the bones.

Gary turned. Faces watched him from the compartment. Eyes on him. And the stewardess raced toward him with her arms outstretched. She was smiling. Her teeth were yellow. Part of her shirt was untucked from her dress and hung loosely about her waist. She opened and closed her hands. Her fingers had fanged mouths on the tips. They opened, closed, drooled. Her eyes were now dark.

"Sit down!" The elderly woman demanded.

"Oh," Gary gasped, blocking his eyes with his arms. The plane dipped sideways. He caught himself on the back of his chair. "No." He struggled to stand.

"Shh, you're fine. Let's sit down," the stewardess had her hands on his shoulders.

He jumped, wheeling away.

She was normal. Her teeth were white. Her shirt was tucked in, and all that covered the end of her fingers was soft, pink skin.

"Let's sit down." Her words were calm, relaxing. "You're fine."

He obeyed. The stewardess helped fasten his seatbelt, pulling it tight around his body. He smelled her shampoo. Strawberry. She stood. She had another drink in hand, which he accepted.

"I must be coming down with something terrible," he said into his lap, eying his opened hands. A jagged cut was slashed into his thumb. It was maroon with drying blood, "Seeing things."

"Everyone gets a little on the edge when flying," the stewardess whispered in his ear. "Don't mind that woman. She's a bit off. You're fine now."

Gary nodded, gathering his thoughts. "My watch. It stopped."

"We'll be there shortly. It's a little after eleven. Better?" She rested her hand on his head. Her palm was clammy.

"Yes. Thank you." He reached for his drink.

"Gary," Emilie said, standing at the top of the stairs. She was wrapped in the blanket. Her words were distant. "You can't do this."

Gary was at the bottom. A dog licked his hand. Their dog. Pauline. A Husky.

"You need help, Gary. You can't run from everything that…"

He crossed the room, stepping around a worn, green couch. The dog followed, panting, sloshing its tongue for Gary's hands.

"What about your job?" She gripped the wooden handrail with her fingers. "You have to go to work. What are you going to tell them?"

He paused. "I quit."

"Gary, you loved working there. What's come over you? Is it me?" She walked halfway down the stairs. The blanket fell from her shoulders and gathered at her feet. She wore a white, laced nightgown. Her frame was slender, and the garment clung to her aging body. A strand of hair hung over her eyes.

He shook his head and opened the front door. The morning sun leaked into the room. Pauline ran anxious circles around his feet. He was still, but his eyes wandered around the front yard and along the winding dirt road that flowed through the trees.

"Do you want them sunny side up?" Emilie eased down another step "Yes," she said, "sunny side up. I know how you like them. Then we can sit outside and…"

He raised an adamant hand. He bent his fingers into his palm.

"If you leave this time, don't ever come back!" She was shrieking. "I can't take your excursions. You disappear, and I don't see you… Then you come back. Not this time. You promised. I won't do it anymore. If you go, everything here is lost. Do you hear?"

He closed the front door behind him.

"Excuse me."

"Yes, Mr. Hinman?" The stewardess looked up from the cart of canned drinks. She was pouring orange soda into a plastic cup. She had her back to him.

"I thought the flight was three hours long?" His arms were

strapped across his belly.

"That's correct," she placed the empty can into a plastic bag attached to the cart. She handed the drink to a young girl in the seat. "Here you are. Orange soda."

"Why is it taking so long?" Sweat dripped down his cheeks.

"We've only been in the air for an hour." She pushed the cart down the aisle. Gary stepped closer. "Would you like something?" She asked a man who was reading a newspaper.

"An hour?" Gary asked himself, running his arm across his forehead. "It's been longer than an hour."

"Shh," a woman ordered.

Gary looked at her briefly.

"My baby is sleeping," she glared.

"Another rum and Coke?" The stewardess looked over her shoulder.

"I know we've been flying for more than an hour." His arms fell from his stomach. "What time is it? Can't I have a straight answer?"

"I suggest you return to your seat and figure out for yourself why it is taking so long. I only serve the drinks." Her face became white. Her smile disappeared from her lips; they were no longer red, they were dry, cracking. "I've got plenty of people to get to."

"What's this?" He mumbled, hugging himself.

"Go sit down." The old woman from before was poking his thigh. She was in the seat next to him. Her scarf had come undone and rested on her lap in a clump. She wore a navy blue dress, and the fur hat was sliding over her forehead. "Some nerve," she coughed, wheezing, jabbing her finger into his flesh.

"Crazy," Gary said, backing away.

At his seat he found another rum and Coke.

He swiped it off the tray, splashing the drink on the window seat. He sat down. Sweat oozed from under his arms, drenching his shirt. His sleeves had fallen again, he pulled them to his elbows and closed his eyes.

"Reading material?" The stewardess nudged his arm. She dropped a book in his lap. "Enjoy." She was gone, pushing the cart. The wheels squeaked.

Before he could read the title, the book fell from his hands. It struck the floor and slid beneath the seat in front of him.

A light above him flashed: Fasten Seatbelts.

He ignored the warning. He returned the tray to its upright position, bent forward, and skimmed his hand under the seat. He felt something cold. Metal. He wrapped his fingers around, wrenching.

"Ow! Let go!" A woman's voice; a hand swatted around the seat, striking Gary.

"Huh?" he removed his arm and sat up. He licked his lips, firing his eyes in every direction.

"You're sick," a young woman stood over him, holding a black purse under her chin. Her square, box-like face was pink. Her lips jerked. She slapped him, and moved on, trotting down the aisle.

"Here you are," the stewardess handed him another drink. She pushed the cart down the aisle. He swallowed.

Gary loaded his suitcases into the trunk of the car. They fit snugly. He deposited a box of Emilie's school papers in the front yard. "Ninth grade essays" was written jaggedly on the cover with a black marker. He slammed the trunk and walked to the driver side door. It was locked. He fumbled in his pocket for the keys.

One stop at the bank, Gary thought, *and then to the airport.*

The front door of the two story, white with green trim house opened, banging against the inside wall. Emilie stood in the doorway. Her hair curlers were loose, leaping from her matted, knotted hair. Stray strands spread across her forehead, ears and neck. An autumn breeze brushed against her, pressing the nightgown to her body. She held a golf club.

"Emilie?" Gary said.

Birds chirped.

"I won't let you leave." Her voice was deep, demanding. She stepped onto the front porch. Pauline came outside with her, prancing on the sagging boards.

Gary slid the key into the lock, turned it, opened the door, and got in the car. He started the engine. The radio blared. He hit the power button.

"I won't let you." Emilie bolted, hurdling the two porch steps, and bounding across the front yard. Pauline stayed, watching, panting excitedly.

Gary hammered the lock on the passenger door.

Emilie's bare feet squashed the wet grass. Her mouth was open, her eyes were glazed, the night gown fluttered from her legs, curlers fell from her hair.

"What are you…" Gary's words stuck in his throat.

The head of the gold club struck the windshield. Spiderweb cracks frosted the glass.

"Emilie!" he shouted, thrusting his foot on the gas pedal. The engine screamed, but the car was in park.

Emilie pulled the golf club from the window. Glass sprinkled inside the car.

"Stop what you're…"

The passenger window crumpled, sagging, and exploded from a second blow, spraying glass, blinding Gary. He wiped his lap, frantic, cutting his hands. The golf club thrust through the windshield again, igniting a burst of falling, sparkling gems.

Gary opened the door. Fresh sores stung his hands, arms, and face. He batted his eyes, blind, and rolled to the pavement.

"You're not leaving!" Emilie hovered, golf club poised over her head. "I won't let you."

"What…" Gary tried to focus. "Emilie! What have you…"

She struck the side of the car with the golf club, denting the metal.

"Stop! I've got to…"

She hit the car again.

"I've got a plane to…"

She hit him. Hit him. Hit him.

Gary jumped, waving his arms. He twisted his head. The plane. He was in the plane. He stumbled from his seat, standing in the aisle. He could smell smoke and his eyes teared. He stood, bracing himself on the seat in front of him, and walked slowly toward the front of the plane. The smoke was misty, invading his sight and coherence. "Again?" He turned. It was the old woman. She was standing in front of him, pointing, "Out of your seat again?" The fur hat dipped over her head, caught on her nose, then dropped, leaving behind curly gray hair.

"Emilie?" Gary gasped. "Is that you?"

"My name's not Emilie. Get in your seat."

Gary darted down the aisle, fleeing the woman, searching for the stewardess. The seats he passed were empty. The plane was empty. First class: empty.

"Mr. Hinman?" It was the stewardess in the front of the plane. She was looking in a mirror, putting on lipstick. She faced him, puckering, smiling. "What's the problem. She adjusted her name tag. Emilie.

"Your name." Gary coughed. Blood. No. His hands were bleeding. Small cuts.

"You're hurt." The stewardess squatted, opened a cabinet, and retrieved a first aid kit.

"What's happening?" Gary leaned against the wall. His head pounded. "Why aren't we in Cleveland yet?"

"Hmm. Let me ask the captain, has been an awful long time." She opened a door leading into the cockpit. "Captain? What's taking so long?"

Gary looked over her shoulder. He couldn't move. He saw himself seated behind the controls, saw himself in a hospital gown with tubes running through his nose and neck, saw machines pumping, saw his eyes closed, saw bandages on his face and hands.

“Should be there soon,” the stewardess closed the door. “Now go take your seat and I’ll bring you another drink. OK?” She smiled. “A rum and Coke?”

“That was me!” Gary was pointing, shaking his arm. His fingers were bleeding.

“Nonsense,” the stewardess caressed his arm, lowering it to his side, “that’s our captain.”

“That was me!”

“But you’re right here, Mr. Hinman,” she was still smiling, licking her lips.

“I saw…”

“Let’s go back to your seat. I’ll get you another drink and some band aids for your cuts.” She pushed him down the aisle. Her smile widened. “You ought to be more careful.”

“That was me,” he eased into his seat.

“I’ll be right back.”

“You’ll be fine, Gary,” Emilie’s voice. He turned to see his wife sitting beside him. She had a golf club in her lap. “I’m sorry for what I did, but now you’ll never leave. You’ll be fine. They won’t turn off these machines. You’ll be fine,” she reached for his face but faded into nothing just before her hand touched his chin.

He felt a kiss on his cheek.

“Here’s your drink,” the stewardess said.

He snatched it from her hand.

“You’re so cute,” she smiled, pinching his cheek. “Let me know if you need anything.”

He drank.

“We’ll be there soon,” the stewardess patted his scalp.

Jeffrey Saucier
UNIVERSITY OF MAINE, ORONO

Directions to Paradise

I was lost. My fingers drummed the leather steering wheel, keeping beat with a bootleg recording of Muddy Waters playing on Maine Public Radio. The jazzy beat and gritty sound of Muddy's voice warmed my mood like cognac. I could picture him next to me, sitting in the darkness, his thick lips dancing over the open slats of a harmonica, while my rusted sedan dogtrotted down the road.

I hadn't a damn clue as to how I'd become so misplaced.

My editor at *Destination Life,* Jack Welleck, gave me directions "that will take you to paradise." But I must have missed a turn. Only trees, millions of pines, flooding the night.

Jack had sent me to cover the potato harvest in Aroostook County. Usually I worked free-lance for small publications, but Jack insisted on making this an assignment. For once, someone wanted me. He'd said it was a landscape that would possibly produce some of the best pictures I'd ever take. Jack, a portly Maine native, wanted my photos to be the feature for the November issue. I took his motivational slop as just that—he was talking about spuds. But the paycheck, even though it was for a magazine with a trivial subscription that lacked prominence, would be decent.

I was singing along with James Brown when I noticed what

I thought was an animal in the road. I flickered my high beams, but the heap didn't move. From a hundred yards away it looked like a fawn, struck and left for dead. I suspected the idiot in the Chevy pickup who had passed me thirty minutes prior. He'd swerved in front of me, tossed a Budweiser out of his window, flipped me the bird, and within seconds his taillights were zig-zagging over a hill. The deer didn't stop him.

I idled slowly down the grade and stopped twenty feet from what I now realized was clearly a human body.

The flesh of her forehead was peeled back, her lips were shredded, one eye was swollen and the other a stationary marble. Her nose was slit, a gash wide and deep, but the blood was dry. Her eyebrows were slender and curved, barely nicked. The right side of her face was resting on her arm, her left ear was torn and her cheek was speckled by pebbles that dug into her sienna-colored skin. Her neck moved slightly, and there was a feeble breath that came from her shredded lips. A necklace dangled from the nape of her neck, attached, a tiny rose pendant made of plastic, imitation rubies.

I was shaking. *What was I supposed to do? Should I move her? How had she survived? What was I getting myself into? Good God.*

My hand moved over her scalp; each finger twitched in a sharp motion as though an electric current rushed through them. No cracks, but her black hair stuck to the bloody paste that had frozen to the pavement. I wondered if she would live. I didn't know where I was, and finding a suitable hospital in rural, northern Maine was not likely. I'd move her, drive fast, and hope she'd make it. Maybe I'd pray.

Lifting her was effortless, but her synthetic pelt coat kept falling off of her narrow frame. Her white and violet boots with fur ruffles, five sizes too big, slipped from her small feet; a gust carried the plastic booties off the road, down the shoulder, into a pile of decaying autumn leaves. After placing her in the back seat, I popped open the trunk, grabbed a blanket from behind my bags and tripod, and tucked it around her.

In the rearview mirror she looked like a trailer park queen and a princess of India melded into one. Her body trembled, and I prayed she wasn't going into shock. I took the car out of park and began to roll down the crumbled road.

I had to save her.

"You're a romantic sucker like all the rest of 'em," she says. "Wearing your heart on your sleeve, and just itching to buy some over-priced flowers or stale chocolates."

Her forehead is smooth, glossy in the light of day, her lips are soft, her nose wrinkles when she squints in the sunshine, her eyes close, safe, her eyebrows are slender and curved, her ears are cute, edible, her checks, velvety, her neck moves a tad and there is a feeble breath that seeps from her lips. A necklace dangles from the nape of her neck, attached, a tiny rose pendant made of sunny rubies.

"Really? Worked on you," I say. She smiles at this, a sure sign of defeat.

"Yeah, I guess. But face it, Aaron…"

"Face what? That I get wrapped up in things. That I want to be sweet. Sure. But, I'm just as afraid of love as you are."

"I'm not afraid, just suspicious." She leans over to kiss me on the cheek. I try to keep my eyes focused on the road, but I look at her anyway.

She wears different clothes, nice clothes, maybe a floral print sundress with sunflowers budding on it, but not boots, instead expensive sandals.

Every Saturday we take a day trip somewhere. It is our way of escaping the severity of grad school. With only one semester left until our master's, the trips are becoming delicate.

"I'm gonna take a nap," she says, "wake me when we get to D.C."

"Sure," I say.

We both enjoy the capital. I bring my camera and she brings

her sketchbooks. She is a graphic designer. A computer nerd who still believes in the power of a blank piece of paper. She worked on two album covers for little-known bands and blueprinted one of the web pages for Maryland University. Not successful in her own eyes, but it amazes me.

"You really want to go to D.C.?" I ask, but she is fast asleep. I look at her again.

How had we met?

I turn the car around.

Her body shifts, and I'm afraid she'll wake, but she simply lets out a small gasp and continues to sleep. Within half an hour the car is parked in a garage down on Pratt Street. I wake her.

As she tries to focus, she asks, "Where are we?"

"You'll see."

We exit the cement slab structure and step onto the cobblestones; she sparks a quick grin and stashes her head on my shoulder.

"The Aquarium? This is where we…"

"Yeah."

She looks at me, a face that says, 'goddamn you are a helpless romantic.' "You are amazing, you do realize that?" she says and then kisses my neck.

We met in the Aqua Shop of the National Aquarium of Baltimore over a year ago. I was looking at a pair of stylish, shark slippers when I noticed her in my peripheral vision. She was trying on sunglasses. Her head bobbed around, trying to see herself in a small mirror above the display.

"They're cute, but too big for your head." She looked at me all goofy. It was a 'who the hell are you' face. "But, these mermaid glasses are *so* you." I grabbed some high-priced, truly tacky glasses, and slipped them on her face. "Look at that. You'll make men melt," I said, making her laugh.

"Oh yeah, well these Poseidon shades would just make you look so charming. Here, try them on," she said, shaking the flimsy frames at me.

"You think? I mean be honest."

"You're adorable."

"Datable?"

"Well, I don't know…"

"You come here often? You go to…"

"Maryland University," she said. "I'm a grad student." She looked at her watch.

"Me too. Hey, you want to grab lunch? I know this great little seafood joint by the Harborplace. On me," I said. Her smile was so coy and pleasant.

"Flattering as the offer sounds, I don't even know your…"

"Aaron Spacks."

"Salila Rani. Really, I don't know about…"

"Salila, what a beautiful name. What's it mean?"

"The Hindu meaning is paradise."

"Well, Paradise, it would be my pleasure to entertain you over lunch at Baltimore's one and only Original Fisherman's Wharf. Ever been there?" I asked.

"Nope," she said.

"You like shellfish?" I asked.

"Yeah, but…"

"Fine. I can take it. Just thought it was my lucky day. You know, finding Paradise, and finding her wearing such cute glasses," I said.

She smiled again and it was at that moment that I knew my pitiful charm had somehow worked.

"They seemed to have changed a lot of the exhibits from the last time we were there," Salila says. She sips on a salty margarita while I munch on some crab cakes.

"I used to love the *Jaws* theme music that echoed in the shark tunnel. It wasn't playing, was it?"

"Nope," she says. "You have some tartar sauce on your lip," she says, dabbing her own lips. She laughs, an inviting laugh.

"Funny, you've had some on your lip the whole time. I just haven't said anything." I laugh.

"You're a brat."

"When's your next project due?" I ask.

"Next Monday. It's going to be a killer."

Our waitress, Shelly, brings us our meals, setting folded paper bags on the table first, then hands over our plates overflowing with crabs, oysters, shrimp, clams and bright red lobster. The table, once a scene of a sunken ship under glass, is now covered with tiny carcasses. Shelly sets two small tins of butter in front of us, gives us plastic bibs and metal picks and crackers. Our refills come next.

"A killer?"

"Yeah. Might have to cancel our day trip."

"What?" I ask, cracking open a lobster tail. We skipped a couple of Saturday excursions in the past, but normally strong hangovers kept us from our retreat. "I thought maybe we could visit, I don't know, my folks next weekend."

"We'll see how much work I get done."

There is a long pause. A question festers inside me like a raspy cough. A ballad, reminiscent of my college days, plays from the ocean mural ceiling while I think. I wait for my throat to just give way to the words.

"What's going to happen to us?" I ask. My meek voice scratches the silence.

"What do you mean?"

"We're a semester away from being human. Right now, and up until now, we've been living an easy life filled with safety nets. Sure we're working our asses off, but it's not real. I'm scared, Sal."

On the smoking side of the restaurant there is some commotion. One lady is yelping, a terrible fear in her squeals. Her husband is choking on something and pounds his chest with a clenched fist. I stand up, panicked. I want to run over and help, but I'd hurt him, break his ribs, I'm sure of it. A waiter scurries to their table, wraps his arms around the old man's stomach and tugs sharply. The hefty woman's arms are flailing in the air. But then, after a few jolts, she is calmed when a mussel surges out of her husband's mouth. The place is overcome with a mad fuss of whispers and 'Oh, my Gods.' I sit back down, my heart still thrashing.

"Damn. I'll be staying away from the mussels. Did you see that? She was terrified," I say.

"You okay?" Sal asks. She takes my hand and rubs my knuckles.

"Yeah. I'll be fine. Where were we?"

"You are so good, you know that?"

"I don't want to lose you, Sal."

"I'm scared too, Aaron. I'm scared that I might be unemployed forever. I'm scared that I'll never be successful. I'm scared of my monestrous, student loans. I'm scared of losing you. We might have to go our separate ways and that, that scares me."

"Our separate ways?" My appetite turns into a sour rumbling in my stomach.

Shelly walks over to see if everything is all right. We politely nod and she moves on to another couple.

"Aaron, face it. You're going places. National Geographic has seen your work and Newsweek is offering you a position in England. Meanwhile, I've done what, a web page for Maryland U. Whooptee-do."

I'd completed two portfolios in the past seven months which I had sent out to be reviewed by reputable magazines. One segment captured images of a battered women's halfway house and the other, ironically, was of the National Aquarium. An editor at Newsweek called one of my pictures of a bruised woman folding laundry touching. "Quality work," he'd said.

"Salila, you are the most amazing person I have ever met," I say. I reach into my pocket and pull out a pair of mermaid shades that I'd bought while Sal was in the bathroom at the aquarium. They are dusty and probably haven't been touched in over a year, but I was lucky that the Aqua Shop still carried them.

I place them on her head. "Now you, Ms. Mermaid Shades, you are going places, and wherever you go, I will be with you."

"Romantic sucker," she says with a smile, wide and welcome.

"Paradise."

We lean over the scraps of our meal. Her lips taste salty, like the sea.

The sign read: ST. JOHN'S VALLEY ESTATE.

I was at an intersection, an indication of civilization. A Mom & Pop store with one gas pump and a large neon poster advertising fresh crawlers, was closed. Opposite the rundown building was a boarded-up potato stand. St. John's Valley Estates rested at the end of a small driveway—two green complexes connected by a glass vestibule. A few lights illuminated the inside, and I suspected that this was our only hope.

I pulled into the cul-de-sac. Concerned I would break her fragile bones, if they weren't already fractured, I lifted her gently from the back seat, then ran up to the entryway, and pounded on the wooden door with the stub of my shoe. My headlights shined on us.

"Somebody answer the fucking door!"

A woman peeked her head from behind a glass column that ran along side the door. I yelled something at her, what, I can't remember, but she listened.

"Oh, Jesus-Mary-and-Joseph. Julie, come quick! It's Rose!"

Rose. She was a complete wound of scarlet.

I carried Rose to a bed near the back of the building, down some government green hallways, past carts of towels and medicine. I expected the frumpy, strawberry blonde to attach IVs to Rose's veins, but apparently she wasn't as injured as I had presumed. Two other women, both with wide, childbearing hips and a thick cloak of baby blue eye shadow, began stripping Rose of her torn clothes. They dampened washcloths and cleaned her wounds with iodine. Within minutes she was covered with butterfly strips and gauze; stable. I stood behind them, observing these three woman perform. It was their craft; they worked painstakingly, like following a recipe.

I snuck out, grabbed my camera, and went back inside. I caught the one named Julie washing Rose's hands, giving me dirty looks. She told me to stop once.

"Don't you respect any privacy? Is this really the place for that?"

"My apologies."

"What are you doing, anyway?" one of them asked.

"I work for *Destination Life*," I said in my defense.

"Like that yellow one with pictures of those Aborigine women, the ones with the saggy breasts and all?" Julie asked her turquoise-eyed counterpart.

"Yes," I said before the other woman could respond.

"Well, I hope you don't plan on making us centerfolds. We want no part of that," one of them said.

"No, these won't ever touch a page. Just didn't want to forget tonight, with all that's happened. I mean no disrespect. I'll stop if you like."

"Just be careful, that's all. She's a delicate thing."

"Certainly," I said, snapping the last of the roll.

"What's your name?" asked the frumpy one.

"Aaron Spacks."

"Anita Trudeau. This here is Julie and that's Margaret Caron. They're sisters if ya didn't ketch on. Where'd ya find Rose?" Anita asked.

"I don't know. I was headed toward"—I reached into my pocket—"Sheridan? And I found her about, oh, an hour ago. She was in the middle of the road."

"Boy, you were a little off. This is Portage. You missed your turn back down by Ashland. Who gave you directions, anyway?"

"My editor. Is she gonna be okay?"

"Yeah, she'll be fine. The blood made it look a lot worse

than it is. We don't have an x-ray machine, but Doc will be by in the morning to check her out. My guess is she has a couple of bruised ribs and maybe, maybe a broken arm, but I'm no doc."

"Should we call the police?"

"Who? Jerome? That's Robbie's uncle, he won't do anything. It's best if we stay clear of that stuff."

A man, Margaret called him Walter, shuffled behind us. His chalky hair was aimed in every direction and he bobbed on the heels of his feet. Walter's eyebrows were bushy, almost as fuzzy as the patches bolting out of his ears like bamboo shoots. There was a large stain in the center of his nightgown. He pointed at me and rambled.

"He's not used to outsiders," Anita said, as Julie and Margaret escorted Walter back to his room.

"What is this place?"

"OSHA calls it a health care facility. We have about twenty folks here. They're old money from New Jersey and Connecticut whose families were sick of carin' for 'em. Walter, he was a big wig at a giant insurance company years ago. He came down with Alzheimer's, oh, say, five years ago. His wife, she's a real gold-digger, sent him up here. She lives in Florida with her boyfriend."

"Interesting. And who's Rose?" I asked.

"She lives down by the ass end of East Branch River with Robbie. He probably did this to her. I mean he's done it to her before. Once or twice I think. That's what I heard from Julie. Her brother is a logger with Robbie."

"What kind of truck does he drive? Robbie, that is?" I asked.

"One of those Chevy getups."

"General Lee orange?" I asked, and it was apparent she'd taken offense. I didn't even realize it when I said it.

"Listen, Mr. Spacks, is it? It was nice of you to pick Rose up. God knows she would have died out there, probably gotten squashed by a lumber rig, but you can go now. Take your fancy camera, and go. We'll take care of her. Like I said, Doc Carson will be here first thing come morning." Anita was blunt, almost rude. I'd crossed an unspoken line.

"I'd rather stay. I've been driving all day."

She raised her eyebrows at me, sighed and said, "I suppose, but don't touch anything, and put that camera away. This ain't Disneyland."

Anita left to tend to more Walters while I rolled a chair close and watched Rose. Her rose pendant necklace caught my eye. I had imagined so much better for her. But, how would it end?

I kissed Rose's hand, careful not to disrupt the bandages and strips of medical tape. I turned. Julie was watching me, but she said nothing, just smiled weakly and walked away.

Her body is spooned against mine. The cotton sheets cover most of us; underneath our naked legs overlap like folded hands. Sweat on my forehead begins to dry with a crisp breeze that slips past the tulips on the sill of my apartment window.

"You want to go to a movie tonight?" Sal asks.

"Sure. What are you up for?" I ask, looking at the digital clock on my nightstand.

"Nothing serious."

"Whatever. I'm easy."

"Are you ever," Sal says. She giggles and her head bobs lightly against my chest. I slap her bum with my left palm.

"Who's the brat?" I ask, kissing her temples.

"So, where we going next weekend? The place where we had our second date?" she asks.

"Your project?"

"It'll get done. You don't remember where we had our second date, do you?"

"Wait. No…it was bowling? Right?"

"Bowling? You dork, we went to Harry's House of Pizza, drank lots of beer, cabbed it back, and then passed out watching, what was it, *Animal House*?"

"God, I hate that movie," I say.

"Bad memories of Northwestern?"

"Don't remind me," I say.

"I still can't picture you as a frat boy," Sal says.

"Enough."

She snickers at my expense. Twelve floors below, on the streets of Baltimore, a pistol shot echoes. We both jerk at the sound and for a few moments are silent.

"Aaron?"

"Yeah."

"You ever wonder what is going to happen?" she asks.

"Sure," I say.

"No. I mean do you ever think about how things could be, then you think about them again, and well, they're totally different? Like what if that gunshot was supposed to hit you or me. What would happen? Am I making sense?" she asks, then turns her head to face me, revealing the rose pendant I bought for her birthday.

"I know exactly what you mean," I say. She begins to crawl up my chest, kissing my skin along the way.

"You're too much," I say, rolling my eyes.

"You can handle it," she says.

"Helpless romantic," I say.

"Aaron. Julie, didn't he say his name was Aaron? Mister, wake up," Anita said, yanking on my sleeve.

"You moved me?" I asked, blinking back sleep.

"You were snorin' awfully loud. We didn't want you to wake Rose."

"How's she doing?"

"Jus' fine. Robbie picked her up about forty…"

"What?"

"Doc said she was fine to go home. He patched her up, felt her bones, looked at her skull and all. Doc said she had a concussion and a few bruised ribs, but nothin' a week's worth of soaps wouldn't cure."

"He let her go back to him? You let her leave? What the fuck is this?"

You let her leave with inbred Robbie...fucking lush Robbie, who tossed her out of his pickup, probably doing around fifty...you let her go back to that, I thought.

Anita was angry. Her oversized cheeks were perspiring and her eyes, two lumps of coal, were staring me down.

"Listen, city boy, you got no right cussin' at me. That's her husband. Just 'cause you had some five-minute fantasy with her don't mean she's yours."

"What?"

"Julie saw you kiss her. You'll be leaving now," Anita said.

"Robbie filled your car up with gas. It was his thanks," Julie said.

"What a kind gesture."

I picked up my camera, brushed my hands over the wrinkles of my blazer, and walked out of St. John's Valley Estates, without a good-bye.

My car started on the first try. I waited for the early October frost to melt from my windshield and looked at the weather vane atop the glass atrium. The 'N' spun wildly in the gusty chill. There was a copper potato on top and it twisted with each puff of Canadian air. I unstrapped my seat belt, opened the door, leaned out, focused and snapped another picture.

I thought for a few moments while driving off. I missed a turn. This wasn't paradise. I latched open the camera, exposing the film, and chucked the other roles into a ditch. No pictures. I headed home, unwanted.

Her forehead is smooth, shiny in the light that permeates the stained glass. Her lips are soft, her eyes are open beneath the sheer material, anxious. Her nose wrinkles when she opens her lips, and her eyebrows are slender and curved. Her checks are supple, lightly covered in make-up. Her hands embrace a simple bouquet of tulips. A necklace dangles from her neck, attached, a tiny rose pendant made of bright rubies.

I wanted her to wear the shades, but she refused.

Then there is her smile and she holds my trembling palms. After that, who knows?

Frank D. Wilkins
INDIANA/PURDUE UNIVERSITY

A Straw Fedora

Toby Callus was sharpening a knife on his ancient, unpainted front porch, humming, "Clementine." He held an Arkansas stone tightly in his left hand and an old, felt green, folding pocket knife in his right hand. The knife was an inheritance, passed down seven times.

The orange midday sun didn't penetrate the rust and the red of the steel porch roof, so Toby was in the shade. He sat on a wooden chair that rested on some of what was left of the floor; multifarious boards of oak and ash had once covered native joists but now, holes gaped. The front porch grew out of the small twelve-by-twenty-foot shack behind it. It had a front door and one front window. Shack and porch lived almost seventeen feet off Highway 51, the one-lane, yellow pavement that could carry a car into Memphis in half an hour. The back of Toby's freckled left hand rested on the frayed and faded blue leg of his bib overalls. A pale blue shirt covered his huge arms and was buttoned tight at the neck just under the pink face and short blond hair of Toby's head. He carefully drew the one blade that was left in the three-bladed relic, in a long, precise, sharpening pattern—out, over and back—out, over and back. Toby had just escaped being born an albino; the Lord had intervened.

Toby's freckled, pink face and pale blue eyes lit up in a wide, silly grin when he saw the man coming up the stepping stones and clay walkway. He was six feet tall, young, lean, blond (too long and curling up), with soft brown eyes, a straight nose, high cheeks and lips upturned in a haunting smile. Toby thought, *he's pretty*, and whistled a greeting, "Howdy miss-tuh Jim." James grinned at Toby; you couldn't look at him, you had to grin at him.

"Have you seen Mamma, Toby?"

"Ssurr, sshe aroun' back with cutten Matt, miss-tuh Jim."

"What are you gonna do with that knife, Toby?" James asked. "Are you gonna have chicken for supper? Mighty hard to eat chicken with only one tooth."

"No ssuh, no ssuh miss-tuh Jim; I'm fixing to make myself well." Now, Toby took a faded blue, dotted bandanna out of his overalls' back pocket. Carefully, he wiped the blade of the old Barlow knife and set the sharpening stone down. He brought the razor-sharp blade up to his mouth, eased the point to the gum over his one tooth— then cut across fast and back across. A tiny, red 'X' dripped blood over his tooth. James watched, mesmerized. Toby pushed the point of the knife into the 'X,' then up over the rotted root, hooked, and quickly flipped his wrist. An orange, black and white tooth hit the weathered, wood porch, and rolled off into the red clay of the yard.

"I rekon I be gummin' chicken in a few days, miss-tuh Jim; your mamma and cutten Matt are havin' quite a visit—been together most morning."

James shook himself out of his trance and headed around the unpainted gray clapboard of Toby's house. "Thanks, Toby, see you."

"See ya later, miss-tuh Jim."

James walked out back of Toby's yard, through an orchard of old intermixed and fruit laden, pear, persimmon and apple trees. Fruit was scattered on the ground under the trees, and starting to rot; they attracted honey bees and yellow jackets. James took long strides, careful of where he stepped, and was just seconds away from getting out of the small orchard and onto the road.

It wasn't soon enough—a honey bee gave up its life and stung James. He grabbed his neck and smashed the already dying bee. "Damn!" James felt for the stinger, and eased it out of his neck. He felt the warmth of the poison in his blood and the itch on his neck.

He reached the yellow and red pavement of the stone corniche and started the walk that would wind his way to his cousin Matt Christianson's small cottage. He thought: *Just a few miles outside of Memphis and I am in another world; it's like a time warp, I have been sent back a hundred years in time. God Almighty, he just cut out a tooth!*

They were all going to Memphis today. Mamma would drive them in the new 1953 Roadmaster. The car was a black beast and the soft, brown upholstery of the high seats would carry them all in comfort. Cousin Matt, Mamma, James, and even Toby would ride along. James loved the city, it fit his personality. Memphis was growing fast, and so was James. They both were changing, entering the modern world. James was entering Memphis State in the fall to study English, poetry, and other liberal art courses. He planned to write and teach when he graduated. Now, he couldn't wait for the rush and excitement of new people. James would be on his own, living on campus.

Paramount in James' thoughts was the visit with grandfather today. The old man was stooped over, just a little, but carried himself with great poise and dignity. James Robert Murchison was the patriarch of the family.

Grandfather had started work at age sixteen as a floor sweeper for the I. C. Railroad; now, fifty-seven years later he still worked there as Head Freight Agent of the Memphis area. He was a man that always had a smile when he spoke, but only spoke when he had something important to say. He tipped his fedora to the people that he passed on the street as he walked to and from work. He didn't drive.

The story James' cousin Mattie told was that his Grandfather had only been mad once in his life. This was when James' mother, Genevive, told him that she was pregnant. Genevive wasn't married. The old man had told her, "Genevive, I am full of shame for the family." When Genevive had her son, she named him James Robert Cherry—taking her mother's maiden name and father's Christian names. Instead of angering Grandfather further, she had pleased him. He loved his namesake, James Robert, as his own son.

James thought of the card he got each year on his birthday, always addressed: Master James Robert Cherry; and in the upper, left hand corner of the envelope: Mr. James Robert Murchison, Illinois Central Railroad, Memphis, Tennessee. There was always a personal note on the card and a dollar inside; then when he turned twelve—five dollars. James had turned eighteen this year and had gotten his last card. Granddaddy stopped sending at eighteen—you were a man then.

Grandfather always wore a light tan suit on Sundays, with a proper fedora and brown and white Nun Bush shoes. He smelled of rose water and glycerin and spoke perfect English in a soft Southern drawl. He was from a different era—a time of manners and dignity and turn-of-the-century prominence.

The smell of cabbage and corn bread and the sight of cousin Matt's white cottage brought James back to the present. He knocked on the front door, didn't wait for an answer and walked in. "It's me."

"Come on back," cousin Matt called in a high, singing voice, "Your mamma's here." James hurried across the small, front room's dark, oak floor in quick steps, eyes on the kitchen door—an open hole gaping in the red roses of the wallpaper. He stepped through the arch into the sunlight yellow of the kitchen. There, at the table, sat his mother and cousin. On a red checkered tablecloth were three lines of playing cards. Knaves, kings, queens and deuces, as well as other cards in random configuration, told his mamma a story. She was reading cousin Matt's fortune.

"Did you get a good reading Mattie?" James joked.

"Now ain't you the handsomest thing! I swear you're a plum pretty boy, just like your granddaddy. I'm gonna go to Memphis with y'all— gonna see the old man too; can't wait to see 'im, the handsome devil."

"James Robert, we will be ready to go soon," his mother spoke softly. "Are you ready?" James looked from his snow haired, plump, Mrs.-Santa-Clause-looking cousin to his mother: as fat as Matt was, Mamma was thin, as white as Matt's hair was, Mamma's was black, as blue as Matt's eyes were, his mamma's were brown, as country as Matt's speech was, his mother's was poised and educated. His mother was four-foot-eleven, eighty pounds—a Cherokee doll.

"Read my cards, Mamma?"

"Why are you holding your neck, James?"

"Just a honey bee. Read my cards, Mamma?"

"Sit down next to Mattie, shuffle the cards, make three stacks from away to towards you, and place them face down." James sat down, took his left hand off his neck, and did as his mother instructed.

"Okay, Mamma."

His mother turned the first and farthest stack over—her small fingers spread the cards out in a line. "Not much here—maybe a short trip, see the ace of diamonds?" Little fingers spread the second, middle stack. "Hum…yes, yes, not much." The queen of spades, she was involved. Mamma spread the third stack slowly, "There you are, James."

"Where?"

"There, the knave of hearts." She moved her tiny fingers and spread the stack more. Then her hand froze. "Sweet Jesus, God Almighty," she whispered under her breath. She saw the jack of hearts was facing the ace of spades, which was upside down. Death, or sickness for sure, for the blond, dark eyed young man or someone close to him. They were bad cards, a bad omen.

James grabbed his swollen neck, started coughing, then gasping, breathing hard, and fell off his chair onto the hard, polished, oak floor. James whispered, "Bee—what—why the hell?" Cousin Matt was down on the floor first, next to him, feeling his neck.

"Genevive, get help! He can't breathe!"

James' mother ran out of the kitchen door and into the orchard yelling, screaming, "Help us!" She saw Toby bent over in the orchard.

"Toby! Toby! Damn it! Toby help, help us!" Toby was in the orchard picking up pears, persimmons and apples. He looked up and saw Genevive waving then started running toward her, fast for a big man. "Msss Genny, Msss Genevive!"

"Stung, the house, the house. Quick Toby. Jesus, help us."

Toby saw cousin Matt in the yard pointing to the kitchen door. He saw James, and the instinct of the back woods took over. Toby reached into his right overalls' pocket as he knelt down over James. He moved James' hand off of his swollen neck and looked for the sting mark. An ancient, green, Barlow knife flashed fast—twice. A small, red 'X' dripped blood on James' neck. Toby looked at James' blue lips, and placed his hands on James' chest. He felt James take a shallow breath.

"Please, Jessuss. Please, Jessuss, in the name of sweet Jessuss." Toby leaned over and sucked blood out of James' neck. He spat and sucked and spat: poison and blood puddled on the dark, wood floor. The swelling of James' neck stopped; slowly it went down a little, just enough so James could keep taking shallow random breaths.

Toby looked up at cousin Matt and Genevive, blood was running down his chin and he gasped out, "Memphis—Mem—Memphis."

Genevive nodded, "Bring him, Toby," as she ran out the egress. Cousin Matt put snuff from her mouth onto the sting and wrapped James' neck with the worn stocking she had taken off her leg.

Toby wasn't waiting, he got up holding James in his arms.

He ran out the kitchen door toward the open, back door of the big, black Buick Roadmaster. He jumped in with James in his arms.

"Jessuss, Jessuss, Jessuss," he chanted. James' mother floored the accelerator, and the giant straight engine moved the black beast forward slowly at first then faster, faster. The Buick ate the road like the hungry Devil ate souls. Today, the Buick had to spare time but eat distance to save James' life. Today, the satan black Buick was an angel of God.

When it was off the corniche and on Highway 51 headed for Memphis, Genevive prayed, "Our Father who art in Heaven…" Then she prayed, "Hail Mary full of grace, blessed art thou among women…" Her prayers blended with the hum of the straight eight Buick's motor. She saw Toby holding James' chest and praying. He was looking up towards Heaven. Genevive started a chant in earnest now, Cherokee words of magic and healing. She sang long unused, shaman words.

Almost there. She saw how James was fighting, losing his breath; then his chest would suddenly jump and he would breathe again. She saw this happen twice—that was enough. She put her hand on James' chest and spoke secret words that could only be handed down from first born to first born. The magic that the ancestors had found, and passed on, encoded among the lines of the Old Testament. The prayer evoked the true name of God that only the angels used. She prayed, "God of Moses. I am that I am. You are called," and whispered the words—the verse, the name, that would heal only once in a generation. She knew that the verse would either heal James' or transfer evil to someone else.

A gurney banged the car, and two black men in white coats lifted James out of Toby's arms onto the cart. "Be careful now, easssy, eassy," Toby warned as he let loose of James.

The day was of morning mist and a light, soft, cool breeze. At the front of the small, white, clapboard church, just in front of the stained glass of the windows and the front door, people gathered and talked before the funeral. Cousin Mattie Christianson, Bob Cherry, Ethelbert Cherry, Effie Murchison, Genevive Cherry and many others stood there. The small crowd was growing.

Genevive looked towards the road and saw him standing in the mist, looking at the church, a marble statue, almost surreal in the whispering white of the mist. The statue lifted the fedora off his head, and walked towards the church, hat in hand, bent a little, walking slowly, painfully. She saw the tears in his soft brown eyes. "I just left, I couldn't miss Granddaddy's funeral, Mamma."

Author Biographies

Katherin Nolte is a twenty-year-old English major at Wright State University. She had her first story published in the summer of 1998 with the *Dayton Daily News* after it placed third in the newspaper's annual fiction contest. She currently has a short story forthcoming in *Happy*.

Eric Lundgren is a bookworm, cellist, and ex-smoker.

Scott Snyder is a graduating senior in the (undergraduate) creative writing program at Brown University. He's been published in *Genre, The Providence Independent, The Brown Daily Herald, The Oakland Review, Clerestory*, and online in *Caffine Destiny*, and *Impossible Object*.

Donna Svatik studies creative writing at the University of Washington. She was born on April Fool's Day. She has lived in Michigan, Colorado, Washington, and the Czech Republic. She's afraid of snakes; but not spiders. She likes building fires. She makes really good crepes suzette. She can crochet a hat for your baby.

Paul Graham, aged 22, graduated from St. Lawrence University, with a major in creative writing in 1999. He is now enrolled in the MFA in Creative Writing Program at the University of Michigan. His fiction has appeared in *Innisfree*, *The Nocturnal Lyric*, and *Abberations*. He has also published poetry in *The Maryland Poetry Review*. He hopes to be teaching college English and creative writing within a few years.

Dan Mancilla is a senior at Western Illinois University which is about three hundred miles from Chicago, his hometown. His favorite writers are Stuart Dybek, Junot Diaz, and Tobias Wolff. He plans to pursue an MFA when he finishes his undergraduate studies. He hopes to end up at Iowa, but he is also considering Western Michigan University, Southwest Texas State, Brown, and Syracuse. Writing awards he has won include the Eula Cordel award for fiction at Western Illinois University: 1997 and 1998, as well as a second place award for short fiction at the Third Coast Writer's Conference which he attended in the spring of 1998.

Jeannette Darcy's first degree was in computer engineering. She worked for IBM and, most recently, for NASA as a flight controller in Mission Control. Her job, officially titled "The Attitude and Pointing Officer," was to point the space shuttle, i.e. to determine which orientation it was to fly (after all, in space you can fly upside down and backwards if you want to). After eight years, she decided to adjust her own attitude by quitting work and returning to school to pursue her writing interests. She is currently working on a creative writing degree at the University of Houston.

Dan Lewis was born in Portland, Oregon, and grew up in Illinois. He is forty-four years old. He graduated in the spring of 1998 from Southern Illinois University at Edwardsville (career change) with a degree in English/ Literature. Several of his short stories have been published: two in *The River Bluff Review*, and one in *Sou'wester Magazine*. He has won SUIE's "The Mimi Zanger Memorial Award in Fiction," three times in five years. His first novel is on a publisher's desk in London . . . they're arguing.

Lisa D. Gerlits was born and raised in Silverton, Oregon. She graduated in 1998 from Lewis & Clark College in Portland, Oregon with a degree in English. This past year she served in an AmeriCorps program working with eighth graders in Northeast Portland. Aside from writing, she loves to paint, travel, cook, tutor, hike, and do photography. She doesn't care what anybody says—she loves the Oregon rain.

George Fountas was born in New York and raised in Florida. He graduated from George Washington University in Washington, DC, with a major in Political Science, in 1999. After encouragement from his sister, Angela, he took a fiction class. He has discovered a new love in life: writing. This story was a product of his first class. It is somewhat autobiographical, although he is not in a circus; he works for the Gap.

Jennifer Anne Vickers spent the first year of her life in Clovis, New Mexico. The rest of her life she travelled a lot—her father being in the Air Force—mainly in Europe because he was stationed in Germany and England for more than twelve years. From that environment she moved to a small town in North Carolina called Elm City—it had only one stop light—and lived there for several months before moving into the city that people called "City on the Rise, Rocky Mount," and then to Greenville to attend East Carolina University, where she completed her BA in English, concentrating in writing and minoring in Ethnic Studies. Last year, her creative nonfiction, "Legs Curl Upwards Toward the Sky," was published in *The Rebel*, ECU's literary and arts magazine.

Cleôn M. McLean was born in Guyana, South America, in 1978. There he lived until he was sixteen years old when he immigrated to the United States. He came to the U.S. on January 21, 1995 with his sister and parents and resided in Queens, New York for eight months. Then they moved to Covina, California, where he graduated from high school. Shortly thereafter he began at the University of California at Riverside, pursuing a degree in Business Administration. After wrapping up his freshman year, he switched to a dual major in accounting and English (creative writing) when he transferred to the University of Southern California, where he is presently a junior.

Risa Nicole Cohen was born in 1972, and raised in historic Moorestown, New Jersey. She moved to the midwest in 1994 and when the immediate shock of living far from any ocean or large body of water wore off, she decided to continue her undergraduate studies in English at the University of Iowa. She has taken full advantage of The Writers' Workshop by indulging herself in critical discussions of her work and the works of many prestigious authors. She graduated in December 1998 and although she misses corn, tornadoes, mayflies and extreme humidity, she is happy to be back on the East Coast.

Ryan Bachtel is a twenty-five-year-old sophomore at IUSB. After high school he joined the Air Force and had the opportunity to travel. Seeing other places and other cultures forced him to reevaluate many of the things he had taken for granted until that time. He took a leisurely interest in philosophy and related literature while serving in the Air Force, and now it is his major.

Clint Connely is a sophomore at the University of Washington. He graduated from Inglemoor High School in 1993 in Bothell, Washington. He attended the University of Washington from 1993 to 1994 until he enlisted in the United States Army. He was honorably discharged in May of 1998 and this is his first quarter back as a full-time student. He plans to major in Education and hopefully become a school teacher or a counselor.

Matt Norman was born in 1977 in Omaha, and will graduate from the University of Nebraska with a degree in Advertising in August 1999. He's enjoyed reading and writing stories since he was a little kid, but really became excited about fiction writing after meeting Stephen King at a baseball game in junior high. After graduation, Matt will begin a career as a copywriter at an advertising agency in Omaha, and he plans on becoming a late-night writer.

Alexis Taylor is a native Texan, but has firmly planted her roots in the sandy beaches of southern California. She has studied creative writing at the University of California, Irvine, and she is close to finishing undergraduate classes at California State University, Long Beach. Her mentors include such writers as Jo-Ann Mapson, Elizabeth George and Raymond Obstfeld. She has completed three novels and numerous short stories. She has won local writing contests in novel, short story and essay divisions.

Aaron C. Reid will graduate from the University of Alabama with a double major in English and Spanish, and a minor in Creative Writing, in the spring of 2000. He was born and raised in Malone, New York, close to the Quebec border (it's near Lake Placid and Plattsburgh). He attended St. Lawrence University in Canton, New York for his first year of college before transferring to Alabama. He has been the senior editor of Marr's Field Journal, an undergraduate literary magazine on the University of Alabama campus, since 1998. He is also the co-chair of the Student Government Publications Committee which is responsible for the production of the Student Handbook. For two consecutive years he has presented short stories at the Sigma

Tau Delta, an English Honor Society, annual convention; first in Anaheim and then in St. Louis.

Jeff Saucier is a senior at the University of Maine in Orono, majoring in Secondary Education with a concentration in English. From Lewiston, Maine, Jeff has taken part in various writing seminars and participated in the Bates Creative Writing Workshop. In 1998 he received the Abby Neese Sargent Creative Writing Scholarship, which is given yearly for excellence in creative writing. He wishes to thank: J. Macri, E. Ford, C. Hunting, D. Sweidom, C. Poulin, L.Eastman, S. Gianattasio, and D. Malinski for the knowledge they have instilled in so many. A very special thanks to Delta Omega Rho Kappa Sigma and his friends and family for their love and support. He is at work on his first novel, *Those Winter Sundays.*

Frank D. Wilkins was fifty-four years old with four grown children when he passed away on April 19, 1999. He had been a building contractor for thirty years before deciding to follow his education. As a senior studying Education at Indiana/ Purdue University in Fort Wayne, Indiana, he had become very active in writing – a dream that had been put on hold for many years in order to raise a family.

Continued from Copyright page

Short Fiction
Judge Information

Short Fiction Judges Needed

Sulisa Publishing will choose twenty-five graduate writing students to serve as Ear! anthology judges. Selection of the year's panel will be based on an application process. The application deadline is December 3, each year.

Judges will be asked to read fifty submissions, each approximately fifteen pages in length, between December 15, and January 15, and to choose the most promising twenty stories.

<u>Prospective Judges will need to provide:</u>

• Proof of graduate student status
• A completed application (provided by Sulisa Publishing)
• A sample of recent work, published or unpublished

Judges will receive two complimentary copies of *Let Go of My Ear! I Know What I'm Doing.*

For more information or an application, please contact us at:

Sulisa Publishing
625 SW 10th Avenue
PMB 388C
Portland, OR 97205-2788
(503) 233-5232
sulisa@teleport.com

Undergraduate Fiction Contest

Writers please provide:

Proof of undergraduate status.
Unpublished manuscripts under twenty, double-spaced pages, that are edited for grammatical errors.
A cover sheet with your name, permanent address, phone number, university, and title of the work.
A $10 reading fee per story (check or money order), payable to Sulisa Publishing.
Keep a copy on a 3.5" disc (in case you win).
SASE (marked as to what you would like sent) if you would like to be notified of work received or of the twenty winning writers.
Winning authors will be published in the year 2000 anthology and will receive two complimentary copies of the book.
Manuscripts can be returned, but only with a self-addressed, sufficiently stamped envelope.

Write or Call for Current Postmark Deadline

For more information contact us at:
Sulisa Publishing
625 SW 10th Avenue
PMB 388C
Portland, OR 97205-2788
(503) 233-5232
sulisa@teleport.com

Undergraduate Art Contest

Artists please provide:

Proof of undergraduate status.
Artwork presented on a color slide, labeled with: your name, permanent address, phone number, university and title of the work.
An entrance fee of $15 for up to three slides (check or money order), payable to Sulisa Publishing.
SASE (marked as to what you would like sent) if you would like to be notified of work received, or of the winning artist.
The winning artist will be featured on the cover of the year 2000 anthology, will receive two complimentary copies of the book and will be invited to submit subsequent work for future, paid projects.
Slides can be returned, but only with a self-addressed, sufficiently stamped envelope.

Write or Call for Current Postmark Deadline

Sulisa Publishing
625 SW 10th Avenue
PMB 388C
Portland, OR 97205-2788
(503) 233-5232
sulisa@teleport.com

Book Order Information

Telephone Orders: 877-233-5232; Please have your credit card ready

Email Orders: sulisa@teleport.com

Postal Orders: Sulisa Publishing
625 SW 10th Avenue
PMB 388C
Portland, OR 97205-2788
503-233-5232

. . . .

Order Form

Please send me _______ copies

Name: ____
Address: ____
City: ____________________State: ___________Zip: ______________
Telephone: ______ - ______________

Number ____ of books @ $12.95 each _______

Shipping ($3.00 for the first book, $2.00 for each additional book) _______

Total _______

Payment:
__ Check enclosed
__ Credit Card: __ Visa __ Mastercard __ Discover

Card Number: ____
Name on Card: ______________________ Exp. Date: _____/_____

Call Toll Free to Order: 877-233-5232

Book Order Information

Telephone Orders: 877-233-5232; Please have your credit card ready
Email Orders: sulisa@teleport.com
Postal Orders: Sulisa Publishing
625 SW 10th Avenue
PMB 388C
Portland, OR 97205-2788
503-233-5232

. . . .

Order Form

Please send me _______ copies

Name: ____
Address: ____
City: __________________State: __________Zip: ____________
Telephone: _____ - _____________

Number ____ of books @ $12.95 each ______
Shipping ($3.00 for the first book,
$[illegible].00 for each additional book) ______
Total ______

Payment:
__ Check enclosed
__ Credit Card: __ Visa __ Mastercard __ Discover

Card Number: ____
Name on Card: ____________________ Exp. Date: _____/_____

Call Toll Free to Order: 877-233-5232